Other Books by Lauren Marie Filarsky

The Star Horses Series

Emma and Starfire
The First Seahorse
Starlight Dancer Saves Christmas

Blood Shadows, Book 1: Khafyri

Breaking Expectations

ENZO
Protector of Humanity

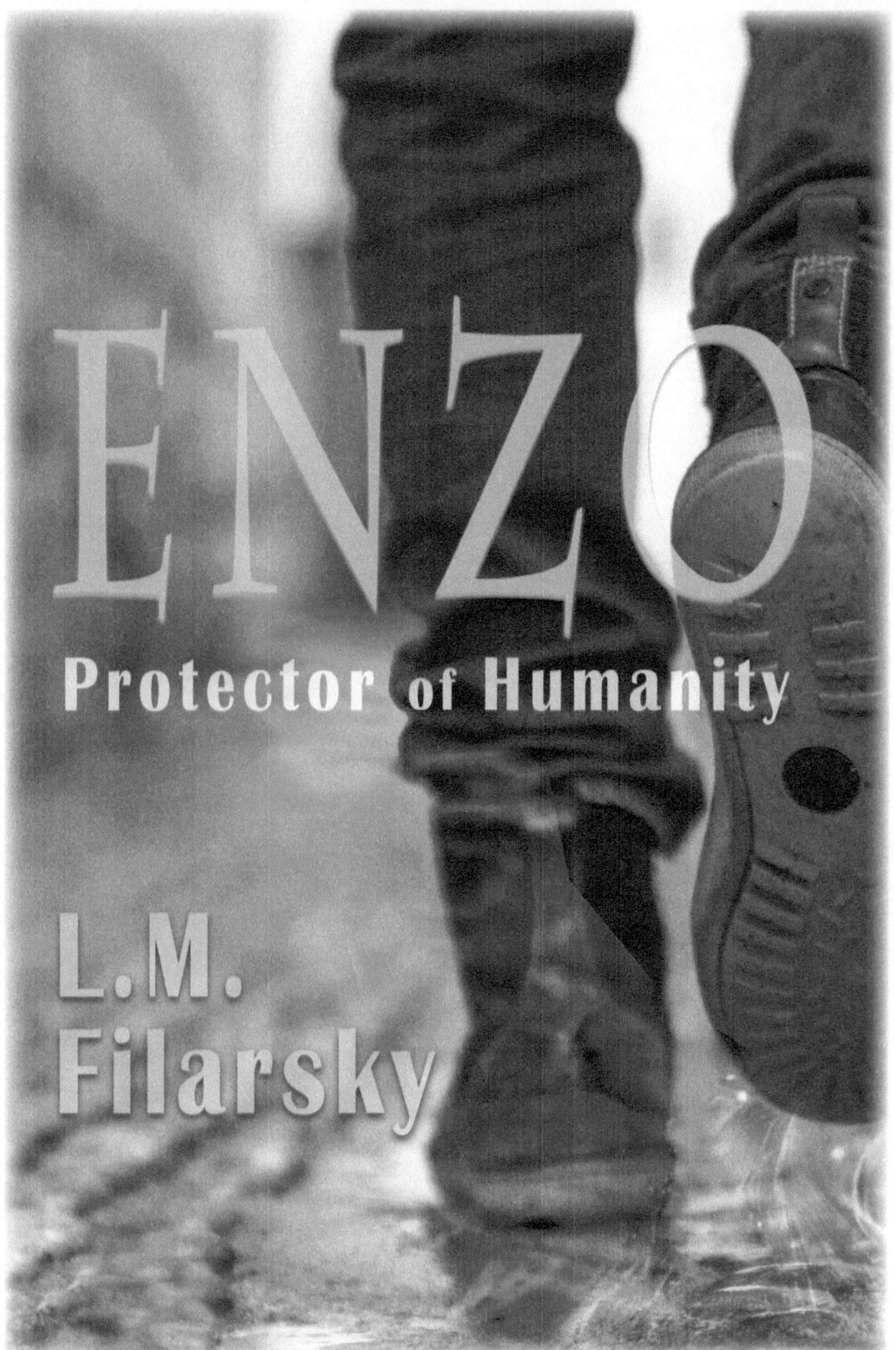

Dusty Rose Books

Bedazzled Ink Publishing Company • Fairfield, California

978-1-960373-71-7 paperback

Cover Design
by

Sapling
Studio

Dusty Rose Books
a division of
Bedazzled Ink Publishing Company
Fairfield, California
http://www.bedazzledink.com

*For Marty, always quick with a joke and an infectious laugh.
You are missed.*

ACKNOWLEDGMENTS

Writing may be a solitary act, but finishing and publishing a novel is anything but. It takes a whole community—of friends, family, and fellow writers—offering encouragement, critique, humor, and the occasional reality check. I'm deeply grateful to everyone who has supported me on this journey.

To the Vacaville Town Square Writers, thank you for years of insightful feedback and kind-hearted roasting. Your critiques have helped shape this book into its final form. A special shoutout to those who read and commented on early drafts of *Enzo*: Betty Lucke, Laurie Rawlinson Evans, Kelly Hess, Sierra Janisse, Cheryl Potts, Rachel Lewis, and Don and Syl Bestwick.

One person that I wish could see this book in print is Marty Markovits. While he read early chapters of Enzo, his constant wisecracks and quips inspired me to write the character Martin—who ended up being far more significant than I expected. I'm sure the irony that the character he inspired is a ghost is making him laugh somewhere.

To my editor, C.A. Casey—thank you again for your careful edits. Enzo is stronger and sharper because of your work.

And of course, to my family. Mom and Dad, thank you for your unwavering support in every project I dream up. And to my brother—thank you for always being game for an adventure, whether in Bay City or around the globe.

PREFACE

(To be removed from the human manuscript)

The following story is true. It is the expanded account of my latest investigative report and, hopefully, is far more entertaining than the dry, tedious facts that I laid out in the formal record. This is the full story—all my triumphs and many flaws. I have written it down so my children (if I ever have any) can understand who I am, figurative warts and all.

But, of course, there is no need for this book to have a single purpose. Despite many objections to my actions, I have decided to submit this to human publishers. Might as well earn a little money from my efforts. It's not like being a Protector pays very much. However, in order to preserve the appearance of fiction for my human audience, I have changed some of the names and descriptions of various locations. The people in this story are all real (a few of them have even threatened to kill me because of how I portrayed them in the following pages). But I can divulge the truth for one simple reason: no ignorant human is going to actually believe any of this supernatural stuff exists.

Verum mirabilius fictionem.

Protector Enzo Thornton

CHAPTER 1

No Good Samaritan Goes Unpunished

PEACE WAS A lot more boring than I'd thought it would be. Everyone said I was crazy. After all, we'd gotten everything our kind had strived for throughout the centuries. The vampires owned most of the blood clinics, so there was no more need to drain living victims. Secret werewolf sanctuaries had been established globally, giving the weres a safe place to turn furry every month, with no risk of accidentally stumbling across a tasty human while they enjoyed their monthly mindless romp. Even the sirens had agreed to focus their womanly charms exclusively on Somali pirates rather than innocent merchant vessels. Every time the sirens' wail lured sailors to their untimely deaths, the high seas actually became a safer place. Win-win.

I'd list all the other agreements with different supernatural species, but, quite frankly, I don't have the attention span to do so. If you really want to know, go read all the long-winded concords yourself. Make sure you wear gloves—a fair number of them are signed in blood. Tradition, and all that.

So why couldn't I be happy when all the peace treaties were firmly in place? I guess part of it's because the motto of my people is entrenched in the root of my being: Protect human life. Others say we've done our job. Being supernatural ourselves, we are able to stand up against the supernatural evils in this world in a way that humans simply cannot. We are the self-appointed supernatural police. Hall monitors on steroids (magical ones, that is), and now all we need to do is oversee the world and make sure the pacts are adhered to by the various factions.

But humans are still kidnapped, murdered, trafficked, enslaved, raped (and God knows what other horrors) on a daily basis. They still need protection. The problem is, the evil creatures they need protection from aren't supernatural. They're human.

Not our problem, our ruling council says. It's human business. They can take care of themselves. Let their police, special agents, and military forces handle the task.

I disagree. We have the power to help them, and it's our duty to protect them. Hell, it's the very name we call ourselves—Protectors of Humanity. Other species call us different names, none of them flattering, but that's beside the point right now.

I decided to take matters into my own hands. If the Council wouldn't act, I would. A supernatural vigilante, you might say, although I had no intentions to function as judge, jury, and executioner. I just wanted to catch the bastards. Let the human courts dole out whatever justice they saw fit.

So it was that I found myself stanching a hemorrhaging knife wound on a human woman, helplessly watching as her attacker ran to a car and drove away in a squeal of tires on asphalt. I could've easily caught him, but that would've meant releasing the pressure on the bloody puncture and allowing the victim to bleed to death. Her life would be the payment for capturing him. Unacceptable. Nothing to do but let him escape and get him another day. I'm not going to lie, though, it was galling as hell to watch him leave.

I freed one red-stained hand long enough to dial 9-1-1 and demand an ambulance ASAP.

It was a matter of minutes that felt like hours before the emergency services vehicles pulled up, sirens wailing in a tone reminiscent of a banshee, lights flashing brightly in the fading blues of twilight. The EMTs quickly relieved me of my duties, bandaging the wound and loading the woman into the ambulance. One of them was kind enough to give me some antiseptic wipes to clean my hands off before they raced toward the hospital.

A pair of police officers approached me. I glanced at them, expertly appraising them in a quick moment. One man, one woman. The male was a few inches taller than my six feet, leanly muscled like a marathoner, and in his late thirties. His skin, hair, and eyes were the medium hues resulting from a well-stirred portion of the American Melting Pot. Hard to even guess what the mix of his ancestry might be. He looked around with the air of a seasoned detective, taking in every detail of the crime scene in a calm, dispassionate manner. He wore authority like a cloak. Not in a pompous, high-handed manner, but a self-confidence that was so ingrained in his core that he couldn't help but project it for all to see.

His partner, on the other hand, was a compact bundle of high-voltage energy. Five-two, early twenties, and every feature on the small side— narrow, angular face and whipcord thin body. Hell, even her black hair was only an inch or two long and a sharp contrast to her pale skin. Her hair did help add to her height, though, as it was short enough to stand on end.

She looked at me with a raptor-fierce gaze. I suppose it made sense, since I was covered in blood at a crime scene, but surely she'd been informed that I had been trying to save the victim's life, not end it. But then, as they got closer, I realized why she was staring at me so intensely.

Shit, I thought, as I instinctively reached for my silver knife, realizing a split second later that I had left all my supernatural weapons behind for this foray amongst the humans. *She's a werewolf.*

CHAPTER 2

BLOOD TRACE

"I'm Detective Marlow. This is my partner, Officer Hawkins," the human policeman said. I forced my gaze away from werewolf Hawkins to look at him. "We'd like to ask you a few questions about what occurred here. What is your name?"

"Enzo Thornton," I replied, flashing a disarming smile, hoping that the appearance I currently preferred would come across as an innocent bystander to him. I didn't want to get dragged into a human investigation. Too much of a hassle, even with my ever-useful get-out-of-jail-free card. I saw him evaluating me—clean-cut white male in his late twenties, dark workout clothes that didn't show much blood despite being currently splattered on the front, and relaxed stance. Although, with a werewolf present, it was much more difficult to pull off an air of nonchalance than if it had been two human cops questioning me. Even if they'd been Gestapo—no big deal for someone like me. Not like a werewolf.

"Mr. Thornton, can you describe what happened here?" Detective Marlow asked.

"I was going for a run," I said. No need to tell him that I was looking for trouble, not exercise. "Saw a man mugging a woman in the alley. He stabbed her with a knife. When he saw me coming, he ran off and drove away."

"Why didn't you catch him?" Hawkins demanded in a fierce voice.

Marlow stopped scribbling in his notebook and looked at her, eyebrows raised in surprise.

Before he could speak, I answered. "The woman was losing a lot of blood. I applied pressure to the wound to keep her from bleeding out, and then called the ambulance."

"But why didn't you do more—"

"Enough, Hawkins," Marlow said, frowning at her.

She glared at me but held her tongue.

Marlow resumed his questioning. "Did you get a look at the assailant? Or his car?"

"Just his back. Shorter than me—maybe five-eight, five-nine. Medium build. Didn't get a look at his face. Drove a dark sedan. Not sure the make or model. Something newish though."

"What about his license plate?"

"No idea. Too dim and too far away."

"If you remember anything else, give me a call." He handed me a business card, which I tucked in my pocket.

Marlow walked away, but Hawkins didn't move, still glaring at me.

"You got a problem with me?" I whispered so the human wouldn't hear, but I knew her keen werewolf ears would pick out my words.

"What are you doing here?" she hissed.

"None of your business." I managed to snap the words out despite continuing to whisper.

"Hawkins, come on," Marlow ordered. His voice seemed unnaturally loud after our near-silent conversation.

"Stay away from me," Hawkins said, a hint of a growl in her voice, before turning and following her partner.

Not one to be denied the last word, I muttered my parting shot so only she would hear. "Nothing you can do to stop me."

I WALKED A few blocks away before I summoned a rideshare. No need to be tied to the crime scene by other humans. Fortunately it was dark enough by then that the blood on my black clothing was no longer visible. Would've been hard to explain it to the driver. Got a quiet one, thankfully. I wasn't in the mood for chatting.

It only took a quarter of an hour to return to my apartment on the other side of the city—rush hour was officially over—and I began collecting an assortment of tools to further my own investigation into the mugging. It was highly doubtful that the human cops would ever be able to catch the bad guy based on the thin evidence and the unobservant witness. That's me, in case you're wondering. And I only play the part of someone who's a run-of-the-mill imperceptive civilian.

I knew the guy I was after drove a black 2015 Mercedes-Benz C 300. He was Caucasian (white hands holding the knife) and had a slight limp in his left leg. Old knee injury, maybe. But I didn't know the face, and I didn't know the license plate. No need to give the other info to the police then. It wasn't specific enough. But it would help me. At least I would know I'd found the right guy when I finally caught up to him.

Before I stripped off my stained clothes and stepped into the shower, I squeezed some of the blood soaking the front of my shirt into a vial. Might be useful in tracking down the mugger. Then I stepped into the steaming shower to wash the rest away in a hot, pink stream of water. No matter how much you are used to getting covered in blood, nothing beats seeing it wash away in the scalding torrent of a refreshing shower. I love modern technology. I can't imagine having to boil water over a fire for a bath, and then sitting in a stew of hot water and your own dirt and sweat. Not to mention any blood picked up along the way.

After my shower, I preheated the oven for a frozen pizza. DiGiorno cheese-stuffed crust pepperoni pizza. Can't beat it. Scrumptious cheesy goodness. Anyhow, I knew I had to kill some time so the human cops could finish up their investigation at the crime scene before I went back. Might as well indulge in some deliciously unhealthy dinner while I waited. Besides, my high metabolism had its uses—I didn't need to worry about calorie counting, or any of that bullshit. If anything, it was occasionally a struggle to keep up with my supernatural energy requirements.

After baking and devouring half the pizza, I returned to the crime scene. No rideshare this time. Didn't want my movements to be tracked back to where the mugging happened. Instead, I ran. Although I'm capable of extreme speeds, I kept my running to a brisk jog—perfectly blending with all the other human fitness fanatics out there.

It took me a half hour to return to the alley where the woman had been stabbed. By the time I got there, all traces of human police were gone. Apparently they had "been there, done that." Gotten all the evidence from the crime scene, and it was time to move on. Not that I blamed them—there wasn't much for them to go on, and it definitely made my job a hell of a lot easier now that the police had abandoned the crime scene. I didn't have to worry about compelling cops or erasing memories.

I pulled out my tracker device. It was a thin black disc, the perfect size to be easily held in the palm of my hand, with a small hole in the center. I carefully poured the small bottle of the victim's blood into the hole and re-stoppered the empty vial. The disc glowed with black light. Mind you, I'm not talking about what humans call black lights. That's just a fancy term for ultraviolet lights. I'm talking about real, honest-to-goodness light that is black. If you've never seen black light before, believe me, it's just as weird-looking as it sounds.

After a moment, three red dots appeared on the tracker. One was far brighter than the others—a heavy concentration of blood, clearly the victim herself. Based on where the spot appeared on the disc, I guessed she'd been taken to Mercy General Hospital.

The other dots were far dimmer—and far more interesting. One was dead center on the disc, indicating that it was where I was standing. It had to be honing onto both the vial of blood in my pocket and the leftovers from the crime scene. The third dot was what I had been hoping for. Another source.

The bloody knife blade, or perhaps even blood that splattered on the mugger himself. Perfect. Time to hunt him down.

I set out at a steady jog, heading toward that third dot. If I was lucky, it would lead me straight to the mugger, who wouldn't know what hit him. A little night-night powder to incapacitate him, then tie him up and dump him in front of a police station for the human authorities to find. Bloody knife conspicuously displayed so they would get the hint to run a DNA test. All in a good night's work.

Of course, I knew it wouldn't be that easy. Life is so rarely wrapped up with such a neat, pretty bow. But it never hurt to hope. After all, I like to think of myself as the eternal optimist—always looking for the silver lining in the looming storm clouds.

As I drew nearer to the target, I habitually checked my weaponry. Silver knife. Check. Wooden stake. Check. Various other tools and devices. Check, check, check. Not that I would need any of my magical weaponry, of course (other than the night-night powder). After all, it was a mere human I was tracking.

Oh, how wrong I was.

CHAPTER 3

A Squeaky Sewer Rat and a Whining Lion

I slowed to a walk when the tracker showed I was within a hundred yards of the blood trace. I looked around. A few blocks of dingy apartments. Next to me was a rusted-out playground, all the swings missing their seats. Just a few lonely chains swinging slowly in the light breeze.

The only people I saw were a block ahead, playing basketball on a communal court under the spotty light of a few tall lampposts. It took only a second of study to see that the lightest person among them was a tanned Mexican. My current pale skin would stand out in this neighborhood like a Grand Dragon at the "I Have a Dream" speech.

I decided to do a quick shift. That's the convenience of being a shapeshifter—it's easy to blend in to any surroundings. Darken the skin, get rid the scruff around the chin, rearrange the facial features, and I was a brand-new black teenager. I figured I'd look a little more innocent if I took a decade or so off my appearance. Give me a bit more of an element of surprise. Not that I really thought that I needed it, but it never hurts to have a little extra help. I thought about shifting to female—humans can be incredibly stupid about underestimating girls—but I didn't have the right clothes to pull it off. Another time.

The tracker dot led me to the second set of apartments. I entered the hallway. No locks, or if there had been a lock, it was broken off long ago. Slowly, careful to make no sound, I advanced down the row of doors, stopping at apartment 112. This was it. I listened at the door. No noise. Perhaps the mugger was asleep.

I took only a matter of moments with my lock picks to trip the simple deadbolt. I eased the door open, wary of creaks from the hinges. No lights on inside. I slipped through the doorway, closing the door behind me, and waited a moment for my eyes to adjust to the dimness. Not complete darkness, mind you, as a streetlight was shining though the curtain-less window.

A quick glance around made me doubt that I was in the right place. Crocheted doilies everywhere. Two cats sleeping on the clawed-up sofa. They opened their eyes and stared at me as I tiptoed though the apartment. A soft snoring came from the bedroom, and when I snuck over to peer inside,

I saw an old lady sprawled on a sagging mattress, another pair of cats curled up at her side.

Just to be sure, I followed my tracker to the exact spot it said the blood should be. The middle of the living room. Nothing there. Damn, I wish the tracker had 3-D capabilities. Clearly I was at the right coordinates, just the wrong altitude. Time to try floor two.

The second floor was equally fruitless. I only had to listen at the door of apartment 212 to know for sure. Screaming baby. Barking dog. Crying mother. That was a rattlesnake's den that I wanted nothing to do with. Give me an old-fashioned beatdown any day before shoving a shrieking infant in my face.

Floor three, though, was a different story. Jackpot.

I listened at the door, pressing my ear to the peeling paint. Voices inside. Loud. Male. Arguing.

"What the hell were you thinking?" Voice Number One was high-pitched, almost effeminate. "You could've blown everything."

"Nobody saw who I was." Voice Number Two was deep, slightly gravelly.

I thought about breaking down the door and nabbing the two guys, but I wanted to hear more. Maybe there was more to the mugging than I originally thought.

"But you were seen in the act!" The voice broke on the last word like a prepubescent teenager. I decided to dub the speaker Mr. Squeaky.

"Just some random guy. No big deal." He sounded more like a Mr. J. E. Jones to me, a bit reminiscent of Disney's dead lion dad. Seriously, though, who puts a scene like that in a kids' movie? And not just once, but in the remake too.

"No big deal? *No big deal?* You have no idea what could happen if the right people catch wind of this."

"There's no reason for anyone to get suspicious."

"Unless she speaks. You didn't even manage to finish the job. She was taken to the hospital."

"Nothing I could do about it. She came after me first. Had to defend myself. Anyhow, I made sure she won't survive. I used this."

"Shit! Give that to me, you moron! Are you *trying* to attract their attention? Besides, she knows the antidote."

"There's an antidote?"

A string of curses rattled off from Mr. Squeaky. It was almost amusing, listening to such a shrill voice muttering curses that would make a troll blush (and, in case you don't know, every other word grunted from a troll's mouth is usually an expletive of some sort). The ending to the tirade caught my attention, sending a flood of adrenaline through my veins. "Damned, idiotic humans."

So. Mr. Squeaky wasn't human. All of a sudden, my night was looking a lot more interesting.

I heard heavy footsteps move across the creaking floorboards, heading toward the front door. "I don't need to take any of this bullshit from you," Mr. Jones said, his deep voice much closer now.

I listened intently, waiting for the right moment. The doorknob turned, and I threw myself into the door, thrusting it into the unsuspecting Mr. Jones as I barged in.

I quickly scanned the dingy room. A forty-something-year-old white guy was sprawled at my feet. Mr. Jones. Across the room, springing up in alarm from a dilapidated couch, was Mr. Squeaky. Damn it all. No wonder he had such a high-pitched voice. He was a sprite. Four feet tall, with the pointed ears and slim build common to all the elfin-type creatures. I might've guessed from the voice, but sprites are usually found in nature settings, not in the middle of a concrete ghetto.

This one was a water sprite of some sort. Pale blue skin, a set of gills on his neck—water sprites can breathe normally in the air—and webbing between his fingers. Probably webbed feet, too, but I couldn't see them behind the sagging ottoman. He was naked, but thank God sprites have no external reproductive parts. One of his hands held a blood-stained knife. The blade was serpentine and had some sort of runes etched along its length. I wasn't able to discern what they were, because as soon as he saw me, Mr. Squeaky turned and punched through the window, using the butt of the knife to shatter the glass.

I lunged across the room, making a grab for the sprite, but he leaped through the broken window before I could reach him. Damn it. Sprites are such a nuisance. So freakin' fast. I heard a splash as I reached the sill and leaned out. An open manhole was in the street right outside the apartments. Sewers. Disgusting but effective. There was no way I'd be able to track a water sprite through the vile sewer water. I may be able to shapeshift, but gills and flippers are beyond me. My kind is confined to strictly human forms. I'd have to be content with questioning Mr. Jones.

Speaking of him, I turned around just in time to see him scrambling out the doorway. "Not this time," I growled, and raced after him.

He was dashing toward the stairway at the end of the hall. Slight limp in his left leg, just like I remembered. Not that a sound human could've outrun me, but it made it mere child's play to tackle him before he made it halfway to the stairs.

We landed with a crash. He spewed curses as I wrenched his arms behind his back and slapped a pair of magi-cuffs—handcuffs with magical-dampening spells—on his wrists. I wasn't too worried about nosy neighbors poking their heads out to see what was going on. Not in this part of town.

"Shut up," I snapped anyway, giving him a good shake. The sprite's escape had put me in a mood as foul as the tunnels he'd fled through.

I dragged Mr. Jones to his feet and spun him to face me.

"You're just some punk kid!" he yelled. "Let me go."

"What were you doing with that sprite?"

At my final word, the man's face drained of all color. "You're—you're a hunter," he stammered. He attempted to step backward, probably to bolt again, but I maintained a firm grip on the front of his clothes.

"Correct," I said. "Maybe you're not as much of a moron as the sprite thought."

"You can't do anything to me!" Mr. Jones protested. "I'm human—you can't touch me."

"Then again, I've been wrong before," I muttered to myself. I gave the guy another shake to get his attention. "You've had dealings with a supernatural creature and, unless I am very much mistaken, a supernatural weapon. You know things that are classified to humans. Therefore, you fall under our jurisdiction. And I most definitely have the right to detain you."

"I want a lawyer!"

I laughed derisively. "You signed away your rights to human counsel the moment you signed up with that sprite. You're coming with me, whether you like it or not. Now, where're your keys?"

"My—my keys?" he spluttered.

Damn, I was going to have to spell everything out for this guy. "Yes, your keys. I don't have a car."

"You can't just take my car!"

I rolled my eyes, not bothering to respond, and patted the guy down. Jingle in the front left pocket. I reached in and pulled out a small bundle of keys. On the ring was a fob with the Mercedes logo. Excellent. I always appreciate riding in style.

I dragged my captive down the stairs and out the door, ignoring his protests and curses. Once outside, I punched the unlock button on the fob. Half a block away, lights flashed on a black car. Perfect.

When I reached the car, I opened one of the back doors, flipped the child safety lock and shut the door, then went to the other side and repeated the process. But before I slammed the second door, I threw the squirming Mr. Jones into the back seat. Not exactly the same as the back of a police cruiser—let alone one of our vehicles, which are strong enough to contain even an ogre—but it would do the job for one wimpy human.

I got in the driver's seat and started the car, taking a moment to appreciate the soft purr of the engine. Sudden revelation hit me—why the hell hadn't I seen the glaring incongruities before? Guess I was too focused on the tracking, the sprite, and the capture. Couldn't see the forest for the trees.

"What are you doing in a place like this?" I demanded. "This car doesn't belong here. Not in this neighborhood. It would be broken into or stolen on a daily basis. Hell, *you* don't belong here. So what were you doing?"

For once, Mr. Jones was silent. Dammit. Typical. Wouldn't shut up when I wanted silence, wouldn't speak when I wanted answers. Oh well. I'd get him into an interrogation chamber soon enough.

Before I pulled away from the curb, I shifted back into my normal appearance. Didn't want to be pulled over by the cops. No, I wasn't worried about racial profiling. Black kid driving a fancy car. Okay, maybe a little concerned. But it was more because my shifted visage was that of a teen not old enough for high school, let alone driving. Better to be safe than sorry on all accounts.

Besides, I would've had to shift back anyway once I reached our command base in the City. Regulations state that all Protectors must use one of their registered appearances while at base—can you imagine how confusing a building full of shapeshifters would be otherwise? You'd talk to a guy in a meeting, eat lunch with another at the mess hall, play basketball with a third, and only when you were in the middle of a poker game with a fourth person would you realize that you'd spent the whole day with the same shifter—just different faces.

"Where are you taking me?" Okay, this guy was really starting to get on my nerves. I don't generally associate such deep voices with such a high volume of whininess, but this guy really knew how to play the wrongfully accused victim.

"To HQ," I said, deciding to humor him. "My home away from home."

CHAPTER 4

SAY GOOD-NIGHT-NIGHT

AS I PUT the car in drive, Mr. Jones flopped over in the back seat, rolling on his back so he could kick the passenger-side window with both feet. Must've been uncomfortable for him to be lying on top of his cuffed hands, but that didn't stop him from banging his size tens against the window.

I slammed the gearshift back into park and turned around to look at him. "Shut. Up!" I roared.

His response was to add to the din by yelling. "Help! Help! I'm being abducted!"

"That's it," I growled. I wasn't about to put up with this racket for the hour's drive to HQ. I pulled out my bag of night-night powder, took a three-fingered pinch of the fine blackish-purple dust, and threw it in his face. It only needed to make skin contact with a human in order to be effective, but headshots always worked faster.

Mr. Jones immediately went limp, his mouth gaping slightly as his breathing evened into a soft snore.

"Much better." I shifted back into drive, pulled away from the curb, and then fiddled with the radio dial as I drove. Needed some tunes for the journey to HQ. The quiet snoring in the backseat was better than the shouting and kicking, but it was already getting dreary. Steppenwolf's "Born to be Wild" was on. Perfect to rock out to during a car ride. I cranked up the volume and headed toward the freeway.

The Protectors' regional headquarters was in Bay City, which (surprise surprise) is a city built by a bay, just over sixty miles from Summerville. Despite the name, Summerville was the worst place to visit during the summer. The dry heat felt like hell itself was vacationing there, though the rest of the year, the climate was relatively mild. Summerville was where I'd made my residence—close enough that it wasn't that big of a deal to drive to the City when needed, but far enough away for me to operate fairly autonomously from the Council. They still didn't approve of me going after human villains, but I wasn't technically breaking any of our laws, so there wasn't anything they could do about it.

Still, easier to keep out from under their noses. Summerville was a much smaller city—only a couple hundred thousand or so, compared to the sprawling million-plus of Bay City—but there were still plenty of baddies for me to pursue. And that wasn't even counting the water sprite who escaped. Or the werewolf cop. What was going on with her? Worth looking into. Weres generally didn't associate so closely with humans unless they had some ulterior purpose. Might be time to use my silver dagger.

The freeway to Bay City was fairly empty this late in the evening. Of course, it was Tuesday. Almost the middle of the week. If it were Sunday—or even Monday—the road would've been clogged with cars returning from a weekend getaway to the mountains. It didn't even matter what season it was—winter brought out the snow-sport lovers, summer the hikers and boaters, and spring and fall catered to those who naively thought that the mountains ever had an off season from tourists. Fridays and Saturdays had equally bad traffic, only it was all the people from the scattered small farming towns heading to the City for a night out on the town.

I reached the outskirts of Bay City nearly an hour later, negotiated the annoyance of the interstate interchange, which required a sudden crossing of four lanes of traffic in order to make my exit onto Market Street and downtown. From the offramp, HQ was only a half-dozen blocks away. Luckily for me, the traffic lights on Market Street are timed, so after one initial red light, all I had to do was stick to the speed limit in order to hit every light at green. It went against my nature to go so slow, but it was better than stopping at every intersection.

And then I arrived. West Coast Headquarters for the Protectors of Humanity. The front of HQ was an old cathedral, the first built in the city. Holy ground is a vital tool in our arsenal. Vampires and a few other creatures of the dark can't enter holy ground, making it a stronghold against them. Although, on the other hand, ghosts are inexplicably attracted to holy ground. Good thing we have other ways to get rid of the nasty ghosts. But the harmless ghosts are usually left alone. There are a few long-term residents of HQ who keep a pact with us: As long as they stay out of human sight, we leave them alone to go about their business.

Of course, to maintain status as holy ground, the cathedral must actually be used as a church. So it is. Hundreds of ignorant humans attend it every Sunday, thinking they are members of the simple Our Lady of Faith Church. The priest and a few of the deacons know the truth, but that is only because it is necessary, mostly in case we need to suddenly explain a dead minotaur or something in the foyer.

But behind the church is where the real work happens. The buildings where Protectors are housed, fed, and trained. It's somewhat between a boarding school and a military base—with perhaps a dash of juvie thrown in, in the case of more troublesome young shifters. Not that I would know anything about that, of course. I was a perfect angel as a cadet.

I passed the front of the church and took a right-hand turn at the corner. Halfway down the block, I turned into the gated driveway leading to our parking lot. I know you're imagining some elaborate, wrought-iron gate leading to our ancient, mystical sanctuary, but the gate was just one of those hinged-bar things like any paid parking lot has. Parking is a highly sought after luxury in the City, and we have to keep unwanted cars out of our lot while remaining discreet. More elaborate, non-human protective barriers are farther in, out of sight of the general public.

A box much like a parking-ticket dispensing machine was to the left of the gate. I rolled down my window and pressed my thumb into the big green button on the front of it. Although it looked like an ordinary button, it was in fact a top-of-the-line DNA scanner, which not only registered DNA, but it also checked for signs of life. In other words, you couldn't just chop off someone's finger (or any other body part) and use it to get past security.

It was a matter of seconds for the box to beep its acceptance of my DNA print, immediately followed by the raising of the gate arm. If an unauthorized person tried to hit the button and get a parking ticket, the display would post the message "Parking Lot Full."

The parking lot itself was bordered on three sides by buildings of various sorts. To the right was the cathedral and the church administration buildings. All what they appeared to be.

Directly ahead was the school, which was supposedly Our Lady of Faith Academy, the most exclusive school in the City, and nearly impossible to get into. Well, technically impossible for humans, since it was a shapeshifter-only academy. It's not wise for young shifters to attend regular human schools, since they have not yet mastered the art of staying in one form all the time. So instead they attend our school, where teachers don't bat an eye if a student's straight black hair turns red and curly when they're angry.

To my left was my intended destination: HQ. A collection of stuffy offices, the ceremonial (pompous) Council Chamber, a delightful arsenal of weaponry, training and sparring courts, some underground dungeons (cliché, right?), and a few interrogation rooms, where Mr. Jones would be spending his time. The parking lot was only half-full, so I was able to get a spot just a few spaces from the entrance for detainees.

Mr. Jones was still snoring in the backseat. Not wanting to have to drag a limp body into the building, I patted my pockets for a vial of sleep-no-more, a handy potion not only for reviving someone who is unconscious, but also for staying awake on little to no sleep. As you might imagine, finals week at the Academy is filled with students overdosing on it, resulting in a zombie-like state of brainless wakefulness. Back in the 1920s, a human actually spotted a Protector overdosed on sleep-no-more, and thus the zombie legend was born. But I hadn't been expecting to revive anyone—I'd been planning on dumping the culprit at a police station—and my search came up empty.

Since it was against protocol to leave a suspect unattended, especially on the grounds of HQ, I couldn't go in search of some handy-dandy potion. Instead I dragged Mr. Jones from the back seat and hoisted him over my shoulders in a fireman's carry, modified slightly due to his cuffed wrists.

The detainee door was steel, reinforced with magical runes to strengthen it so that even a troll couldn't break it down. Supposedly it is able to withstand dragon fire as well, but I'll believe that when I see it. Another DNA scanner awaited me at the entrance. Shifting my grip to maintain a hold on Mr. Jones, I pressed a thumb against the pad. The scanner beeped and the door swung open as a computerized female voice said, "Welcome home, Enzo Thornton."

I snorted derisively. "Home indeed."

CHAPTER 5

WHY CAN'T ANYTHING EVER BE EASY?

Have you ever gone somewhere and the first person you see is the absolute last person on the face of the planet that you'd ever want to encounter? One of those people who you despise so much that if you were given the choice of either letting them win ten million dollars or you going twelve rounds with Mike Tyson, you'd be smiling through broken teeth on the way to the hospital?

Well, that's how I felt about the shifter walking down the hallway toward me: Jake Jonson. Or, as I liked to call him, Jake the Snake, Jake the Jerk, Jake the Fake. Our rivalry went way back, all the way to the first year of schooling, when he intentionally tripped me in front of my childhood crush, Zoe Anna—Zoanna, as she preferred to be called. I went sprawling face-first into a garbage can filled with leftover cafeteria food. And believe me, school food for Protectors is no better than that for humans. Yuck.

The next day, I retaliated by "accidentally" kicking him in the crotch during soccer. Our relationship has only deteriorated from there.

"What has the Enzyme dragged in this time?" Jake asked with a sneer.

I was saved from immediately answering when a translucent head popped upside-down through the ceiling between us. "Did I just hear the start of my favorite entertainment?" the head asked, smirking.

Remember how I mentioned some ghosts are long-term residents of HQ? Well this was Martin, a ghost who'd been around long before I was born. He delighted in mischief, to the point that he was occasionally accused of being more of a poltergeist than a ghost. Whenever Jake and I clashed, Martin was there on the sidelines, egging us on. If he could've eaten popcorn, I'm sure he would've been scarfing it down as he watched the show between us, but sadly for him, the lack of a corporeal form barred such buttery treats.

Martin floated down through the ceiling, righting himself as he did so. If you want to know what Martin looks like, think of a semi-transparent Santa Claus—fluffy white beard, a bit corpulent, and a big smile, although Martin's grin is usually a bit more mischievous than the classic jolly Santa look. Also, Martin wears blue jeans and a green flannel shirt—the clothes he died in— not a white-trimmed red suit, although that doesn't stop him from floating outside every Christmas Eve, trying to convince as many children as possible that they saw the real Santa.

Of course, the Protectors try to keep Martin indoors and out of sight. But despite their many ghost-capturing devices, Martin is wily enough that he always manages to escape for his Christmas Eve romp around town, simultaneously inspiring and terrifying small children throughout the City.

"Any news, Martin?" I asked, ignoring Jake. If you want the best HQ gossip, Martin is the man—I mean ghost—to go to.

"Zoanna's back from her trip to Scotland," Martin said slyly, giving me a suggestive wink. "Another kelpie sighting in the loch—sounds like Zoanna really went above and beyond with covering the whole thing up. Maybe you two can exchange war stories while you're both here."

I scowled. Martin knew I was over my childhood crush. All I wanted was to be friends with Zoanna. I swear it.

Jake laughed derisively. "Still aiming out of your league, Bozo?"

"Shut up, Jake-ass," I said, aiming my scowl at him. "At least I've never dated my cousin."

Jake flushed an unhealthy shade of mottled red. As a teenager, it had been a major setback for him—and a huge victory for me—the day that he discovered that Joyce, the girl he'd been lip-locking for a month, was actually a second cousin on his mother's side. He'd never live that incident down if I had anything to say. It didn't even matter that second cousins only shared a smidgen of DNA—kissing a cousin of any degree of relation was great ammunition in our feud.

"We never knew we were related," he snapped. "But it's better than making out with a pixie."

So, he'd heard about that little escapade. Oh well, I could still make this swing my way. "Just a lost bet." And several regrettable shots of tequila, though I saw no need to mention those. "Still, kissing outside one's own gene pool is better than kissing too closely within it."

While we'd been trading shots, Martin had been floating between us, his head whipping back and forth as if observing ping-pong volleys, a wide smile splitting his face. "What about the time when—"

Whatever inflammatory incident Martin had been about to recall was cut off by an authoritative voice bouncing down the corridor, accompanied by the sharp tap-tap of heels on hard floor. "Jonson. Thornton. What is going on here? Martin, go away."

With a last smirking wink in my direction, Martin floated back though the walls and disappeared. Even he didn't want to face the wrath of Councilor Jennifer Ainsley. Tall and thin, with salt-and-pepper hair and dressed in a classy navy pantsuit, she was every inch the imposing authority figure.

"Just came to relieve Geoff of his duties, Councilor," Jake said. "Found Enzo carrying some random person inside."

Ainsley turned her steely gray gaze on me. I struggled not to flinch under the weight of the look—she'd been principal of the Academy while I'd been a student, and it had been many a time that I'd borne the wrath of that glare. And faced the consequences she'd doled out.

"Well, Thornton?" she asked briskly. "What are you doing? That is a human, is it not? And you are aware of the statutes limiting humans access to this building?"

"Yes, Councilor," I said, fighting to keep snarky quips from escaping my mouth. I knew they'd just get me in a world of trouble with the no-nonsense Ainsley. "I caught this human conspiring with a sprite."

Jake snorted. "Hardly a reason to bring a human to Headquarters. You should be brought up on charges."

"Not when this human is guilty of stabbing another," I said. Jake opened his mouth to protest, but before he could get a word out, I played my trump card. "With a supernatural blade."

Jake hesitated, but Ainsley didn't. "You have this weapon with you?" she asked.

"No, the sprite has it," I replied stiffly.

"He escaped."

I couldn't quite tell if it was a question or not. "Yes."

"How is he connected with this human?"

"I don't know," I confessed. "That's why I brought him here. To interrogate him."

Councilor Ainsley thought for a minute, then gave me a curt nod. "Very well, carry on. Jonson, I believe you have somewhere to be?"

"Yes, Councilor," Jake said. He shot me a look of pure loathing behind Ainsley's back before leaving down a side corridor.

I started walking toward the interrogation rooms, still lugging the unwieldy and unconscious Mr. Jones. To my surprise, Ainsley walked next to me, her heels making a loud click-click with every stride.

"I would like to watch your interrogation," she abruptly said.

"Yes, Councilor." There was no other response I could give.

"And, Thornton, I am going to make sure that you adhere to *all* Protector protocols."

Of all the luck. Shit. Screw it. Damn it all to hell.

"I've heard some worrying reports of your willingness to throw aside all tradition and rules," she continued, as my internal tirade of curses kept going, getting more elaborate and vulgar with every word. "But I expect you to do everything proper tonight. That means no magical compulsion of the suspect."

Well, there went my easy night. Guess I was going to have to do this interrogation by the books after all. What's the point of having magical methods of persuasion if you are only allowed to use them on supernatural species? Surely it wouldn't hurt to use a compulsion stone or some loose-tongue on a human villain. Talk about bureaucratic ineptitude. All the rules we put into place in order to protect humans could really backfire in the almost non-existent cases where we had a human suspect. The regulations only survived because the Council didn't care what humans did to each other—just what the supernaturals did to magic-bereft humans.

"Yes, Councilor," I repeated. It was going to be a long night.

CHAPTER 6

TONGUE-TIED

THE INTERROGATION ROOM that I took Mr. Jones to was similar to what you see in every cop TV show: rectangular table with steel chairs on either side, one wall mostly filled with a one-way mirror, and a cheap surveillance camera in a corner. Of course, those human police rooms don't have optional high-intensity UV lights, a magically enhanced four-inch steel door, and nozzles recessed in the ceiling that, depending on the species contained within the room, could shoot out a wide variety of devious concoctions—silver nitrate, garlic oil, holy water, or antifreeze, to name a few.

I dumped Mr. Jones in the chair facing the mirror and unlocked the magi-cuffs. Body language is a critical factor in conducting a productive interrogation, and most people use their hands unconsciously when they speak. It's very useful to help determine if someone is lying, hiding something, nervous, et cetera, et cetera.

The observation room adjacent to the interrogation room had a standard kit of various potions and artifacts. I grabbed a vial of sleep-no-more, wishing that the small bottle contained loose-tongue instead. I sighed, and Ainsley gave me a sharp look, as if guessing my thoughts.

Too bad it was a banned substance. Interrogations would be so much easier. You know how alcohol lowers inhibitions and often makes people babble while drunk? Loose-tongue acts in a similar manner, although it doesn't affect coordination, intelligence, or ability to form a coherent sentence the way booze does. It just turns off a person's ability to shut their trap, while simultaneously decreasing their ability to lie. But there's all the rules we have to follow—can't force someone to testify against themselves, and all that other crap.

I returned to the interrogation room, leaving Ainsley in observation. Mr. Jones was slumped back in the chair, mouth wide open and drooling slightly. I uncorked the sleep-no-more and poured three drops onto his tongue. By the time I had re-stoppered the vial and taken a seat across from him, Mr. Jones was awake, albeit disoriented, and blinking slowly as he looked around the room. His gaze finally settled on me, and recognition—and a hint of fear, I was pleased to see—sparked in his eyes.

He opened his mouth to speak, but I cut him off before he could begin. "What is your name?" I asked coldly.

Apparently the change of scenery from a ghetto apartment complex to a no-nonsense concrete interrogation chamber caused him to finally recognize that cooperation might be in his best interest. "Peter Newell. And I want a lawyer."

"Well, Mr. Newell, you aren't going to get one. According to Section 192.3 of the treaty governing mundane/magic relations, any human knowingly using supernatural artifacts to harm another loses any rights and privileges given by human governments. Furthermore, Section 118.6 allows us to detain and question any human colluding with a supernatural being." Damn, I'd been pissed when I had to memorize over a hundred major supernatural laws before I was allowed to work as a Protector. But, even though I hated to admit it, the knowledge could be useful at times.

"Now, who was the woman you stabbed?"

"Don't know what you're talking about. I haven't stabbed anyone."

"How do you know that sprite?"

"What's a sprite?"

"That naked blue guy you were talking to."

"Don't know what you're talking about."

Dammit. So much for this guy being cooperative now. I paused, took a deep breath, and did my best to impress upon this guy the seriousness of his situation.

"Mr. Newell, I currently have enough evidence to throw you in jail—that's our jail, not some dinky human one—for a very long time. Unless you cooperate, I will do so. However, if you tell me about the sprite and the dagger you had, I will be lenient with you."

"Don't know about any dagger."

"All right, then. Your choice." Maybe a night in the slammer would loosen his tongue. We still had a banshee locked up down there—a sleepless night of listening to wailing would be good for this idiot human. And it would give me a chance to follow up on the lead with the stabbing victim. Maybe if I heard her story, I could get a bit more leverage on Mr. Jones—I mean, Newell. Hard to remember the guy's real name instead of the one I'd facetiously dubbed him.

I yanked him to his feet, pulled his arms behind his back, and slapped the magi-cuffs back on. Holding him by one arm, I led him out the door and down the hallway toward the steps to the basement dungeons. As we passed the door to observation, Ainsley stepped out. "Make sure you question the victim, Thornton."

Duh. I was already planning on doing that. It rankled to merely say, "Yes, ma'am," and continue down the corridor.

The steps down to the dungeons were reminiscent of a horror movie—narrow and twisting, with the faint echo of the wailing banshee audible from the cells below. Newell tried to balk when he heard the howls, but I jerked him forward.

Down, down, down we went. Lower than your standard basement—had to have a thick buffer of earth to keep certain inmates from being able to escape. The banshee's screaming petered out while we descended. Finally we reached the barred entrance to the dungeon itself. Jake was sitting at the administrative desk, which was situated in a soundproof booth to keep the guards from going mad listening to the inmates. Crap. I'd forgotten that he'd been on his way to start guard duty when I saw him earlier.

He looked up from his computer screen when he saw me enter, and he opened the booth window. His mouth curled into a sneer. "Entrails," he said curtly.

"Jape," I replied stiffly. "Got another prisoner for you."

"Put him in number five."

I pulled Newell down the corridor of barred cells and stopped at his assigned one. After removing his cuffs, I pushed him inside. "Enjoy your stay," I said, then turned to leave.

As I exited the dungeon past the scowling Jake, a voice shouted out over the renewed screeching of the banshee. "I want a lawyer!"

CHAPTER 7

Fed, Creds, and Fled

I DECIDED TO drive Newell's Mercedes back home. Not like he was going to get a chance to report it stolen, and it saved me the hassle of trying to check a vehicle out of the motor pool. I probably would've been denied one, since my case was far from high-priority. Even though it wasn't completely mundane, as the mugging initially appeared, it took more clout than I currently had to be issued a car.

By the time I made it back to my apartment, midnight had long since passed. I was exhausted—the late hour and the excitement of the day, not to mention the energy expenditure of two shifts, had drained me. I set the alarm on my phone and crawled under the covers, ready for sleep to take me.

But it didn't. I was caught in that frustrating state of being too exhausted to fall asleep. All my mind could think of was how tired I felt, how late it was, how fatigued I would be in the morning. It wouldn't just shut up, shut off, and leave me to the peaceful bliss of unconsciousness. Questions bubbled up. Who was Peter Newell? How did he know a sprite? What was the dagger? Who was the mystery victim? Was she really a victim? And what on earth was a werewolf doing as a police officer?

Beep Beep Beep. I jerked awake. At some point, my questions had apparently drifted into dreams—the last image I remembered was a snarling gray wolf, bloody saliva dripping from its fangs as it lunged toward me. Practically the Siberian Uprising all over again, only in the dream, the wolf and I had been alone, not surrounded by the battling, dead, and dying.

I staggered out of bed and made a beeline to the kitchen. Coffee. Need it. Now. Water, filter, grounds, punch the button, and it's started. By the time I'd taken care of personal needs and dressed in a navy suit, the heavenly scent of fresh coffee filled the air of my one-bedroom apartment. I poured a cup and opened the fridge, ready to scavenge for breakfast. Leftover pizza. Delicious.

I briefly considered how to prepare my feast: cold, microwaved, or properly reheated? A glance at the clock showed it was seven-thirty, probably way too early for visiting hours at the hospital. Good, I had some time to do things right. I turned on the oven. Did you know that reheating pizza in the oven is the best way? Microwaving it, while quick and convenient, leaves you with a soggy slice. But a few minutes in the oven restores a fresh, crunchy crust.

While I waited, I browsed the internet, curious to see what the news had reported on last night's mugging-slash-stabbing. It would be nice to at least have the name of the victim, so I wouldn't arrive at the hospital completely clueless. Nothing. Apparently a near-homicide was an all-too-often occurrence around here. Not newsworthy. But some actress got breast implants. That made headlines in five major papers. Apparently big boobs captivate readers better than a stabbing. Not gonna lie, though. I checked out the pictures. Definitely a major improvement.

After I'd finished my wonderfully nutritious breakfast, I grabbed my FBI creds—badge and ID—and put them in the inner pocket of my suit jacket. Although I'm not an FBI agent like the credentials say, they technically aren't fake. They're actually issued by a compartmentalized branch of the FBI that deals in super-secret information. You know, like secret, top secret, et cetera? Well, super secret is a special classification of information specifically tied to the supernatural (hence the cheesy name). The super-secret branch of the FBI issued creds to Protectors so that we could go about our business relatively unhampered by human authorities.

Once ready, I locked up my apartment and drove to Mercy General Hospital. I was really getting spoiled with Newell's Mercedes. It would be a shame to have to give it up. The Protector motor pool cars are, for low-level lackeys like me, complete crap. Granted, the Councilors have some pretty sweet rides (with chauffeurs, no less), but I had no desire to enter politics. And, if my current situation continued, I was unlikely to rise within the regular ranks of defenders either. Hard to get a military promotion when all the supernatural species are sworn to peace. Not that I really cared. I had my own, self-assigned, mission.

The nurses' station was staffed by a frazzled-looking woman in her mid-forties. Must be a busy day at the hospital. "Can I help you?" she asked.

"Agent Thornton, FBI." I flashed my creds as I spoke. "I'm here to see the stabbing victim from last night."

"Jane Doe?"

I was surprised—I'd thought the woman would've been lucid enough to at least provide her name. "She didn't have any ID on her?" I asked.

The nurse stared at me, blinking in confusion, then sudden understanding lit up her face. "Oh! No—she told us her name is Jane Doe."

"Really? And you believed her?" I cocked an eyebrow, skepticism heavily coloring my voice.

"Her driver's license said the same thing," the nurse snapped. "Some parents like to make jokes out of their children's names."

"What room is she in?"

The nurse turned back to her computer and slowly typed and clicked. I guessed she was deliberately taking her time, making me wait in retribution for irritating her. I understood. I got that sort of reaction frequently. My extra superpower is being able to annoy almost everyone around me.

"Room 259," the nurse finally said. "Down the hall to the left."

"Thank you." See, I'm not a total asshole—sometimes I try to be polite.

When I got to the room, it was empty. Had the nurse purposefully sent me to the wrong place because I'd implied she was a few eggs short of a carton? But since so many other things about this whole situation didn't add up, I decided to double-check the room before going back and berating the nurse.

A medical chart on a clipboard hung from the foot of one of the two empty beds in the room. A quick look showed that it was for patient Jane Doe. Stabbed in the gut. Went into surgery last night to sew everything back up. This was all written in medical jargon, of course, but I'm translating to normal English. Nothing indicated that Jane Doe shouldn't be here—no scans scheduled or anything.

Well, I still had my tracker. Boy Scout motto was applicable to supernatural situations—be prepared. I pulled it out, plus the vial of blood from the night before. The vial was empty—just a faint residue on the glass. I went to the cupboard-sized bathroom and filled the bottle in the sink, swirling it slightly so the blood mixed with the water. Hopefully there would be enough to activate the tracker.

Carefully, I poured the pink liquid into the receiving hole on the tracker. Nothing happened. Crap. There wasn't enough blood left for the device to work. Yes, I know that DNA could be taken from that minuscule amount, but I wasn't trying to run a DNA test, I was using a magical tool that relies on blood magic. And for blood magic to work, you need enough blood.

Plan B—track her down the old-fashioned way. I returned to the nurses' station. This time, the nurse on duty didn't look up at me. Still grumpy, I guess.

"Jane Doe isn't in her room."

"Really?" the nurse asked, mimicking my skeptical tone from earlier. Dammit. Should've been nicer. "Are you sure?"

"Medical chart is there, but her bed is empty," I said.

"She must've been taken in for a scan or something," the nurse replied. "It's not like she could've just gotten up and walked away. Not in her condition."

"You haven't seen her, though?"

"No. Now, if there's nothing more, I'm busy."

I debated continuing the argument, but decided I'd have better luck elsewhere. "Where is the hospital security room?"

"First floor."

It took a bit of sleuthing to find the security headquarters—it wasn't boldly labeled the way all the medical departments were—but I finally found it. Flashing my badge granted me access to the security cameras. I selected the footage from the hallway where Jane Doe had been staying and played it backward. There was me, going in and out of the room ten minutes ago. A few minutes of nurses patrolling the corridor, a patient rolling down the hall in a wheelchair, a janitor mopping the floor, all in octuple speed. There—a woman exiting Room 259. I paused the video and checked the timestamp. 2:23 am. Crap. Should've come straight here instead of going home to sleep.

Jane Doe was dressed in a hospital gown. Her left hand was pressed against her side—against her bandage, I assumed. I used the rest of the hospital's security cameras to track her progress to the exit. Despite the fact that she passed a few night-shift nurses and janitors along the way, nobody confronted her or tried to stop her, even though it was clear from the footage that she should not be up and about.

When she left through a side door of the hospital, a white panel van was waiting for her. Couldn't see the plate number—looked like it had been intentionally covered by something. She gingerly climbed in, and the van sped off.

Now what was I going to do? My only lead had vanished into the night. Guess I'd have to go back and take another crack at Newell.

As I left the security room, I was distracted, focusing on my conundrum instead of my surroundings. I turned a corner, heading toward the main entrance, and ran straight into the werewolf.

CHAPTER 8

WOES OF THE MISSING DOE

THE WEREWOLF JUMPED back as if scalded. My hand instinctively darted to the concealed silver dagger strapped to my left forearm, but I stopped before actually drawing the blade. We froze, staring at one another, and at that moment I realized there was another person watching us.

It was Detective Marlow, the human cop from the night before. He looked back and forth between his partner and me, plainly wondering why we were reacting in such a strange fashion. Slowly, as if by mutual unspoken consent, Hawkins and I relaxed from our crouched, tense stances.

"Mr. Thornton," Marlow said. A slight frown creased his brow. "What are you doing here?"

I decided to go for honesty—mostly. Might be helpful to have some human backup for the investigation, and it could give me an opportunity to figure out why a werewolf was acting as a police officer.

"I'm looking for the stabbing victim, Jane Doe," I began.

"Why?" Marlow asked.

"FBI." I flashed my badge.

To my surprise, Marlow wasn't content with the cursory glance the nurse had given my creds. He examined it carefully. I would have been offended that he didn't trust that I was an agent, but it would've been a bit hypocritical of me, considering I wasn't.

"Why didn't you mention this last night?" Marlow asked, once he'd finished looking at my ID and badge.

"It didn't seem relevant at the time," I replied. "Since then, I've come across new information that ties Ms. Doe to an investigation under my jurisdiction."

Hawkins shot me a sharp look, but Marlow didn't see her reaction. "What investigation?"

Time for one of my favorite words. "Classified."

Marlow's frown deepened into a scowl. "And you're going to expect full cooperation and information from us, without sharing any of your own intelligence, right?"

"Correct." I flashed him an apologetic smile. A little niceness in this situation would hopefully go a long way to prevent future stonewalling. There's a big difference between inter-agency "cooperation" and inter-agency cooperation. "Nature of the job. Wish I could tell you, but I'm sure you understand."

"Have you looked at the security tapes yet?"

"Yes, and I can share that info with you. Ms. Doe left her room at 2:23 am. She was picked up by a white panel van. Plate number obscured."

Marlow gave me a long look. Undoubtedly considering whether I was lying about the license plate.

"Feel free to check for yourselves," I said nonchalantly.

Marlow nodded. "I will. In case you missed anything." And in case he could catch me in a lie. "Any leads on the suspected mugger?"

"No." I suppose I should've felt a pang of conscience over lying to him about Newell, but I didn't. The cops would undoubtably waste hours searching for the guy I already had in custody, but the supernatural element of the case meant I had to keep Newell to myself. "What about you?"

"Nothing. We were hoping to get answers from Ms. Doe today."

"Welcome to the club," I muttered.

Throughout our conversation, Hawkins had been silent but restless, shifting her weight from foot to foot. She stood a half-pace farther from me than her partner, out of his sight. I briefly wondered if she was going to bolt to the door. Visibly unhappy about being near me. Was it a natural aversion to a species that routinely killed rogue members of her kind, or was it because she herself was one of those rogues and was afraid of being found out?

"Have you issued a BOLO for her or the van yet?" Marlow broke through my reverie.

"No." I paused, intentionally hesitating, and glanced to either side before continuing in a lower tone. "To be honest, it would be damaging to my case if the BOLO came from the FBI. If you don't mind, I'll let you run point on this one—just keep me in the loop as to what is going on."

Marlow looked suspicious—not often that one agency would willingly give up their rights to be lead on a case. Especially not feds. I could practically see the cogs turning in his head, although he retained his air of quiet thoughtfulness. "Very well. I'll put out the info."

"Here's my card, for when you need to get ahold of me." I produced an official-looking FBI business card from my pocket. The cell number was mine, and the office number even went to the Bay City FBI field office—to the super-secret division, naturally. All legitimate. Of course, at Bay City, the agents would transfer the calls to Protectorate HQ as required. But the caller would still think they were talking to the FBI.

"Very good," Marlow said, pocketing my card. "We'll be in touch."

He shook my hand then walked past me, on the way to the security room to double-check the footage. Hawkins followed him, keeping the width of the hallway between us. I stepped back, giving her even more space. Didn't want to be caught in too close of quarters with the were. I kept an eye on them—well, her—until they rounded the corner. Then I left the hospital, plotting my next move as I returned to my borrowed car. There was only one logical choice—I had to return to HQ, not only to re-interrogate Newell but also to do a little research on the werewolf cop.

CHAPTER 9

Aren't Friends Supposed to be Supportive?

TRAFFIC WAS LIGHT going to the City. Midday, smack dab between rush hours. I mulled over everything as I drove. Marlow was putting out a human BOLO. Good, but not enough. I needed to send one out through the Protectorate network. Might pick up on something that slid past the human authorities. After all, occasionally a witch scried something pertinent to our cases.

And it never hurt to send information to our goblin informants. They loved getting gold, whether it was from selling a stolen unicorn foal or from selling information to us. They weren't picky about the source of their income, as long as it was yellow and shiny. As informants, goblins were surprisingly honest. They knew the value of a trustworthy word, even though in other situations I trust them about as far as I can throw a troll. They'll lie to their widowed grannies if it means a profit.

I went through the main door when I arrived at HQ, instead of the detainee door. Newell could stew for a bit longer while I took care of other business. First I went to the computer lab and logged onto the Protectorate network (yes, we've joined the twenty-first century of technology, despite mostly dealing with ancient creatures). I put out my BOLOs—white van, Jane Doe—despite the fact that I knew they were so generic that they were likely to turn up diddly squat.

After I'd completed my cyber tasks, I logged off and went in search of Scott Avery.

Scott was a nerd, plain and simple. He admitted it—was proud of it, in fact—and anyone who spent more than two seconds in his company knew that to be true. Scott and I had been friends since we were twelve, when he and his family moved here from Wales. Being the new kid, with a funny accent besides, Scott was immediately the target of the resident bully: Jake. My nemesis. So, naturally, I took it upon myself to defend Scott. Not because I was being altruistic, but because by that point, anything Jake hated was a thing that I had to love.

But it turned out that friendship with Scott had come with enormous benefits to me. He didn't let me cheat off his homework (c'mon, what are friends for?), but he did help me out time and time again with the ridiculous amount of knowledge he had stuffed in his enormous brain. I swear, the guy was a walking encyclopedia of random but useful trivia. Currently he was overseeing a lot of the various local supernaturals—kept him busy from the safety of HQ. Scott wasn't exactly suited to be a field agent, but perhaps he would know about my mysterious werewolf policewoman.

The computer lab was next-door to the library—a good starting point for finding Scott—but when I entered, he was nowhere in sight. I headed upstairs, where the archives were kept. The dusty, musty tomes were horrendously boring for someone like me, but for Scott, they were more enthralling than a naked harpy (and, in case you didn't already know, wings plus curves equals bow wow). To be honest, Scott would probably not even notice a naked harpy dancing the Samba in front of him if he had some long-lost scroll to peruse.

I took the stairs up—no elevators in the building. They interfered with the various spells that had been cast to shield HQ. The archives were just as I remembered: dark and stuffy. Between all the ancient manuscripts present, there were clearly several forms of mold growing. Hopefully none were too dangerous to breathe in.

A light gleamed from an end row. I headed toward it like a moth to a flame. Success. The last row of bookshelves contained not only hundreds of ancient manuscripts but also Scott, sitting cross-legged on the floor as he read a crackling, crumbling parchment scroll.

"Scottster," I said softly. Scott jumped, as he's liable to do when startled, which, to be honest, is quite frequently.

He looked up from the document he'd been perusing. "Enzo! What are you doing here?"

"What everyone does in a library," I said. "Looking for information."

A puzzled frown creased Scott's eyes. "Looking for information in a library?" he asked. "Last time I checked, the only things you read were the daily comics and the top five articles in Google News."

"Ha, ha," I replied. "You know it's the top ten."

Scott smiled, frowned, then smiled again. Sarcasm was a difficult language for him to decipher. It was a wonder that we'd remained friends over the years, since sarcasm was one of my mother tongues.

"Have you heard anything about a werewolf working as a police officer in Summerville?" I asked, cutting to the chase.

"You mean Cora Hawkins?"

I stared for a moment. I hadn't expected Scott to have heard much more than rumors, let alone the werewolf's name. "Yes," I finally replied. "What do you know of her?"

"Turned a year ago." Scott eyebrows creased slightly. Irritated or trying to recall information—I couldn't tell which. "Maintained her job as a member of the Summerville Police Department."

"So she was a cop before she was a were?" I interjected.

Scott blinked, pausing for a few seconds as he resettled. "That's what I just said, wasn't it?" he finally asked. "Anyhow, Cora has been an upstanding citizen since then. Flown under the radar, as far as I can tell."

"Any reason why she'd be twitchy when she saw me?"

Scott gave a short bark of laughter. "Seriously, Enzo? Come on, I thought you were supposed to be so much more worldly than me, what with being out in the field instead of stuck in the archives. Any supernatural being is going to have reason for treading carefully when dealing with an unfamiliar Protector. Isn't that what we've been working for all these years?"

"Sure," I said easily. "But something seems off to me."

"Why? Because there is peace instead of fighting? Is it really so hard to believe that a were is just trying to continue a normal life?"

"Yes, it is hard to believe," I retorted. "Weres usually aren't content to remain peaceful. The wolf inside fuels their aggression."

"Don't blame a whole species for the actions of some members."

"Literally every single werewolf I've ever encountered has tried to kill me."

"Because you were hunting them!"

"I was only hunting them because they'd killed someone—or many someones."

Scott threw up his hands and made a frustrated noise. "Again, you've only encountered aggressive weres. That doesn't mean that there aren't peaceful ones out there."

"I'll believe it when I see it."

"Maybe you already have seen it."

"Doubtful."

"Guilty until proven innocent, eh?"

"In the case of werewolves, yes."

"Jeez, Enzo, I know you have some personal reasons to distrust werewolves, but still, how did you get so prejudiced?"

I mentally skipped past the incident Scott referenced. Didn't want to think about it. Not right now. Instead, focus on the less horrific cases. "Sixteen wolf hunts," I snapped. "One where a woman killed her own children. You ever seen what a wolf can do to a six-year-old? I have."

We were interrupted at that moment by a boy dressed in an Academy uniform. "Excuse me, Mr. Avery, but Mr. Williams sent me to find you. He's still waiting on that record of the 1507 Goblin War."

A look of guilt and embarrassment crossed Scott's face. "Tell him I'll be there right away."

As the boy left, Scott carefully rolled up the scroll he still held. "Forgot I was supposed to take this to Williams. I only started reading to make sure it was the right one. Guess I got caught up in it." He slid the rolled document back into its protective tube. "See you later, Enzo."

I followed at a more leisurely pace as he scurried off down the aisle. At the end, he turned around for one last parting shot. "Give the werewolf a chance! Who knows, you might actually make a new friend."

He was gone before waiting to hear my response. "Fat chance of that," I scoffed anyway. How could a Protector be friends with a killer?

CHAPTER 10

BANSHEE'S WAILS AND MUGGER FAILS

AFTER MY FRUSTRATING and pointless talk with Scott, I decided to take another crack at Newell. Maybe he would finally give me some information. So down the long, long staircase to the dungeon I went.

Geoff Durham was on duty at the guard-slash-sign-in desk. He was a Protector in his fifties. Used to be an active-duty field agent, but after a hydra bit his arm off, he decided to transfer to a job with less life-threatening action. He regrew his arm, of course (what's the use of being a shapeshifter if you can't shift away pesky wounds?) but it took over a week of painful recovery for his digits to all function properly again. His two young daughters helped seal the decision to go off field duty, I think. Not because he suddenly worried that he'd die and leave them fatherless, but because they were quite vocal about how revolting his regrowing arm was. I'll admit, I was on their side—for a couple days, it looked like Geoff had a giant earthworm attached to his shoulder. Disgusting.

"You brought in a loud one, Enzo," Geoff said by way of greeting.

"He say anything good?" I asked.

"Just whined about everything every time I made my rounds. Too noisy. Bed too hard. Food inedible. Not that I can blame him on the last bit. Prisoners' food is crap. Kept asking for a lawyer, even though I told him fat chance."

"Nothing about a sprite or a dagger?"

"A sprite? Hell, Enzo, what are you doing going after one of them? Pacifistic naturalists, the lot."

"Not this one," I replied. "There's something else going on here."

"Well, best of luck figuring it out. Let me know what you find."

"Sure," I said absently, already on my way to take Newell out of his cell.

Peter Newell didn't look like the same healthy middle-aged man I'd thrown in the dungeon the night before. His eyes were bloodshot, ringed by dark circles. "This is torture!" he cried out when he saw me approach. "It's unconstitutional!"

As if to emphasize his words, our captive banshee let out a wail. I stuffed my fingers in my ears. "Don't like your accommodations?" I yelled over the screeching. "I'm here to give you another chance to get out of this hellhole."

"Bleep you!" Newell responded.

No, he didn't actually say the word "bleep." There are just some lines that I draw when recording or translating certain messages. Insert your favorite curse word here (or, if you don't have a favorite, read that line as "darn you").

I slid open the cell door, grabbed Newell as he tried to make a futile run for freedom, and slapped another pair of magi-cuffs on his wrists. "Time for round two," I growled, dragging him toward the dungeon entrance.

Back to the interrogation chamber. As I pulled Newell down the hallway, Councilor Ainsley appeared. Was she keeping track of everything I did? Dammit. Should've kept Newell away from HQ. Could've strung him up over a pit of alligators or something. Fear is a great motivator. But laws sure can be hinderances when trying to get information from an obstinate suspect.

"Thornton," Ainsley greeted me with a short nod. "Find out anything else yet?"

Why was she asking me in front of the suspect? Newell would know he had the upper hand if he found out that Jane Doe escaped. A lot of my leverage would disappear.

"A few interesting bits," I replied vaguely. "I'll tell you later."

"I'll be watching your interview again," Ainsley replied, heading toward the door to observation.

Of course she would. Just one more needless complication in my life. I yanked Newell's arm with more force than necessary—receiving a small cry of protest in response—and went back into the interrogation room.

I took Newell's cuffs off once the door was closed. "Have a seat," I ordered.

Newell complied. "I want a lawyer."

"And I want to make out with Scarlett Johansson. Unfortunately, neither of us is going to get what we want." I paused. "I could get you a cell in solitary. Out of earshot of the banshee."

Temptation was clear in Newell's bloodshot eyes. "And a reduction of my sentence."

I shrugged. "I'll see what I can do."

"I demand—"

"No, Mr. Newell, you *demand* nothing. This is the best offer you are going to get from me. Now, tell me who the sprite is, or I will throw you back into the dungeons and leave you to rot."

Newell sat silently, a stubborn expression on his face.

"That's it." I stood and grabbed Newell. As I began putting the cuffs back on, he finally cracked.

"Wait, wait, I'll tell you! Just keep me away from that stupid banshee."

I rolled my eyes behind Newell's back. Classic, the bad guy folding when I called his bluff. So classic that every cop show out there had a scene just like this in practically every episode. The only difference was there weren't any banshees involved in the TV shows, at least to my knowledge. Maybe in a *Supernatural* episode or something. I don't know. Don't keep track of those types of shows—too much like real life, except riddled with laughable errors.

We returned to our seats. Newell's shoulders were slumped in defeat. "The sprite's name is Finian. He approached me with a business proposition. He wanted me to sell some potions for him."

"Why would he come to you for that?" I prompted.

"I'm a drug dealer."

I'll admit, that took me by surprise. I looked Newell up and down. Clean-cut (well, he had been clean-cut before spending the night in the slammer), middle-aged white guy in a polo shirt and jeans. Looked more like a used car dealer than a drug dealer.

"You?" I asked skeptically.

"I teach at Summer High. English. Some of my students are my clients."

Disgust filled me, even as the pieces of the puzzle fell into place. Summer High was the roughest of the high schools in Summerville. A Mercedes was out of a teacher's salary. Would've been easy to make a little money on the side. Teachers are rarely suspected of doing such a thing, despite the popularity of *Breaking Bad*.

"Tell me everything."

Slowly, bit by bit, Newell laid everything out. He'd become a teacher because he knew how strong tenure was—nearly impossible to fire a teacher once they'd achieved that holy grail. But a teacher's salary wasn't exactly lucrative, and he needed an extra source of income. Pot had been his constant companion in college, and it was an easy step to start dealing once he realized how much money could be made by providing it to students.

"It's not like marijuana is that bad of a drug anyways," Newell said. "It's not like I was dealing crack or something."

But his herbaceous exploits attracted the attention of the nature-attuned sprite, Finian, who was looking to make a profit off the human population that was overwhelming his native habitat. When in Rome, sell magical hashish to the Romans.

"It was just some innocent potions. Help them focus during exams. Give them a little extra strength on the football field. Make their crush interested in them. No harm done. I didn't think it was that big of a deal."

Newell's story made sense—mostly. There were still a few important unanswered questions. Including the big dial M for mugging.

"What about the woman you knifed?"

Newell looked ashamed. "She was Finian's partner. She was the one who brought the potions to me."

"And so you stabbed her for it?" I asked skeptically.

"She started blackmailing me, demanding a bigger cut. Threatened to go to the school board and tell them about the weed I was selling students. Would've ruined me."

"And that's why you attacked her? To protect yourself?"

"No!" Newell shook his head vigorously. "Well, yes, it was to protect myself. But she attacked me first! I was just defending myself."

I had to admit, the story did correspond with what I'd overheard between him and Finian. I still needed to confirm some details, but everything seemed to line up. Newell was a first-class SOB, but in a mundane way, not a magical one. The supernatural was apparently just a sideline gig for him. If I was lucky, I might be able to turn him over to the human authorities and wash my hands of him. Focus on the supernatural target instead.

"Why would a sprite have a human partner besides you?" I asked. "Was she another dealer?"

Newell looked surprised. "You don't know? She's the one who made the potions for him. She's a witch."

CHAPTER 11

Does She Weigh Less Than A Duck?

A WITCH. THAT certainly was an unexpected development. Witches can be incredibly difficult opponents—or seriously easy, depending on their level of education. The trick was figuring out how strong and talented of a witch I was up against.

Not all witches are bad. In fact, witches are invaluable to us. They spell many of the artifacts we use on a daily basis—my tracker device, for one—and brew the ever-useful potions and powders in our arsenal. But a rogue witch could be quite a tricky opponent indeed. Not like I could just tie her to a stake and burn her or drown her in a ducking pond.

The revelation that Jane Doe was a witch did clear up my confusion about the hospital security footage. She must've cast a small misdirection or misperception spell to keep the hospital staff from noticing the severely wounded patient staggering to the exit. It also explained why Finian had said that she had an antidote to the magic knife. Speaking of which . . .

"What was the knife you used to stab her?" I asked.

Newell grimaced. "I'm not sure, exactly. Finian had it. I thought it looked interesting, with all the runes etched on the blade. When I asked him about it, he said it was a mortal blade—the smallest nick would kill its victim within a week. Sounded valuable, so when Finian wasn't looking, I stole it."

"And he didn't notice it was missing?"

"Apparently not. It was in a crate with a bunch of other objects."

"What sorts of other objects?"

"I dunno. Weird-looking amulets and stuff. Didn't know what any of it did, so I left it alone."

Was Newell really as dumb as he seemed, or was he just pretending? I continued questioning, but apparently he was going with the old "that's my story and I'm sticking to it." I wasn't able to catch him in any lies or inconsistencies. Bugger even claimed the crate had been in the dilapidated apartment—gone by the time I arrived, of course.

"Tell me more about the witch," I finally said. "What's her name?"

"Jane Doe. Or, at least that's what she said her name was. I figured it was a cover."

Dammit. Couldn't catch a break. Wish I'd gotten at least a better name.

"What types of things could she do?"

Newell looked at me as if I'd grown an extra head. "She was a witch. Isn't that enough? She told me she'd turn me into a newt if I got on her bad side. I avoided her as much as possible. Just took the goods, gave her the money, and got the hell away."

Able to transfigure someone into something else. Middle-level magic. If she'd told the truth to Newell, she wasn't a novice, at least. And that was the type of transformation that didn't just "get better" over time.

"Did you see her perform any witchcraft, or was it all just talk?"

Newell looked down with a shudder. "She . . . she cast some sort of spell on me once. Felt like getting kicked in the nards by a horse or something. Not something I'd ever want to experience again."

I repressed a sympathetic wince. "Why did she do that?"

"I wanted more money. Felt I was getting shortchanged, since I was the one taking all the risks."

"And yet you still managed to stab her? How the hell did that happen?"

"I think that knife had some sort of protective properties. She shot lightning at me, but it split to either side, like there was a force field around me or something. It was like nothing I've ever seen before. Scared the piss out of me."

Crap. I really needed to get ahold of that weapon, to see what it could do. It was exactly the sort of artifact that we didn't want to see in enemy hands. It needed to be confiscated and locked up in our vault. And Jane Doe's ability to conjure electricity wasn't something to be scoffed at either. I wasn't going to be able to take this witch on alone, despite how much my pride hurt to admit it.

It seemed to me like Newell was playing out his usefulness—he'd only been on the side of whatever the hell was going on, not the center of the action. I wanted the sprite and the witch, not their lame human counterpart.

"Are you willing to write a confession about attempting to murder Jane Doe?" I asked.

"Attempted murder? Bleep that," was Newell's response (see earlier comment about replacing the "bleep").

"It's either attempted murder and a human jail sentence—life with a possibility of parole—or whatever my people decide to charge you for here. Beginning with attempted murder with a mortal blade. Followed by collusion with a sprite and the selling of magical potions to humans. I can guarantee that there will be no parole offered to you. Just a lifelong sentence with whatever other prisoners we have—including our current banshee representative."

A long moment of hesitation, followed by, "I'll take human prison." Surprise, surprise. "What do you need from me?"

"Just write a confession." I slid a pad of paper and a pen to him. "A thoroughly mundane confession, mind you. Then I'll see about transferring custody."

Newell began scribbling on the paper I'd given him. Game, set, and match. Or so I thought.

CHAPTER 12

Not My Problem Anymore

I HAD DECIDED that Newell wasn't worth wasting Protectorate resources on detaining. Room, board, medical care, et cetera, can add up in a hurry when it comes to housing convicts. Besides, by Protectorate laws, he was only guilty of selling a few minor potions and being in possession of a magical artifact—the dagger, which I couldn't even prove was magical, since the sprite Finian had absconded with it. Not that I was going to tell Newell that his sentence would be light if administered by us. Let him think that I had the power to lock him up and throw away the key.

Believe it or not, my trump card—the attempted murder—wasn't even punishable by our laws, despite the use of a magical blade, since it was human-on-human (witches are simply humans with the knowledge of how to use magic) violence. AKA "their problem."

So it was time to make it their problem. I stepped out of the interrogation room while Newell was writing his confession. Ainsley left observation as soon as I'd made it to the hallway. "See to it that the transport of the suspect goes by the books," she ordered, not waiting for my reply before turning and striding off.

"Yes, ma'am," I said to her retreating back, then fished Marlow's card out of my wallet and punched in his number.

Only one ring before, "Detective Marlow here," came through on the line. Guy was punctual.

"Detective Marlow, this is Agent Thornton."

"Agent Thornton, what can I do for you?" All formalities observed from both parties.

"I have your mugger in custody. Man by the name of Peter Newell."

A pause. "You sure he's the right guy?"

"Yes. Evidence plus a confession all point to him. I'd like to turn over custody to you."

"Why?"

Again, not expecting cooperation or sharing between agencies. Were human law enforcement agents really that competitive? Couldn't they see that they could get so much more accomplished by working together? Okay, granted, I hadn't exactly been forthright or completely honest with Marlow, but that was a completely different situation.

Time for another lie. "To be honest with you, Newell is just a petty criminal. Not worth the FBI's time."

"What about his connection to your case?"

"Nothing significant. Found out what I needed to know."

"So you already interrogated him?"

"Yes."

"I'll need a transcript of that."

"No can do. Need to know. Classified."

I could practically feel Marlow's annoyance in the silence on the line.

"I spoke to the agency less than an hour ago. They didn't mention anything about you having a suspect in custody."

So, Marlow did his homework and checked to make sure my story of being an agent panned out. Guy was thorough. A bit of a pity that I'd have to continue to lie to him.

"Compartmentalized intel," I said easily. "Phone guys don't have the same clearance as the field agents."

Another irritated silence.

"If it's any consolation," I continued. "I can give you his written confession. Everything you need to lock him up for a long time."

A sigh. "Better than nothing, I suppose. Should I come pick him up from the FBI office?"

"No need." Not to mention the FBI agents would have no idea who he was talking about. "I'll bring him by your station. Be there in about an hour."

"I'll be here." *Click*. Dammit—a bit of a power play to be the first to hang up.

I returned to the interrogation room, where Newell was putting the finishing touches on his written confession. Once he'd signed, I picked up the paper and skimmed over it. Good—he'd admitted all the mundane crimes, while leaving any hint of magical activity out.

I gave him a hard stare. "I'm taking you to the police station now. Under no circumstances will you mention anything about magical or supernatural activities, species, or artifacts. Any attempt to do so, and I'll transport you back here and lock you up next to the banshee for the rest of your miserable life."

Newell looked sufficiently scared to not say a word, but threats and promises weren't enough to meet Protectorate security protocols. I took a small container of chewable tablets out of an inner pocket and gave him one.

"What's this?" he asked apprehensively, staring at the tiny orange pill in his palm as if it were a cobra.

"It's called tongue-tie," I said. "It will prevent you from speaking—or writing, drawing, communicating in any form—anything to do with the supernatural. Now take it."

Thankfully, Newell popped the tablet into his mouth and vigorously chewed without a fuss.

We didn't have any pills to alter or delete memories—the human brain is much too complex and delicate for that—but preventing communication was the next best thing. I could've possibly tried using a compulsion device to obscure memories, but there was an off-chance I'd need to question him again, and besides, he'd been involved in the supernatural for a while now. It would be easy for a stray memory or two to sneak past a compulsive block.

Once Newell had swallowed—and I checked his mouth, to make sure he wasn't faking—I cuffed him and led him outside to his Mercedes.

"What are you doing with my car?" he whined as I pushed him into the child-locked backseat.

"Seemed fitting to chauffeur you in it." I smirked. "Besides, you got any plans for it? Not like you're free for a road trip."

"But it's mine. You can't keep it."

"Yeah, well, I'll leave it at the police station when I drop you off. Their problem then. Won't need it after that anyway."

Newell sulked in the back seat throughout the hour-long journey back to Summerville. I ignored him, blasting the local rock station to make the drive go by faster. At least he was quiet and didn't complain about my music choice.

Finally I pulled up in front of the Summerville Police Department. Before I got out, I decided to give Newell one last run-down.

"Now, what's your story?"

"I was strapped for cash. Saw a woman who looked rich alone in an alley. Tried to mug her, but she fought back. Accidentally stabbed her in the fight."

"And?"

"And that's it. She was just some random woman. Not a—" Newell's voice suddenly choked off. "A—"

I grinned as Newell struggled to speak. The tongue-tie was doing its job.

"What is Harry Potter?" I asked. "Muggle or wizard?"

"A wizard." Newell's face in the rearview mirror looked shocked. "Why could I answer that but not say Jane Doe is a—" A strangled squawk ended his sentence.

"Fiction versus truth," I said. "The tongue-tie just keeps you from revealing the true supernatural world."

Time to take Newell in. He came without protest, although I still kept my hand wrapped around one of his arms, just in case he decided to stupidly make a run for it. In an unexpected show of wisdom, he meekly walked into the station.

"Agent Enzo Thornton," I announced to the front desk officer. "Here with a detainee for Detective Marlow."

The officer, a Filipino woman in her early thirties, gave me an evaluating stare as she picked up her desk phone and punched an extension. Brief conversation, a short wait, and then Marlow entered through the door to the squad room.

"Agent Thornton." He gave a brief nod.

"Detective Marlow." I echoed the greeting. "This is Peter Newell. He's confessed to mugging Jane Doe."

And with that simple sentence, I condemned myself to the seemingly endless protocols of transferring custody of a suspect. You'd think it would be easy, but you'd be wrong. Very, very wrong.

After an eternity of paperwork, I was free to go. As promised, I left Newell's car at the station and grabbed an Uber home instead. Damn, wish I could've kept that sweet ride. Back to being carless.

Once in the comfort of my apartment, my stomach adamantly let me know that I hadn't eaten since breakfast pizza. Since a rummage through the fridge proved fruitless—well, technically not, since I had a couple of oranges in the bottom drawer—I decided to order Chinese takeout. Quick, cheap, and easy—there's even an app for it. Didn't even have to make a phone call, and thirty minutes later my egg foo young, eggplant pork, and steamed rice arrived hot and fresh.

I'd been flipping through channels while I waited for the food to arrive, finally settling on a *Big Bang Theory* rerun. Always good for a laugh, and the main characters reminded me of Scott a bit.

But tonight I couldn't stay focused as the guys quibbled over whether Batman or Superman would win in a fight. My mind kept jumping back to Finian. Needed to catch that bastard. Of course, by now he could've disappeared into the depths of the nearby canals or be looking for another human contact to sell potions for him. No way to know for sure.

It might make my job easier if I found another sprite to question, but sprites of all sorts are notoriously reclusive. I'd probably have no more luck finding an innocent sprite than the one I was looking for. And it wasn't like I could call in any underwater reinforcements—besides water sprites, merpeople are the only sentient aquatic species in North America, and mers are a strictly saltwater race.

I finally decided to go back to HQ and do some more research on sprites. They were generally peaceful species—i.e. ones I didn't have to deal with much—so I didn't know much about them other than the basic facts. Time to do research. Ugh. Maybe Scott would be able to help out. He knew the contents of the library better than he knew the names of his cousins. And he only had four cousins.

The other thing I needed to look up was our registry of witches. It's not a mandatory signup list, but we do try to keep track of any magical humans around. Might be able to find a clue to the identity of the mysterious Jane Doe.

Resigned to a day devoted to research, I went to bed early. At least I'd gotten one bad guy off the streets, even if it was just a human. It was a start.

CHAPTER 13

Spoke Too Soon

PUBLIC TRANSPORTATION. I'D rather get in a wrestling match with a Yeti than deal with the nightmare of public transport, but the loss of my temporary wheels meant that I had to resign myself to a train car packed full of tired, grumpy humans on their way to tedious jobs. At least it was a train, not a bus. Didn't have to deal with all the traffic that was visible through the train windows, clogging up the interstate on the way to Bay City.

I willfully ignored the suspiciously colored stain on the last remaining seat when I boarded. Not old urine, not old urine, I told myself. On second thought, considering this was public transportation, old urine might not be the worst bodily fluid present. Thankfully the seat was dry and I couldn't pick up any odors other than the seriously overpowering aftershave on the guy next to me. No wonder the seat was empty. Apparently he didn't know the meaning of the word moderation. More is not always better.

An hour and a half later, my nostrils numb and destroyed by the oppressive scent next to me, I gratefully joined the throng of people pushing their way out through the train doors and up the escalators to the streets above. Compared to the train ride, the scent of exhaust and cigarette smoke permeating the sidewalks was a refreshing breath of fresh air.

A brisk five-minute walk brought me to the doorstep of HQ. I went around the cathedral to the Protectorate building, straight to the main library entrance. It was a door I'd only used a handful of times in my life.

But before I could begin my search for Scott, I ran into a pleasant surprise. Zoanna. What fortunate timing. Okay, maybe it was an exaggeration to say I ran into her, but she was briefly visible before disappearing into a row of books.

"Hey! Zoanna!" I called at a loud whisper. I thought I'd been quiet, but I still received a "Shhh" from the librarian sitting behind her central desk. I ignored the reprimand and hurried in the direction Zoanna had gone.

She was perusing the shelves halfway down the row, biting her lower lip in thought. Her dark hair was pulled back in a ponytail, and she wore jeans and a form-fitting green t-shirt.

It's funny how the significance of physical looks changes when members of a species can vary their appearance at will. Anyone and everyone could be supermodel gorgeous if they so desired. But Zoanna had a modest appearance—she wasn't the type to turn guys' heads as she walked down the street. No makeup on her smooth golden-bronze skin, a small bosom (not that I looked), a body shape more straight than curvy, and warm brown eyes, not a bright, contrasting green or blue like she could've had. I thought she was beautiful.

"Hi, Enzo," Zoanna said quietly when she saw me. "How's it going?"

"Not bad." No need to recount all my sprite and witching woes. "I heard you went to Scotland. How was that?"

"Busy," Zoanna said with a small laugh. I love her laugh. "Nessie IV decided to be social. Popped up right next to a tourist boat and posed for pictures. As the Scots say, it was a bloody nightmare. Thank God the British Protectors were able to intercept the boat and delete all the pictures before they went online."

"So why were you called in?" I asked. "No offense, but don't different regions usually keep things in-house?"

Zoanna rolled her eyes. A bit sassy, as always. I liked that.

"C'mon, Enzo, you know I specialized in aquatic beings. Made sense for me to check out a kelpie. Not to mention all the other beauties of the Scottish Highlands. Have you ever been?"

"No need, so far."

"It's not about *need*—it's something everyone should experience at least once in their life."

"Speaking of aquatic beings," I said, not so subtly changing the topic of conversation. "What do you know about water sprites?"

"Solitary, vain, and mostly peaceful," Zoanna said. "But formidable opponents when they've set their minds on something. Why do you ask?"

"I'm trying to track down a sprite that's selling potions to humans."

Zoanna winced. "Good luck with that. Sprites are tricky, and they're good at covering their tracks."

"Tell me something I don't know," I muttered.

"Sprites are vulnerable just under their gills."

"What?" Where did that come from?

"It's something you don't know, correct?"

Dammit. She had me there.

My cell phone rang, cutting into our conversation. I glanced at the screen, intending to send the call to voicemail, but saw that the caller ID said, "FBI Reroute."

"Crap," I muttered. What perfectly inconvenient timing. "Sorry, Zoanna, I need to take this."

"Later, Enzo."

I regretfully watched her leave as I answered the call. "Agent Thornton speaking."

"This is Officer Cora Hawkins."

Seriously? My first good conversation with Zoanna in months was being interrupted by a werewolf? Could my day get any worse?

Apparently it could.

"Peter Newell has escaped," Hawkins said.

CHAPTER 14

CALL TO MANY ARMS

"I—ER—WHAT?" I fumbled for words, my brain struggling to find traction after my thoughts being knocked so completely off track. "How did he escape?"

"Nobody here is sure, but I know he used magic."

"How?"

"You screwed up. You should've realized he's a warlock."

I felt like I'd swallowed a boulder. How could I have missed such a key detail? I hadn't even considered running tests on Newell—I was too caught up with finding the witch Jane Doe and the sprite Finian to consider that Newell might be a magic user too. He'd seemed so ordinary, so stupidly human. But I'd been the idiot for underestimating him.

Time for damage control. I needed to know if any humans had witnessed any magical activity, and cover it up if they did. This investigation was turning into a nightmare for me.

"What happened? Any witnesses? How do you know it was magic?"

"Obviously magic by the lack of evidence." Thank God. No evidence to cover up. "All the security footage was wiped. Even Newell's booking records disappeared. The locks on his cell and the door out of the jail were unlocked, no signs of tampering. The rest of the police think it's an inside job, but the cops on duty that night have spotless records. Only plausibility in my mind is that Newell's a warlock."

"I agree." I said the words with extreme reluctance, still trying to come to terms with my massive blunder. A warlock in custody, and I'd blithely handed him over to human police.

"How did you miss that? It's not exactly a minor detail."

"Same way you did," I said. "Warlocks are human, so it isn't immediately obvious that they have supernatural abilities. Their magic is external, not internal."

"But you knew what I was, and I recognized you. And I was born human."

"I'm not human, even though I look it. And your supernatural abilities are internal, even if they aren't innate. The werewolf curse became a part of you when you were bitten. But warlocks get their magic from purely external sources."

A pause while Hawkins apparently digested the information. "What's your plan?" she finally asked.

I had no plan, but I didn't want to admit it. One thing though—I needed to report this. And I needed to get backup. This case had too many supernatural elements for one Protector to handle alone. And I still didn't have a clue as to what was actually going on.

"I'll get back to you," I said vaguely. "I need to tie up some things here first."

"But—"

"Later." *Click.*

I hurried in the direction Zoanna had gone—maybe she'd be willing to partner up with me. Silver lining in the thunderheads.

Before I could find her, an alarm sounded, followed by a message on the intercom: "All available Protectors report to the briefing room. Immediately."

Shit. Something big must be going down. The alarm and call to action wasn't unheard of—in my ten years of service, I'd heard it at least a dozen times—but it was rare, and it was bad. It could mean anything from a rabid sasquatch on a rampage in a small Washington town to a rogue dragon starting wildfires in the Sierra Nevada mountains. No guesses what it was this time. If Newell was causing magical mayhem I'd get into a world of trouble. But if I could quietly recapture him, there shouldn't be serious repercussions for me. I think. I hope.

I filed into the briefing room after two older Protectors. The room was fairly empty, only twenty or so people inside. It had stadium seating for over a hundred, with rows of seats facing a projector screen that dominated the far wall. Not surprising that there were so many empty seats, since most Protectors were assigned out in the field, managing and overseeing various territories. Spotting Zoanna seated in the front row, I quickly claimed the chair next to her, even though I was generally a back-of-the-class type of guy. Easier to stay out of trouble there.

"What's going on?" I asked. "Heard anything?"

Zoanna's response was cut short by Counselor Ainsley striding to the front of the room. All the low chatter immediately silenced.

"There's been a kraken sighting less than twenty miles off the coast of Santa Cruz," Ainsley said with no preamble.

Shit. That meant Zoanna was sure to be involved, what with her specialty in aquatic beings. So much for my hope that she'd be able to provide backup with my whole messy situation. I refocused on the situation at hand as Ainsley continued the briefing.

"So far, one human vessel is involved. A fishing boat, the *Sea Demon*"—apparently Ainsley didn't see the irony in this name, since she continued without a pause while I stifled my laughter—"has been capsized by the kraken. We were able to intercept its distress call and prevent the Coast Guard from responding. A team of merpeople is on the way to assist. Our mission is to rescue any human survivors and relocate the kraken. If necessary, we will use lethal force. However, as krakens are endangered, it is preferable to use non-fatal measures."

The way she said it, you'd almost think that krakens were easy to kill. But with a mantle a hundred yards long and tentacles five times that length, krakens were decidedly on the "hard to even piss off, let alone kill" list. It was definitely an all-hands-on-deck situation.

"Everyone not involved in critical work will assist with the kraken relocation. Is there anyone here unable to help?" Ainsley finished.

I was torn—I wanted to help with the kraken, not just because I'd be working with Zoanna, but I needed to deal with the Newell situation ASAP. Reluctantly, I raised my hand. I was the only one.

"Thornton?" Ainsley asked.

"May I speak to you in private, Councilor?" No need to confess my blunder in front of the rest of the Protectors present. Especially not Zoanna, now that there was no chance of her coming on board my investigation.

"Thornton, I don't have time for dramatics. Say what you need to now, or remain silent."

So much for that idea. "Counselor, I just found out that Peter Newell escaped from human custody. There is evidence that he is, in fact, a warlock. I believe it is critical to pursue him with no delay."

"Why didn't you mention this before?" Ainsley asked sharply.

"I just found out, Counselor. I was on my way to report it when the call to arms sounded."

Ainsley gave a curt nod. "Very well. Avery, you will assist Thornton in his capture of the warlock."

"What?" came Scott's startled response from the back of the room. As far as I knew, it was his first field assignment.

"All Protectors are needed to deal with the kraken, but I can't send one of us against a warlock alone. You are the logical choice for backup. Everyone else, prepare to move out!"

The commotion of everyone chattering as they left the room drowned out Scott's stuttered protests.

"Good luck, Zoanna," I said as she hurriedly rose.

She shot me half a smile. "You too, Enzo. Don't get cursed into oblivion."

I grinned. "Well, if I do get hexed, I'll have you to kiss me and break the spell."

Zoanna rolled her eyes, as I'd intended. "You'd better hope that's not your cure. You'll be a long time waiting."

"But some things are worth waiting for." I winked to take the seriousness out of my words, although in truth, they were more heartfelt than I cared to admit, even to myself.

Scott was suddenly at my side. "Enzo, what the hell did you get me into? I'm no field agent!"

"Don't fret, Scottster," I said. "Just a little routine investigation and arresting. Nothing you can't handle." White lie combined with encouragement. Hopefully a formula for success.

CHAPTER 15

Witches and Warlocks and Sprites, Oh My!

I STARTED FILLING Scott in on everything that had happened so far as the room emptied around us. Scott's eyes got wider with every word I spoke.

"A sprite, a witch, and a warlock?" Scott finally asked. "What's the plan?"

"There isn't one," I confessed, then tacked on a "yet" when Scott looked as if he was going to start panicking.

"Enzo, I'm a researcher, not a field operative. I'll be totally useless to you."

"Good thing we need to start with some research," I said. "I need to find out anything about any water sprites living in the canals around Summerville. Maybe even the Blue Lagoon or Lake Fruitina. Plus see if there are any records for magic users in Summerville. I was actually on my way to find you when the alarm sounded. This is right up your alley."

Scott took a deep breath and ran a hand through his ginger hair. "Okay, let's start in Records."

"Lead the way."

I mentally steeled myself against a long, tedious, pointless day. After hours upon hours of poring through dusty books, we had no more useful information than when we started. Although I did learn that Summerville had been the seat of power for the infamous conjurer Henrietta Henderson a little over a hundred years ago. Not that that info helped us any. So much for the library being a comprehensive record of the known supernatural world.

Time to switch tactics—even Scott had to admit that his beloved books didn't have the answers this time. "Maybe we should go to Summerville and do some investigating there," he said as he closed yet another leather-bound tome with a thunk. "Most of this is past records. Nothing to do with the present."

I let out yet another yawn. "Anything to get me out of this damn Records room."

I went to shelve the book I'd been perusing. "Careful!" Scott scolded, upset over my rough handling of the old book, but I'd already shoved the book back into its slot, and I didn't care.

"Let's head to Summerville. Pack a bag. You can stay with me until we figure this out."

Scott gave me a look like a kicked puppy as he went to gather some clothes for a multi-night visit. I didn't take it personally; I knew he was upset about leaving his routines and precious library, not sad to be forced to stay with me.

The train ride back to Summerville was mostly quiet. The only time we broke the silence was when Scott would begin a not-safe-for-public question. Damn. No wonder he'd never passed the tests to be a field agent.

"So, Enzo, where was the last time you saw the sp—"

"—Spectacled bear? Saw one in the Bay City Zoo a couple of months ago."

A few minutes later. "Have you had any encounters with witches before?"

"Only on Halloween. Dressed in black, cute caldrons or pumpkins for candy, usually carrying a broomstick."

"What about the warlock?"

"Aren't they usually called wizards? You know, Harry Potter and all that?"

Between the redirected conversation and the glares I shot his way, Scott eventually got the message to shut up about anything supernatural while we were on the train ride. Seriously, how does one spend so much time in our culture and not pick up on some basic security details?

We made it to Summerville at last. Only a half-hour walk from the train station to my apartment. One bedroom. Not suitable for guests that weren't of the female persuasion. Fortunately an REI store wasn't too far out of the way, and we were able to stop by and pick up a blow-up mattress and sleeping bag for Scott.

Once we'd obtained the necessities and arrived at my apartment, we were faced with the same conundrum of the night before—no food. I quickly ordered a pizza from the local delivery joint. Scott was surprised.

"I've never ordered takeout," he announced.

"Seriously?" I couldn't believe it.

"No point. Just got my meals from the cafeteria. All paid for."

I shuddered as I recalled that institutional food. It was the mark of a true non-foodie to be able to live on that crap. Even fast-food cheeseburgers were more appealing. Maybe Scott could tolerate it better because he was from the UK—they don't exactly have a reputation for five-star cuisine in the British Isles.

Scott and I hashed out a few more details of our mission as we ate. I was mostly interested in what he knew about the werewolf Hawkins—I hadn't had a chance to quiz him before.

"How do you know her?"

"Met Cora a little under a year ago," Scott said between bites of Hawaiian pizza (yes, pineapple is a valid topping). "She'd just gone through her first change. She was at HQ, trying to come to terms with what happened and what her future would bring."

"Why was she at HQ?" I asked. "Isn't that the type of thing that a new were's pack helps them with?"

"Generally, yes, but Cora didn't want anything to do with the pack that turned her. Blamed them for ruining her life."

"She was turned against her will?" That was a surprise—most new werewolves willingly underwent the bite that transferred the curse. And if a wolf bit an unsuspecting victim, our kind came in to administer justice. "Why didn't I hear anything about it? I don't remember any sort of wolf hunt a year ago."

"There wasn't one," Scott said. "It was deemed an accident. No need for punishment."

"But still, a wolf so careless as to be near a human during the full moon—"

"Wasn't their fault," Scott interrupted. "Cora and her ex crossed the fence into one of the wolf sanctuaries. Pack had no idea any humans were on their land before they shifted. When the pack found them—" He grimaced. "She's lucky to be alive."

We ate pizza in silence for a few minutes as I mulled over what this new information meant. "So what did you have to do with her?" I finally asked.

"Not much—just told her that it was possible for life to go on mostly as usual. Helped her figure out a full-moon sanctuary."

"You mean she doesn't go to the Summerville Werewolf Sanctuary?" Horror colored my voice. "Jeez, Scott, don't you realize how dangerous that is?"

"Haven't you been listening to anything I said? She doesn't want anything to do with the pack. So she goes to Headquarters instead."

"What?"

"I got permission for her to turn in one of the cells. After all, they were designed to contain werewolves, among everything else."

It made sense—but was also surprising. Who in their right mind would prefer to be locked in a six-by-eight concrete cell instead of running free on a hundred, fenced acres?

"So what's the plan for finding Newell?" Scott asked, breaking my reverie.

I winced. Crap. Still needed to figure that out—if only I hadn't turned Newell over to the human police. Now I needed to make sure that all evidence of any supernatural activity was kept off police radar (pun intended). And recapture the bugger. If only I'd realized he was a warlock when I'd questioned him—or at least spent more time collecting information about him. I'd been too focused on the witch, Jane Doe. Just what Newell intended by telling me about her. And I'd taken the bait—hook, line, and sinker.

"I don't know," I admitted.

"We could ask Cora for help," Scott said.

"Do you have any idea how far that goes against protocols?" I snapped.

Scott looked shocked at my outburst. "But, Enzo, you're the one who's always saying protocols are too restrictive."

"In most cases, sure, but to add a werewolf to a Protectorate investigation? Not a good idea."

"But the humans are already involved—it might be helpful to have supernatural backup."

I shook my head in denial of the sense of Scott's suggestion. This mess was too tangled as it was. It would only get worse with a werewolf thrown in the mix. I needed to try and reduce outside involvement on this case, not add more complications. Especially werewolf complications.

CHAPTER 16

What Cops Hate More Than a Criminal

BY THE FOLLOWING morning, I still hadn't decided how to handle the police involvement with Newell. Besides not wanting to work with werewolf Officer Hawkins, I really didn't want to tell Detective Marlow about the existence of the supernatural—the paperwork involved in giving a human super-secret clearance caused a headache equivalent to a hangover, brain-freeze, and sucker punch all rolled into one horrendous hit. Not worth it. Plus, I knew next to nothing about him, so I couldn't even say if he would be a good candidate for super-secret clearance.

But I'd stupidly gotten the human police involved by turning Newell over to them, and now I needed to fix the problem I'd created. As quickly and secretly as possible.

First things first, though—clothes.

"You don't have a suit?" I asked Scott incredulously.

He gave me a mirrored look. "No. Why would I need a suit?"

"To pass as an FBI agent." A more pressing concern suddenly struck me. "Scott, you do have FBI creds, don't you?"

"Yes," Scott said. He pulled out his wallet and showed me a card. "Well, I have this. That's the same thing, right?"

It was Scott's super-secret clearance card, issued by the US government, which all American Protectors have.

"Crap." No suit, no creds. Even worse, still no plan. Time to improvise. "No, that's not the same, but we can make it work. I'll be FBI, and you'll be a consultant helping me. Just wave your super-secret card and say 'classified' if anyone asks you who you are or why you are investigating. But you still need a suit."

I quickly googled the hours of the nearest Men's Wearhouse. Open at ten. Too late for me to go—I needed to be at the police station at the start of normal business hours and bluster my way through the day as an all-important FBI agent.

"Scott, you're going to have to go buy a suit yourself. You have a Protectorate credit card?" He nodded. Good. Not another unnecessary complication. "Text me when you're changed, and I'll let you know where to meet me."

"How do I get to the store?" Scott asked.

"Take the bus."

"Which one?"

I blinked and stared at Scott for a minute. How had he managed to live in Bay City for so long and not know how to use public transport? Talk about being a sheltered bookworm.

"Use the map app on your phone. It has a 'transit' setting. It will tell you all the buses you need to take, what time they arrive, and where you need to get off. Just follow the directions."

"Okay," Scott said, looking nervous.

"I need to head out now. There's a coffee shop around the corner if you want to get some breakfast." I rummaged through my junk drawer and found my spare apartment key for Scott. "Lock up before you leave. And Scott, remember: Do not, I repeat, do *not* say a word about anything supernatural in front of any humans. Got it?"

"Yes."

"See you in a few hours."

On the way out the door, I grabbed my briefcase—it helped make me look official, and it was stuffed with all sorts of useful items, both magical and mundane. Never know what might be needed on a day like today.

I spent the bus ride to the police station trying to come up with some sort of course of action. By the time I disembarked, I had a few ideas cobbled together, but nothing definite. I'd have to wing it then. That was all right— I'm the king of bullshit and making stuff up on the spot.

"Agent Enzo Thornton, FBI," I told the officer manning the front desk. "I'm here in regards to the escape of Peter Newell."

The next couple of hours were spent in tedious fact-checking, made even more wearisome by the fact that all the police officers were extremely displeased to see me. They would've been irritated to have an FBI agent poking around in any of their cases, but the fact that Newell's escape was professionally embarrassing for their department only served to compound the innate tension between various law enforcement agencies.

Security footage was missing, as Hawkins had said, and the techies assured me there was no sign of tampering in their system. No surprise there, if magic was involved.

Next I questioned the officers that had been in the building at the time. All three looked haggard—being suspended without pay for circumstances that are completely beyond your comprehension will have that effect. Getting interrogated by the police chief one day and an FBI agent the next day definitely didn't improve their emotional health.

The testimonies of the three all lined up with Newell being a warlock. They'd seen nothing out of the ordinary, heard no sounds of a breakout. Every nuance of their stressed body language fit with them being honest cops.

Once I'd dotted all the i's and crossed all the t's of the procedural bullshit, I decided that my next step in tracking down Newell was to search his house. When I let my intentions be known to the police, I was informed that Detective Marlow and Officer Hawkins were already there. Just what I needed. This investigation was turning into more of a nightmare with every passing hour.

Scott texted me while I was on the bus to Newell's house. He'd bought a suit. Great. One more task checked off the to-do list. I sent him Newell's address and told him to meet me there.

Crime-scene tape blocked off the entrance to Newell's ranch-style house on E Street. I had evaluated the neighborhood as I'd walked from the nearest bus stop—upper income middle class houses. Probably out of a single teacher's budget. Most families in the area had to have either a bigger breadwinner or two working adults in the household to afford this lifestyle. Not that it was fancy, it was just too much property with too-nice houses for a lone teacher. Lined up with Newell's alternate income.

Not that knowing Newell said something truthful was all that reassuring. The most clever liars realize that they need some basis in truth in order to make their lies convincing. The trick is unravelling true information from false.

I ducked under a yellow-and-black ribbon blocking the open front door and looked around. The living room was open and austere. A mahogany leather couch, nice big 4K television, plenty of electronics hooked up to the TV. Newell was living the good life, at least as far as I could see.

"Hello?" I called into the seemingly empty house.

Sudden footsteps coming down the hallway. Hopefully the Summerville PD had alerted Marlow and Hawkins that I was coming. If not, I sure as hell hoped they didn't have a "shoot first, ask questions later" kind of attitude. Although, in the case of the werewolf, would it be "bite first" instead?

That type of musing would have to wait, as the officers in question made their appearance.

"Agent Thornton, was it?" Marlow asked. Calm and collected, as I was beginning to expect from him.

"Correct. I'm here to recapture Peter Newell."

"Any idea how he escaped?" Despite his placid tone, Marlow's eyes were sharp. Too sharp.

"Haven't the foggiest," I lied. "Must've been a glitch in your security."

The glare Hawkins gave me only served to compound my guilt over lying to this seemingly honest cop. But I couldn't tell Marlow the truth. There were too many repercussions.

At that moment, Scott made his entrance. Wearing—I kid you not—a plaid suit. Navy with dark turquoise lines—like a Scottish kilt and a traditional Western suit had a baby. A tacky, fashion-challenged baby. Nothing could scream "nerd alert" more than the clothes Scott had on. I should've gone shopping with him, to hell with needing to follow all police protocols.

There was nothing left to do but try and salvage the situation. "This is Scott Avery," I introduced. "He's a special consultant with this case."

Scott smiled and flashed his super-secret card. "Classified," he said.

Crap. Just when a whole lot of common sense would've done more use than hastily given instructions. Why me?

CHAPTER 17

Getting a Chick's Name and Number

IT TOOK A fair bit of dissembling to un-ruffle Marlow's feathers. Added to the longstanding enmity between police and FBI was now this new player spouting one of the most annoying words in the world (if you're on the receiving end of it, that is). If only Scott had played it a bit cooler during the introductions. But there was no turning back time, despite conspiracy theories that it was magically possible, and so we'd have to move forward with what we had.

Scott's strange attire ended up being beneficial—the plaid suit plainly showed that Scott wasn't fully in touch with practical reality. A bit of communication weirdness naturally fit with that territory.

I noticed that Hawkins had relaxed slightly when she saw Scott, and he gave her a small smile. Marlow didn't notice it—he was too busy paying attention to me—and, thankfully, Scott didn't strike up a conversation with her. The small blessings in life.

"What have you found so far?" I finally asked, bringing our motley group back to the task at hand.

"Officers searched the house yesterday. Found around a hundred pounds of marijuana, plus several containers of unidentified powders and liquids. On-scene Marquis tests showed some really weird results. Turned bright blue for a couple of them. Never heard of that before. Everything was taken to the lab for further analysis. Should find out in a couple of weeks what they are," Marlow said.

Crap. The humans had Newell's magical potions. I needed to get my hands on them before they completed their tests. Who knew what the lab results would show, but I knew it wouldn't be good for the sake of magical secrecy.

The silver lining was that I had two advantages. First was the ever-present backlog in police labs. There was no way they'd even begun their analysis yet. Secondly—"I'll need those samples transferred to the FBI lab instead," I ordered.

The warring expressions on the two faces before me was almost comical. Outrage and resigned irritation clashed on Detective Marlow's face, but

Hawkins's expression—was that relief mixed with her innate anger? Huh. She knew—or at least suspected—that I was rerouting the potions because they were magical and threatened to expose the mundane world to the supernatural. And she apparently didn't want the magical truth of the world to be revealed. Unlike some supes, who wanted magic to be out in the open so they could become supernatural rulers over the humans.

Although I supposed her behavior now lined up with what Scott had told me the night before—she kept herself mostly separate from the supernatural, retaining a normal human life as much as possible.

"You'll have to fill out the forms back at the station to get the evidence transferred," Marlow finally said.

"You find anything more today?"

"Nothing yet. We've only been here a couple of hours though."

Only a couple of hours. Great. Most likely another long, boring day. But I couldn't leave the search to the human police, in case they missed—or worse, discovered—anything else magically incriminating in Newell's house.

"Drug dogs were here before," Marlow continued. "They didn't alert on anything other than what was already collected."

"Doesn't matter," I said, then immediately regretted it as Marlow jumped to the correct conclusion.

"So if you're not looking for drugs, what are you hoping to find?"

I had a split-second internal debate as to whether I should brush off his question as "classified" or give him something more concrete—without giving any clues to the magical aspect of the case. With Marlow's wits—and my luck—he'd take an inch of intel and make a mile-long leap in logic. I finally decided I had to give him a smidgen of information. Might be useful in the long run. Nothing too truthful though.

"The FBI is investigating Newell's possible connection to the theft of some unusual historic artifacts. Quite eccentric and valuable items."

Marlow frowned. "And that's classified?"

I shrugged and gave him an apologetic half smile. "That's all I can tell you."

"And if I ask what exactly was stolen and where it was taken from?"

My smile broadened to a wide grin. I was back on solid footing and knew exactly how to answer. "Classified." Not that I even knew what Newell might have lying around. But I'd know it when I saw it.

Marlow let out a sigh of frustration. "Figures."

"Look in his office," Hawkins suggested. "There was some weird stuff in there." She raised her eyebrows significantly.

My hopes lifted somewhat—apparently the werewolf had seen something that would be of interest to us.

"We'll start there," I said, masking my excitement.

"Second door on the right."

Scott followed me down the short hallway to the indicated door, which hung open. I peered inside before entering. Jackpot.

The office was fairly austere, making the magical objects exceptionally conspicuous against the background of IKEA furniture—computer desk and printer stand, bare except for a couple stacks of papers (no doubt the police had confiscated the electronics), basic black office chair, single bookshelf against the wall. It was the bookshelf that caught my immediate attention. More specifically, it was the objects resting on its shelves that grabbed my notice.

I opened my briefcase, pulled out two pairs of disposable gloves, and gave one set to Scott. Not that we needed to be concerned about fingerprints, but we did have to keep up appearances as legit FBI agents. I snapped on my own gloves then approached the bookshelves slowly, examining their contents as I did so. Mostly filled with novels, binders, and paperwork one would expect of an English teacher. But the middle shelf housed some books I'd be surprised to find on any summer reading list—a handful of leather-bound grimoires. Sitting next to the spell books was a variety of objects that were likely magical in nature: a cat skull, mortar and pestle, obsidian knife, and an assortment of labelled vials and flasks: hemlock, wolfsbane, nettle. That sort of thing. Spell-casting and potion ingredients. I even spotted eyeballs of a crocodile and blood of a hen.

In the center of them all was a grapefruit-sized crystal ball—not a standard clear or cloudy white crystal, but instead a translucent stone of blended pale teal and purple colors, with internal facets of various sizes that gave it a fractured appearance despite its smooth surface.

I didn't recognize the stone; glancing at Scott to see if he knew what it was, I saw that Marlow had followed us down the hall and was watching us from the doorway. Had to be extra circumspect with him looking on so closely.

"You recognize that stone from the list of missing objects?" I asked Scott, hoping that he would both understand my underlying message—what was the stone, and was it dangerous—and remain discreet at the same time. It was a tall order for my secretive-challenged friend, but for once, Scott was up to the task. Mostly.

"Yes, it's a fluorite crystal," Scott replied. He picked it up and turned it slowly in his hands. At least that answered whether or not it was dangerous to handle. "But not just any crystal. See that half-moon sigil etched there? This is a stone that was associated with African witch trials about a hundred years ago. It was stolen sometime around then."

I was surprised—had I inadvertently told the truth about stolen artifacts? "We should take all this in as evidence," I said, grateful that my briefcase was stocked with FBI evidence bags.

The grimoires were what interested me the most—essential to see what sort of spells Newell had access to—but we also needed to figure out the magical attributes of the other stuff. Since Scott and I couldn't discuss anything important in front of the human, we performed the laborious process of filling the evidence bags and writing down all the pertinent information on each one. And no, that wasn't just for show—even Protectors need to keep a clear chain of custody, although thankfully it was only for the sake of properly investigating a case, not from a need to defend our every action in a courtroom.

"African witch trials," Marlow broke the silence. He was standing closer, practically looming over us, but at least he was only looking, not trying to touch anything. "And what about that knife? Chinese? Those are odd-looking yin yang symbols. I thought they usually had a dot of color in the opposing sides."

I looked to where he was pointing. The obsidian knife had a pale handle, likely made of bone, which was marked with a series of small circles next to where the grip joined to the smoothly faceted ebony blade. I picked up the blade to examine the markings and nearly cursed aloud. The symbols were composed of two red and white teardrop shapes curved into a circle, almost identical to a yin yang other than the fact Marlow had noted—the colors were solid. I knew what they represented—a drop of blood and a fang. The emblem of one of the creepiest supernatural species out there. Vampires.

"Might be Chinese," I lied nonchalantly and bagged the knife.

"So this is what you're looking for?" Marlow asked. "Stolen stuff that looks like it belongs on the set of *Hocus Pocus*?"

I decided to roll with the turn of events. I put down the evidence bag with the knife and faced Marlow. Hawkins, I saw, was standing in the study doorway, watching from a distance. I sighed in annoyance. "Fine, I'll read you in, as much as I can."

Marlow looked startled, though he quickly composed himself. Not every day an FBI agent is willing to disclose details of a classified assignment.

"We are part of an operation tracking the sale and movement of eclectic black market art items, many of which, as you can see from the items here, have to do with ancient witchcraft, magical rituals, and witch trials." I paused, trying to sort out what more I could say.

"What about the mugging? How does that fit in?" Marlow asked.

Crap. How to explain that, and my presence there, when it was pure coincidence?

"We had been tracking Jane Doe as a member of the smugglers' ring. She and Newell met, I assume to complete a transaction, but something went wrong."

"That's an understatement," Hawkins muttered under her breath.

"Why did you turn Newell over to us?" Marlow asked.

"After interrogating him, we had reason to believe that he was a low-level fence, not worth pursuing. The attempted murder charge was more significant. But based on his escape, he was more important than we originally thought and worth the risk to the smugglers to break him out of jail. It was a mistake," I admitted, though for different reasons than what I could confess.

"And why wasn't a guard placed on Jane Doe?"

Dammit. Could I look any more incompetent? I wished in vain that I could tell the truth, if only to salvage a bit of my reputation. Not like I had any reason to suspect she was a witch at the time. "Another mistake," I said stiffly.

I was rescued that moment by Scott, who had finished bagging the last of the evidence while we'd been talking. "We should take this back to HQ to see if we can find anything else about it," he said.

"We need to check the rest of the house first, see if there's more stolen items," I said.

"So tell me," Marlow interrupted. "Does this sudden revelation of information mean that you plan on working with us?"

I couldn't see a way out of it, despite all the complications of working with a werewolf while trying to keep a too-smart, too-observant human in the dark about the truth of the world. But I had to admit that a plain police investigation might be invaluable in tracking down Newell and Doe.

"I think that would be advantageous," I said.

"Very well, Agent Thornton. Let me give you my personal cell number."

"If we're going to be working together, we can dispense with formalities," I said. "Call me Enzo."

Marlow nodded. "Raymond," he replied.

"Scott," my fashionably challenged friend chimed in.

"Cora," Hawkins said from the doorway.

And quickly thereafter, I found myself not only on first-name basis with a werewolf, but I also had her phone number saved in my cell. What other fresh hells was this case going to bring?

CHAPTER 18

BREAKING BAD . . . MAGIC

WHEN WE HAD finished searching the rest of Newell's house, Scott and I collected all the evidence. I snagged a duffel bag from Newell's closet so that we could unobtrusively carry everything on public transportation. Marlow watched with a frown as we walked away from the house, no car of our own in sight, but fortunately didn't ask any questions. I needed to remedy our car situation before he figured out that we were using the bus to get around, something no true FBI agent would do.

Before leaving Summerville, we headed to the police station and confiscated—I mean, requisitioned—the rest of the evidence the police had collected, minus the marijuana. Didn't need that. Getting the evidence took another stack of paperwork and waiting about an hour. If only police work could get done as quickly in real life as they showed in cop television shows. I'd especially appreciate being able to do a music montage to get through all the boring bits of investigation and analysis.

Once we'd gotten everything, we were finally free to go back to HQ and get started on the monumental task at hand. Of course, I was stuck with lugging around the heavy duffel bag, which was nearly bursting at the seams with all the spell books and vials of unidentified potions.

On the train to Bay City, Scott pulled out one of the grimoires and read during our trip back to HQ. I figured it didn't really matter that he had it out in public—his reading material was no odder than his plaid suit. Well, in for a penny, in for a pound. I grabbed another and started slogging my way through the Latin and various complicated diagrams.

I'd barely finished a quarter of one book, and Scott was midway through a second, when we reached our stop. Once we'd gotten off the streets and into the eavesdrop-free halls of HQ, we broke the silence.

"Find anything unusual?" I asked as we headed toward the second-floor labs.

"Just basic spells," Scott said. "You know—levitation, fire-starting, healing, love potions and whatnot. Nothing sinister so far. What about you?"

"A lot of the same. Did see a misperception spell. Could've been what Newell used to escape undetected."

"Aren't those tricky to pull off?"

"Are you boys going to try your hands at witchcraft?" Martin interrupted, materializing from the wall to our left. So much for not being eavesdropped on in headquarters. I'd briefly forgotten that the walls often contained ghostly ears.

"Just looking for a decent ghost-banishing spell," I joked. I knew Martin would figure out what we were up to sooner or later, but I preferred that it would be later. Much later. I didn't want everyone to know of my blunders, and as soon as Martin found out, every Protector would know. Annoying as hell to have a resident ghost who loved to gossip.

Not that his penchant for collecting and distributing information couldn't come in handy at times. "You hear anything more about the kraken relocation efforts?" I asked, both to distract Martin and to find out what Zoanna was up to.

"There's been a few complications thrown into the mix," Martin said. "Turns out the kraken is female." He paused expectantly.

"So what?"

"She had babies with her, that's what. And a fishing boat netted a bunch of them. Thought they were some type of squid."

"Bloody hell!" Scott exclaimed. "She must've gone on a rampage."

"Bloody is an understatement, from what I've heard. She sank the ship that killed her babies. No survivors. And since then, she's targeted other ships. Apparently, she sees them as a threat to her remaining offspring."

"Crap, that's terrible," I said. Krakens only give birth once a millennia— every effort would no doubt be taken to save the kraken mother instead of killing her, despite the human corpses she'd recently left in her wake. The response team would be kept busy with her for a long time. No chance, then, of getting any more backup for my problems anytime soon.

"Thornton! Avery! What are you doing here?" Councilor Ainsley interrupted.

"You boys will need to fill me in later," Martin said under his breath as he faded back into the walls. (Well, is it really "under his breath" when he doesn't actually breathe? I'll leave that question to the philosophers.)

"We found some grimoires and other potential magical artifacts at the home of the escaped warlock," I replied. "We were just taking them to the labs for testing."

"Carry on, then. And make sure to report all your findings." Ainsley didn't wait for a reply; she continued past us, her heels beating a military march into the floor.

"Yes, Councilor," I said anyways. Nobody could complain about *my* manners, at least.

We went to an empty lab and got to work. Well, that is to say, Scott got to work. I've never been exactly an academic, lab-geek guy. Sue me. Instead, I plopped down the duffel bag of our spoils at one of the black-topped tables adjacent to where Scott was setting up. Then I stayed out of his way as he went to various cupboards and pulled out a wide variety of beakers, round flasks, glass tubing, and an assortment of liquids and powders. The lab was designed just like a college lab—a fume hood in one corner, an emergency shower in another corner, rows of tables for partners to work at. The countertops on the perimeter of the room contained plenty of sinks, Bunsen burners, microscopes, and all that other science-y stuff.

The only difference was that half the ingredients in the stockroom were things that any sensible human scientist would say were either useless, nonsense, or nonexistent. Oh, and there was a griffin skeleton suspended from the ceiling.

Before long, Scott had a network of complicated-looking glassware and bubbling liquids set up. The *pièce de résistance* was a large spherical glass container, into which he put the cat skull that had been among Newell's things. In the meantime, I had slogged through another half-dozen pages in the grimoire I'd been reading. See? Not totally useless.

"Enzo, look at this." Scott broke through my laborious translation of a dragon-taming spell. Rubbish, it was; besides the fact that dragons were critically endangered and now legally protected against being used as guardians, it was absolute nonsense that a dragon could be subdued by a few herbs and some random botanical items—including dragon fruit, of all things.

"What is it?" I asked, relieved to set the grimoire aside for the time being.

Scott pointed to the cat-skull container, which was half-filled with a murky green liquid and emanating gray smoke. "This only happens when an object's been used in a spell to commune with the dead."

"Newell was doing necromancy?" Of all the things I wanted to encounter when dealing with magic, necromancy was definitely at the bottom of the list. Not because a necromancer was any more dangerous than other spell-casters, but because, at its core, the act of enslaving a dead spirit to do your bidding in the world of the living was disgustingly foul.

"No," Scott said. "No necromancy. Just communication with spirits."

"That's a relief. Anything else?"

Scott grinned. "See those tiny flashes of light in the smoke? That means that this was used recently. There's a lot of magical residue attached to it still."

"And?"

Scott gave me a look of exasperation. "Did you pay any attention at all in our magi-chem lessons? Spell-casters have a unique magical signature. Like a fingerprint. And there's enough here to isolate Newell's magical profile. Once I do that, we'll be able to pinpoint any location where he uses magic in the future."

"How long will it take?"

"A day or two."

"That long?"

"You think you could do it any faster?"

I scowled at Scott's impish grin.

"It's not like there isn't a lot more that needs to be done while you wait for me to finish. You could deal with the other artifacts."

"Great." I picked up the crystal ball and looked at it, halfheartedly hopeful that its faceted interior would reveal the rock's hidden secrets. It didn't, of course, but I was fortunate enough to have an encyclopedic friend.

"No need to test that. I already know what it does," Scott said.

I waited a few seconds for an explanation, but none seemed forthcoming—Scott was focused on using an eyedropper to add a fluorescent blue liquid to the smoking globe. "So what's it do?" I asked when Scott finally finished. "Allow you to see the future?"

"Like I said before, it's from the witch trials in Africa." Scott carefully weighed a gram of white powder and added it to his concoction.

"And that's significant because?" I prompted.

"Well, there's always been a lot of superstition in African tribes. They believe witchcraft to be real, and they're terrified of it. Historically, witches have been heavily persecuted. And despite the fact that the witch trials have spanned decades and claimed the lives of hundreds of supposed witches, the African trials are not nearly as famous as the ones in Salem. But just like Salem, it's the innocent humans that get killed—any halfway decent witch can easily elude their non-magic persecutors."

"Interesting history lesson, but what's that got to do with the stone?"

"It was used as a communication device. One of the warlocks was undercover with the persecutors. He was able to pass on intel to others when he knew their communities were going to be targeted."

"So it's a magical phone."

"Basically." Scott returned to his work, and I pulled the next magical items out of the duffel bag. Mortar and pestle. Boring staples of any magic-user's kit. Nothing to be learned from them. I set them aside, then took out the potion-making ingredients from Newell's house and the potions we'd confiscated from the police and piled them on Scott's table for him to deal with. There was only one item, besides the grimoires, left in the bag, and I reached for it with great reluctance.

The vampire dagger. At the very least, I knew what it was—one of the five identical blades given by the original vampire to the five people he turned before his death. Those five vampires became the heads of the modern vampire factions—noble houses, as the vampires call them—and the daggers were symbolical (and bloodily ceremonial) to them. So how the hell had Newell come to possess one of them?

"You know anything about a vamp knife being stolen?" I asked Scott.

"No," he said, eyeing the knife with the same puzzlement I felt. "And you'd think that would be something we'd have heard of. The theft of something of that importance would've caused an uproar in whatever faction it was stolen from."

I looked at the knife with distaste. Only one way to get answers. I needed to interview a vampire.

CHAPTER 19

Old Enemies and New . . . Friends?

THE COVEN OF vampires in Bay City was led by Nolan Blair, youngest of the five vampires in the original generation—he'd been turned somewhere in the late thirteenth century, as compared to his eldest brother, who predated Christ. Despite his late arrival on the supernatural scene, Blair ruled one of the strongest modern vampire empires, spanning all of North and Central America. He spent his time traveling, checking in on his local deputies throughout his domain, and it was just my luck—or maybe misfortune—that he was in town. I'd never met one of the first vampires, and I'd never wanted to. But he was my best chance at finding out how Newell had obtained the knife.

Making an appointment to speak to a high-ranking vampire is a ritualistic affair. I left Scott in the labs and went to the courier room, which stocked the parchment and quill pens that I needed. The good thing about ritual is that it provided the correct wording of the message, so I didn't need to be creative, just formally write: "Honorable Lord Blair, I request the honor of an audience to discuss a matter of great importance to the noble and bloody House of Draxivar. With all due respect, Protector Enzo Thornton."

The message was quickly written in black ink, but when it came time for me to sign, I pricked my finger, allowing a few drops of blood to fall into an empty inkwell. Then I dipped the quill and signed my name in blood. Damn vampires.

I left the note with one of the couriers—poor Protectors-in-training, tasked with all the drudgery as they worked their way to the coveted rank of field agent. I'd done my stint here as well—at least it got me out of HQ fairly often, unlike working in the library, records, labs, or the dungeon. Although, the worst thing about working in the dungeon wouldn't have been dealing with the prisoners, it would've been working with Jake. Bastard had found his calling in tormenting the condemned. Speaking of the devil . . .

"Fix your mistakes yet, Enzy?" Jake's mocking voice sounded down the hallway. "Or are you still trying to recapture the warlock? You know, the one you had in custody. The one you handed over to the humans, like the idiot you are."

It burned that Jake's taunts were in line with the self-recrimination I'd been feeling the last couple of days. What he said was true; there was no denying it. For the first time, I was at a loss for a retorting quip.

"Didn't Newell spend the night in the cells here?" a familiar female voice asked.

I turned in shock to see Cora Hawkins, wearing civilian clothes of blue jeans, green tank top, and white "Visitor" sticker, coming up behind me.

"Yes." At least I was able to manage that one-word reply.

"Surely Jake saw him sometime during his stay here," she said.

My surprise kept me puzzled. "Yes, he was there when I booked Newell." Suddenly it clicked. I turned back to Jake. "You're one to talk. You didn't realize he's a warlock either."

"Wasn't my job to do that," Jake said, though I could hear the triumph leaving his voice. "Not my responsibility to do your job for you."

Thankfully that last, weak jab was the best Jake could manage, and he left quickly after the parting shot.

I looked at the werewolf. "What are you doing here?"

"I'm here for the truth," she replied. "Obviously you couldn't say everything in front of Raymond. But if we're going to be working together, I need to know what's going on."

"Right," I said, then asked the most important question. "How do you know Jake?"

"I come here and change in the cells at the full moon. I've seen him down there. He's an ass. An even bigger ass than you."

I decided to let that remark slide by and take the moral high ground instead. "Thanks for helping put him in his place."

A flash of surprise filled Hawkins's sharp brown eyes before she masked it. "You're welcome," she said gruffly. "Now, tell me what's actually happening."

"Let's talk somewhere else." Who knew who else would show up if we chatted in the hallway. Martin, no doubt, looking for the latest gossip. Possibly Ainsley, ready to micromanage me again. Since I didn't particularly fancy running into either of them, I led Hawkins back to the lab where Scott was still working.

"Hey, Scott," Hawkins said as we entered.

Scott put down the beaker he'd just picked up. "Hi, Cora," he said with a wide smile. I looked back and forth between them. That was just friendship, right? "Sorry, I need to keep working on this. It's at a critical stage where I can't leave it unattended." Without waiting for a response, he turned back to his project. That was the typical Scott I knew. I'd been imagining things.

Hawkins and I sat at a table out of Scott's way. "Now, tell me the truth."

I quickly summarized everything that had happened from the moment I'd stumbled on what appeared to be a mugging of a normal human woman, not a warlock stabbing a witch. How I'd tracked Newell to the apartments where Finian the sprite escaped. Why I'd thought that Newell was just a low-level drug peddler, and not worth my time to keep in magical lockup. My screwup with not recognizing that he and Jane Doe were magic users. And finally, I explained what all the artifacts were that we'd taken from Newell's house.

"So when are you interviewing the vampire?" Hawkins asked.

"Hopefully tonight. But I won't get a response until after the sun is down. Shouldn't be too long now."

"And that meeting will be here?"

"No. All of HQ is on holy ground. Vampires can't stand it. Not to mention that a high-ranking vampire like Blair would never consent to meeting with a mere Protector like me in a place anywhere other than his own territory. So I'll have to go to him."

"Alone?"

"Yes. Everyone else is dealing with a kraken issue. Scott's my backup and, as you can see, he's busy."

Hawkins stared thoughtfully at me for a minute. It was the calmest I'd ever seen her; quiet contemplation, instead of the jittery ready-to-fight attitude that I'd come to expect from her.

Despite noticing her change in attitude, her next words completely blindsided me. "I'll come with you."

CHAPTER 20

Roll with the Role

"WHAT DO YOU mean, you'll go with him?" Scott had apparently been paying more attention to our conversation than I'd thought. "It's too dangerous. You're not a Protector."

"So?" Hawkins bristled. "I've been a police officer for five years, and I'm a werewolf. I've been in a lot more dangerous situations than you have, Scott."

"No, you misunderstand me," Scott said placatingly. "It's not a matter of skill; it's a matter of legal protection. Enzo is a Protector, and if the vampires lay a finger on him, it will mean war. Even if they manage to win, their ranks would be decimated. It's not worth the risk. But you're a werewolf, and a lone wolf at that. A werewolf with a pack is under the pack's protection, so vampires will steer clear, but they've been known to go after individuals before."

"And you great *Protectors* wouldn't do anything about that?" Hawkins spat.

"There isn't much we *could* do. Vampires are damned clever—they've been getting away with murder for centuries. If they decided to do anything to you, they'd be sneaky about it. Make it look like an accident, or make you vanish without a trace. And our hands would be tied, since you aren't human. Protecting humans is our priority." Scott looked ashamed as he said the words. "I'm sorry, Cora, but it's best if you stay away. Don't let the vampires know you even exist."

"There is another option." I couldn't believe I was saying the words. Only the thought of going into the vampires' lair with absolutely no backup made me continue to speak. "We could get her deputized. Make her an honorary Protector. The vamps would have to treat her the same as one of us."

"Is that even possible?" Hawkins asked skeptically. "I'm a werewolf, not a shapeshifter."

"It's not completely unprecedented," Scott said, gaining enthusiasm as he spoke. "There's never been a wolf Protector before, but there have been a few other non-shifter species that joined the Protectorate. Let me think . . . Brognir

Hammerfist was a dwarf, then there was Lady Aliandre of the fae, and that centaur, what was his name?"

"No need to recite all of them," I broke in. Scott would continue until he'd named every last one if he was left unchecked. "The point is that there's precedent. I'll get her deputized, and you can stay here and finish your project. Our priority is still tracking down Newell."

Before we left the lab, I snapped a quick picture of the dagger on my phone. Didn't want to bring the actual blade to the vampire coven—no doubt they wouldn't want to let us take it away with us, and it might still be useful in our investigation.

Since Ainsley was the only Councilor currently in residence, I had to go to her in order to get Hawkins deputized. All the other Councilors were at a retreat in the Swiss Alps. Lucky bastards. Granted, they were meeting with Councilors from across the globe to coordinate international relationships, so it wasn't a complete holiday. Still, not like it was in the Mojave Desert or some other godforsaken place.

Ainsley was in her office. A curt "Enter" greeted my knock on her door. Such a warm and fuzzy person. Didn't even appreciate my rendition of "Shave and a Haircut."

"Councilor, I am here to see about getting Officer Cora Hawkins sworn in as an honorary Protector," I said. No need for small talk.

"Deputize a werewolf?" Ainsley asked, studying the were in question. "*You,* Thornton? Why?"

"Officer Hawkins has been helping my current case, acting as a liaison to the police department." Okay, that was stretching the truth a bit. It was more like future truth than current truth, but Ainsley didn't need to know that. "As part of the case, I need to interview Nolan Blair. Scott is currently busy working on evidence in the labs, so I thought it prudent to bring backup."

"Are none of our own available?"

"No, Councilor. Every active field agent from Headquarters is busy with the kraken situation."

"What about Jonson? He is registered active duty, even though he spends his time in the dungeons."

I stared for a minute. Was she seriously suggest I work with Jake, my mortal enemy? I'd take a hundred werewolves as partners before I worked with that idiot.

Ainsley waved a dismissive hand. "Yes, I realize that was a foolish notion. The two of you would get on like a cobra and a mongoose. All the mice would escape while you were too busy going after one another. Very well, Officer Hawkins will be your partner."

"Thank you, ma'am," Hawkins said. "I'm honored."

I turned my head to look at her. *Honored?* I hadn't gotten the impression that she felt very highly of Protectors. Oh, right. That was it—she didn't think highly of Jake or me. Well, good for her. Showed that half her judgement was correct, at least.

"Cora Hawkins, werewolf and officer of the Summerville Police Department," Ainsley said formally. "Do you swear to protect human life, to do everything in your power to guard innocent humans from any and all supernatural threats?"

"I swear," Hawkins vowed.

"Then by the power invested in me by the Council of the Protectors, I declare you as an honorary Protector of Humanity. Honor that title, and we shall honor you as one of our own, from this day henceforth."

"Hip hip, hooray," I said, not a hundred percent sarcastically. I now had a werewolf partner. Well, at least I maybe had a buffer for when I went into the lair of the bloodsuckers.

We left Ainsley's office, and I took Hawkins to the storerooms. "What are we doing here?" she asked, looking at the shelves and racks of various clothes, pieces of armor, and other tools of our trade.

"If you're going to act as one of us, you need to look the part." I showed her the official field uniforms: black pants and long-sleeved tops. Moisture-wicking, tear-resistant, stain-repellent. All that good stuff. "Pick something out and get changed. I'll wait outside."

It was a short wait. "What about you?" Hawkins asked. "You staying in that suit?"

"No, I keep clothes in my quarters here. Not that I stay here much," I said. "You need any weapons?"

"I have my gun and taser out in my car."

"Go grab them. I'll meet you at the dining hall. You know where it is?"

She nodded and left.

I walked slowly to my room, weighed down by dark thoughts. How the hell had I ended up with a werewolf partner? I couldn't believe I had suggested it. Then I thought of the proposed meeting with the vampires. Right. Between the bloodsuckers and the wolves, the vampires definitely won the creepy and deadly contest. And Hawkins didn't seem that bad. For a werewolf, that is.

My room was just as I had left it, only the bed was made and everything had been dusted and vacuumed. Gotta love the staff of brownies at headquarters. Kept everything in tip-top shape, only requiring never-ending bowls of cream in return.

I quickly changed and dropped my dirty clothes on the floor. The brownies would have them dry-cleaned and hung in the closet by the time I returned from the meeting with the vampires. If I returned.

Don't be so damn pessimistic, I chided myself. You've gone through worse. A vampire's no harder to beat than an ogre, and you beat four of them with Zoanna. And a were is capable of holding their own against a vamp.

By the time I made it to the mess hall, I'd mostly worked my way out of my bad mood. It was a good thing I was feeling more optimistic, because one of the couriers showed up as I was making my way down the buffet line. He handed me an envelope of heavy parchment. I pulled out the message and read the flowery script: "On behalf of my noble master, I am honored to invite representatives of the Protectorate to his Bay City home tonight, at the stroke of midnight. —S.P."

Of course it had to be midnight. Immortal creatures sure loved their time-honored traditions. They couldn't see how cliché some of them had become over the centuries.

Hawkins was already seated at one of the long tables when I finished filling my plate. I dropped my tray across from her and handed her the note. She read it while I started eating. "So, midnight tonight?" she said when she finished. I could hear the tightness in her voice, although she was keeping her tone lighthearted.

I grunted in return, keeping my gaze on my food.

"What's your problem with me, Enzo?" Hawkins suddenly demanded, anger in her voice.

I looked up, surprised at her outburst, meeting her fierce eyes. "Nothing."

"Liar. I've seen how you act with Scott, and I know him. He wouldn't be friends with an asshole. Yet ever since we've met, you've acted like you'd like nothing more than to see me fed to a flock of starving griffins. If we're going to work together, I need to know that I can trust you."

"Trust works both ways," I snapped. "I've dealt with dozens of your kind that were trying to kill me. So forgive me if I'm not full of sunshine and rainbows over working with a werewolf." No need to tell her the rest of the truth. That was enough.

"So I'm being blamed for the actions of people I've never met? That hardly seems fair. Does that mean I should blame you for all the werewolves *you've* killed?" Hawkins challenged.

I scowled. Her words sounded uncomfortably like Scott's. Accusing. What if they were true? I felt the glare leave my face, my body deflating under the weight of her righteous fury.

"You're right," I admitted, forcing the words through my teeth. "I shouldn't hold you accountable for others' actions. I should judge you by yourself."

Hawkins looked flabbergasted. Clearly not expecting me to admit a fault. "So . . . what now? Wipe the slate clean? Start over?"

"If we can." I gave her a rueful grin. "If *I* can. I'll try to be on my best behavior, but—" I shook my head, unwilling to go on. But I had to. "I didn't tell you the complete truth before. About why I feel so strongly about werewolves. You see, when I was ten, my mother had a meeting with a pack of wolves to discuss the boundaries of a new full-moon sanctuary. Supposed to be routine, nothing dangerous. But they betrayed her. Murdered her under a banner of truce. Since then—" I forced my eyes to remain dry.

"Enzo, I'm so sorry," Hawkins said, empathy filling her voice. "I can't imagine what you went through."

"My father was devastated. Threw himself into work. I rarely saw him after that. Still hardly ever see him. He's usually abroad—in Austria, right now, or Australia. Hardly matters which. But every time I hunt down a werewolf, I think, maybe this one is the one who killed her. Maybe I'm getting justice for her. But I never know—nobody ever found out which of the bastards murdered my mom."

"If you ever find out, I'll help you hunt them down," Hawkins said, with sharp venom. "Nobody should have to go through that pain."

An unexpected warmth filled my chest. I forced a laugh, trying to lighten the mood. "If the murderer is also a female werewolf, would that make it a bitch fight?"

I grimaced in pain as Hawkins kicked my shin under the table. "Asshole," she muttered.

"Always," I said with a genuine laugh. "I'll try to be nicer. Honest. But I've spent so much time hating werewolves, that there's something deep inside of me that wants to fight every time I see one. I won't be caught unaware like my mother was. I can't let my guard down. But I'll have your back. Promise."

"Partners, then?" Hawkins asked, holding out a hand.

I took it. "Partners. At least until the vampires drain us dry."

CHAPTER 21

Unleash the Dogs of War

ONE OF THE only good things to come out of the mess of my investigation was that I finally had a reason to check out a car from the Protectorate motor pool. At last, my own set of wheels. It was only a Honda Civic—silver, four-door, basic—not nearly as sweet of a ride as Newell's Mercedes, but I didn't care. Didn't even matter that I'd have to return the car as soon as the case was done—the loss would be alleviated by my eventual success.

At eleven-thirty, Hawkins and I left HQ and drove toward the ritziest part of Bay City, ready for our midnight rendezvous with Blair. Traffic was nearly nonexistent this time of night, and far too soon I was parking in front of Blair's hilltop mansion, wishing futilely that I could postpone this meeting indefinitely. Though I'll say one thing for the vampire: he certainly knew how to live the good life.

I got out of the car, my nerves tingling as we approached the gate to the vampires' lair. It was strange to feel so jumpy. I'd staked plenty of vampires in my time as a Protector, although I'd never entered their coven before. Never gone into a situation where I knew I'd be hopelessly outnumbered. Of course, I'd never had an energy-charged werewolf at my side before, radiating edgy tension. That didn't do anything to help me stay calm.

Nobody guarded the wrought-iron gate in the eight-foot rock wall surrounding the property. I tested the handle. Unlocked. "Ladies first," I told Hawkins with a grin. She rolled her eyes and walked through the gateway.

I followed, closing the gate behind me, and got my first good look at the vampires' home. Three-story Victorian house, painted in bland pastel blue and white, illuminated by spotlights placed strategically in the flowering gardens. Not exactly something you'd expect from the creatures who ruled the night. But at least it wasn't a mausoleum.

Barking—no, yapping—suddenly assailed us as a pack of Chihuahuas raced around the corner, small shadows bouncing off the walls and ground from the various light sources.

"What the hell?" Hawkins exclaimed.

"Don't move," I hissed, standing stock-still as the tiny canines approached and vigorously smelled our shoes, still yipping in between the sniffs. "We're here by invitation," I said louder, addressing the Chihuahuas.

"Since when do tiny dogs scare you?" Hawkins was clearly baffled, but at least she had listened to me and was standing still.

"These aren't any normal dogs," I said. "They're hellhounds."

"Hellhounds?" Hawkins asked skeptically. "I know Chihuahuas get a bad rep, but they aren't exactly dangerous. What, did one bite you when you were little?" She laughed. "Hey, little doggies, it's okay. There's nothing scary about you, is there, little cuties?"

"Arroof!" one of the dogs nearest her bellowed, far too deep and loud for its tiny lungs. In a move too fast for the eye to follow, it grew into a snarling black-and-red beast the size of a pony.

Hawkins's hand flew to her gun.

"Don't!" I warned before she could draw it. "That'll only piss him off."

"Crinitus!" a voice called from the doorway to the mansion. "You know better than to transform in front of guests unless ordered."

Despite the danger facing us, I couldn't help but think, *Who on earth names their hellhound Fluffy?*

Crinitus growled again. To call the creature a hellhound was a bit misleading—in its true form, it only vaguely resembled a canine. More like the unholy offspring of a grizzly and a demon. But the massive creature was obedient, at least. With a last rumbling snarl, he shrank back into an innocuous-looking brown Chihuahua.

"All of you, go away," the man continued. "These are expected guests."

I looked at him more closely. Human, and flamboyantly so. He wore a dark paisley suit with a silver and navy pattern—even more eye-catching than Scott's plaid suit but, unlike Scott, he managed to pull it off in a way that made it seem fashionably chic.

The pack of tiny hellhounds trotted back into the dark. Only Crinitus looked back over his shoulder, a hint of annoyance and hunger in his glowing eyes.

"I'm Protector Enzo Thornton. This is my partner"—I'll admit, those were still hard words to say—"Cora Hawkins."

"Welcome, welcome, Protectors," the man said, coming down the steps toward us and giving an expansive bow. "My master is expecting you. So sorry about the hounds; they can be a bit hmmm . . . overprotective . . . at times. But they mean no harm to those here in good faith. Please, come in. I am Sergio. I serve my master in all his mundane activities, and I will be honored to escort you to him."

"Not Renfield?" I muttered under my breath. I didn't mean for Sergio to catch the words, but his hearing was sharper than I expected.

"Renfield? No, no, of course not. Renfield's descendants serve in Europe, with my master's eldest brother. Although, my father's sister's husband was a Renfield. I, however, am a Promus. We have served Master Blair since the time of his creation."

We were quickly ushered though the entryway and asked to give up any weapons. I surrendered the pair of silver daggers strapped to my forearms (would've been extremely tacky to bring a wooden stake on this trip), and Hawkins relinquished her gun and taser. Despite our compliance, Sergio patted me down, though he was apologetic as he did so. "So sorry, but you must understand, my master's safety is of paramount importance. Not that we have anything to fear from our friends. Protocol, you know."

Once Sergio had professionally frisked Hawkins as well, he escorted us up the sweeping staircase and though an opulent pair of doors on the second floor. Probably had been intended as a ballroom at the time of its construction, but the vampires had repurposed it as a throne room. Nolan Blair sat at the far end of the chamber on a raised dais, his throne an elaborately carved chair. Made from wood, not bones, thank God.

Every muscle in my body was taut as Hawkins and I approached under the raptor-sharp gaze of a dozen vampires lounging around the room. Even if I hadn't been disarmed, there were too many to take on in a fair fight. Would need a holy-water hand grenade or something to even the odds. I heard the doors swing shut behind us. Surrounded by vampires, with a werewolf as my only ally. Even though I knew I was protected by an ironclad treaty, at that moment the treaty felt no more protective than the sheet of parchment it was written on.

When we'd reached an appropriate distance from the throne—close enough to speak without raising voices, but far enough to be well out of reach—Hawkins and I stopped and bowed. The sheaths on my forearms were uncomfortably empty.

"Master, it is my great honor to present to you Protectors Enzo Thornton and Cora Hawkins," Sergio announced with a bow, much more flourished and graceful than our own had been.

Dressed in a three-piece, tailored black suit—definitely not off the rack—with a royal blue silk tie and vest that complemented his sapphire eyes, Blair was an imposing figure on his throne. Somehow the blackness of his attire lent an elegance to his contrastingly pale skin. His blond hair was fashionably tousled—that exact balance of being perfectly styled while appearing completely effortless.

"Welcome, Protectors," Blair greeted, his voice carrying a slight accent that I couldn't place. Most likely a compilation of the many languages and dialects he'd used through his centuries of . . . life? Death? Undeath? The debate is still open as to exactly what to call the immortal vampires.

I couldn't help but stare at his teeth as he spoke. Looking for fangs. What I saw instead was completely unexpected. And completely ridiculous. Nolan

Blair, one of the five descendants of the original vampire, had braces. I couldn't help myself—my tightly strung nerves, combined with the absurdity of the situation, startled a laugh out of me.

I tried to disguise it as a cough, but I could tell by the flash of irritation in Blair's eyes that he hadn't been fooled. Crap. I was going to get us killed. Exsanguinated by a brace-face vampire. I bit my lip, barely managing to suppress another burst of somewhat-hysteric laughter.

"Does something about my appearance amuse you, Protector?" Blair asked.

"Forgive me," I said, bowing even lower than before. Partly to show deference, partly to hide my face while I composed my expression. "I meant no offense."

"Intended offense or not, tell me: What do you find funny? I enjoy a good joke. What is it you laughed at?" Blair demanded.

Hawkins shot me an unnecessary look of warning. I knew exactly how much trouble I was in. Offend the vampire by refusing to answer, or offend him by telling him that he was the butt of the joke. Well, it was never in my nature to keep my mouth shut.

"I'm sorry. It's not really funny, exactly. I was just surprised."

"To see a vampire with braces?" Blair cut in.

"Umm . . . yes."

To my complete relief, Blair only sighed with annoyance. "Yes, it is quite incongruous. And quite annoying to deal with. All these modern inventions, modern *orthodontics*." He spat out the last word like a curse. "Back when I was created, it was only natural for people to have crooked or missing teeth. But now—now they cause my prey to notice that I am different. They draw attention, and I must rectify the situation."

"But what about those invisible braces?" I couldn't help but ask. Now that the immediate fear of retaliation had passed, I couldn't keep my curiosity at bay. Hawkins elbowed me in the ribs. Hard. But it was too little, too late.

"And have my fangs punch a hole through them anytime I forget about the damn things? I have to go to a human orthodontist—none of my kind are interested in taking the time to learn how to fix teeth, not to mention the difficulties of taking classes only at night. At least with these brackets, I can claim that I ate toffee or something when I accidentally pop one off." Apparently this was a sore subject for Blair, and he had no problem with ranting at length.

I simply nodded and smiled politely—no more laughter. Perhaps establishing this rapport with him would help in future situations.

"Can you imagine how degrading it is to be lectured by some *human* about dental care as though I was no more than an impulsive child? Almost makes me want to—" He broke off sharply, as though suddenly recalling exactly who his audience was. "But of course I would never act in a fashion that would go against the spirit of the accords."

"Far from me to accuse you of such a thing," I said politely, though the words felt stiff coming out of my mouth.

"Now, what can I do for you, Protectors? It is not often that your kind visit my home. And for one of you to be a werewolf—most unusual."

"Officer Hawkins and I are working a case that has necessitated the cooperation of the Protectorate and the human police department. We are here following a lead."

"A lead? Surely you are not here to accuse one of mine from being involved in any sort of criminal activity. I assure you, I am most strict with keeping my people in line."

And making sure that they weren't caught when they did break the magical and mundane laws. But it wasn't like I could say that aloud.

"Not in the least," I said instead. "We merely recovered an item that we believe may have been stolen from you."

I reached into my pocket. Immediately all the vampires in the room tensed, leaning forward. Ready to attack. Freezing in place, I said, "I'm just reaching for my phone. I'm unarmed."

Blair waved his hand impatiently, and the vampires relaxed. Mostly.

I pulled out my phone, careful to make no sudden moves, and opened up my photos to the picture of the vampire dagger.

"Does this belong to you?" I asked, tilting the screen so Blair could see.

Rage twisted his face as he hissed, fangs extending to their full, deadly length. The terrifying effect was only slightly spoiled by the *twang* of breaking rubber bands as the braces on his canines popped off.

"Where did you find that?" he snarled.

"So it is yours? When did you lose it?"

Blair glared at me. I stared impassively back, though my heart was thundering in my chest, ready to burst through my ribs. Sweat beaded on my palms.

After a long moment, Blair's face relaxed, his fangs retracting. Well, not really retracting, just magically reshaping to appear as human canines.

"Yes, it's mine," he finally said. "It was stolen several months ago, along with the rest of the contents of a shipping crate of mine at the Bay City Port."

"Why didn't you report it?"

He laughed derisively. "You say that as if you Protectors would have done anything about it. You don't care about doing anything for us; all you do is protect your precious humans. We take care of our own problems. Now, tell me: Where did you find that?"

I shook my head resolutely. "I can't tell you that. It's part of an ongoing investigation."

Blair's eyes sparked in anger. His jaw clenched, but before he could speak, Hawkins cut in. "I assure you, we are doing everything in our power to capture the thief. He will be punished for his crimes in accordance with the law. And rest assured, we will return your dagger when it is no longer needed for our investigation."

"And when will that be?" Blair snapped.

"Soon," I promised.

Blair scowled. "Very well. But find this thief quickly, or my people will have to take this matter into our own hands."

"But—" I elbowed Hawkins into silence as she opened her mouth. I knew exactly how futile it was to try and convince vampires to follow the supernatural law. Their centuries of immortality allowed them to perfect the art of appearing to adhere to the law while still doing whatever they wanted.

"Thank you for your time," I said with a bow. Hawkins bowed as well, her back stiff. "We'll be back with the dagger soon."

"See that you are."

Together we turned and left the room. Quickly. I won't say we fled the vampire den, but we certainly didn't mosey as we descended the stairs and retrieved our weapons before exiting.

"Well, that was fun," I said as we passed through the wrought-iron gate.

Hawkins only stared at me skeptically, eyebrows raised.

I grinned. Danger past, ready to get back to the investigation. "Still glad you volunteered for this?"

"Ask me in another week," Hawkins muttered. "If you haven't gotten me killed by then."

CHAPTER 22

TERRIFIC TERRAFORM

THE RIDE BACK to HQ was mercifully short, punctuated only by yawns from both Hawkins and me. The late hour, combined with the draining of adrenaline after we left the vampires, left me completely exhausted.

"You want to stay in a guest room?" I asked as I pulled into the parking lot.

"No, I'll head home. Got the day off tomorrow."

"You sure? It's no problem."

"Who are you, and what have you done to Enzo?" Hawkins demanded, a note of amusement in her voice.

"Well, you did say you come here for the full moon transformation," I said. "I was just going to throw you into your usual cell."

"That's more like it." Hawkins gave a tired laugh. "Thanks anyway, Enzo. Let me know if you find out anything more."

"Sure."

"Say goodbye to Scott for me."

"Sure." What? But Hawkins was gone before my tired mind could form a question for her.

Despite my fatigue, I went to the lab before going to bed. As expected, Scott was still there. Hard at work—if you consider snoring at a table, using an open grimoire as a pillow, to be work.

I gently shook him awake.

"What? Enzo? What's going on?" Scott's sleepy confusion manifested itself as questions, without waiting for a response from me. "How'd the meeting with Blair go? Is Cora okay?"

"Yeah, everything's fine. She went home. Said to tell you bye," I replied. "Now go to bed. You can keep working in the morning."

"I'm fine. This is important," Scott protested, though his bloodshot eyes betrayed him. "We need to track down Newell before he tries to kill anyone else."

"You're useless to me if you can't think straight," I said. "Bed. Now."

"Yes, Mother," Scott grumbled.

I heeded my own advice and followed him to the dorm rooms. Another day of trying to figure out this mess was going to come far too soon.

SATURDAY MORNING. WEEKEND freedom. Day off. I wish. Instead I headed straight to the labs after breakfast. Scott was already there, reading. His cat-skull contraption was still emitting gray smoke, only now the liquid surrounding the bone was neon pink.

"How's the tracking going?"

"Fine so far," Scott said. "Needs to simmer for another six hours. Then it will be done—one way or another."

"What do you mean? There's a chance it won't work?" After all our efforts, could we really lose the one slim lead we had?

Scott shrugged. "It'll probably work. But this isn't just science. It's magic too. Sometimes weird stuff happens."

"And the only way to tell is once it's finished?"

"Yep."

"Great. Plenty of time to read the spell books while we wait to see if we're screwed. And I just love reading Latin." Okay, maybe I was laying it on a bit thick with the sarcasm. But this day was setting up to be boring as hell. Where's a good knock-down, drag-out fight when you need one?

As I pulled a grimoire out of the stack, a thought occurred. "Did you get a chance to examine the vampire dagger yet?"

"Yeah. Couple of fingerprints. I sent them to Cora to run through AFIS. Nothing else though—no magical residue."

"So it'd be all right to give it back to the vamps?"

"I suppose. Why, you looking forward to going back there?"

I shuddered. "Not in the slightest. But Nolan Blair really wanted that dagger back. And I figure the sooner we give it to him, the more likely he will be to feel good about us in the future."

"Currying favors, eh?"

I was surprised by the note of censure in Scott's voice. "Of course. Why not? Who knows when it'll be useful to have a powerful vampire indebted to us?"

"I suppose."

We returned to our reading in silence. More boring spells. How to cure boils. How to cause boils. Plague of frogs. Swarm of locusts. Finding magical repositories. Finding fresh water. Blah, blah, blah. Nothing that indicated a war-mage, necromancer, or anything else very dangerous. A mixed blessing— didn't appear that Newell would be a tough opponent, once we tracked him down, but also quite tedious labor. I'd always wondered how spell-casters managed to do the useful bits—kill a zombie with a word, turn lead into gold, shoot lightning from their fingers. You know—interesting stuff.

"How do you know when your thing's done?" I asked, taking a short break when I finally finished reading the grimoire. Only five left to go, and Scott was already on his fourth. Hopefully I'd only have to read one more. There is only so much Latin I can read before feeling the urge to jump out a window.

"The reactive agent will change color again," Scott replied. "Red if it works. Black if it's a dud."

Not wanting to think about the possibility of failure, I pulled another tome from the stack of unread books and flipped open the heavy leather cover. It was written in English. An older version of the language, to be sure— not quite Shakespearean, but definitely before the invention of dictionaries. What? Why wasn't it in Latin?

Puzzled, I looked at the books that Scott had been going through. With a mounting sense of indignant outrage, I realized that they were all in English too. Just a few Latin phrases scattered throughout. No wonder he'd been outpacing me.

"This is ridiculous!" I exclaimed, disgusted. "How the hell did I get stuck with the only Latin grimoire?"

Scott looked up with a laugh. "It's *all* Latin? Really? You should have said something earlier. We could've switched."

"Too late now," I grumbled, going back to my reading. Despite not needing to translate anymore, I didn't progress much faster. Spent too much time looking up at the potion every few minutes, waiting for it to change. Like the proverbial non-boiling watched pot, the liquid stubbornly remained a bright, bubbling pink.

Lunchtime came and went, but Scott and I stayed at our work. I didn't want to miss a second's opportunity of tracking down Newell, and Scott's six-hour finish time was getting closer, one agonizing second at a time.

At last the color changed. Getting darker. "Red, not black. Red, not black," I muttered to myself in a weird sort of prayer. If this lead didn't pan out, I wasn't sure what the next step in the investigation would be. More research, most likely, and I was already going stir-crazy to get back into the field.

To my relief, the potion deepened to a ruby red. "Perfect," Scott said. He carefully poured his strange liquid creation into several test tubes and sealed them. Time to track down Newell.

"So, how does this actually work?" I asked.

"It'll activate any tracking device," Scott said. "Only problem is, since it's magically linked, not blood-based, nothing will show up until Newell actually uses magic. But once he does, the residual aura should allow us to track him for a while—at least an hour, maybe more."

"We'll need to use the Terraform," I said. "Then we'll at least be able to tell if he's skipped town."

The Terraform. An amazing blend of modern technology and ancient magic. When it's not in use, it looks like a ten-by-ten teak table, taking up most of the floorspace in its room. The only hint as to its magical origins are the runes carved into the four-inch vertical apron bordering the plain tabletop. But when the Terraform is activated, the flat surface transforms into a three-dimensional map of anywhere in the world, showing streets, landmarks, terrain, you name it. It's even hooked up to Google Street View to zoom in for a closer look.

The Terraform room was empty when Scott and I arrived. Perfect. I'd been somewhat worried that we might encounter Ainsley there, analyzing the movement of the kraken and the Protectors sent to relocate it. But, lacking an overbearing Councilor, we were free to go about our task of tracking down Newell unhindered.

Scott poured one of the tubes of potion into the funnel-shaped receptacle in one corner of the Terraform. It used the same basic spells as my tracker disc, although rather than merely showing relative distance and direction, the larger device was able to overlay the beacon on a detailed map. Once Newell used magic, we'd see exactly where he was.

Unsurprisingly—though still disappointingly—the Terraform remained blank. Nothing to track yet. Dammit. Who knew how long this was going to take. Hopefully Newell was the type of warlock who used small bits of convenient magic throughout the day. Making his five o'clock shadow disappear instead of bothering with a razor. Summoning car keys instead of looking for them. That sort of thing. It would seriously help shorten our waiting game.

With a resigned sigh, I turned back to the unread grimoires we'd brought with us from the lab. Might as well get something useful done while we waited for results.

A score of boring spells later, and one at last caught my eye. "Braking the Curss of the Fulle Moon: A Waye to Overcomm the Werr-Wolfs Spelle." Could it actually work? I'd never heard of any method to keep werewolves from turning into dangerous, uncontrollable animals at every full moon. Sure, you could lock them up, contain them, but there was no way to *tame* them. They lost every shred of their humanity during that one night a month.

"Enzo, look!" Scott exclaimed. Of course. Just when I was getting to something interesting.

But what was happening on the Terraform was even more intriguing. A red dot appeared at the center of the flat surface. Quickly, like a time-lapse of a spider spinning webs, black lines spread out around the red spot. Straight lines, with ninety-degree intersections and a few moderate curves. A city map, with Newell somewhere within.

Smaller details started filling in as the edges of the map continued to expand. Street names, a tree-covered park, shopping centers. All very familiar to me. I grinned. I knew exactly where Newell was.

It wasn't until a large cursive scrawl appeared across the entirety that Scott figured it out. Of course, he didn't live there, so I didn't expect him to know the area as well. "That's Summerville," Scott said. "He didn't leave after all."

I met his broad smile with a wolfish grin of my own. My prey was in sight. "We got him. No way he can escape now."

CHAPTER 23

LOCK 'N' LOAD

"IT WORKED!" SCOTT exulted. "It actually worked. Let's go!"

For once, I was more forbearing than my academic friend. Time to do the wise thing and prepare before we leaped into an unknown magical situation. We needed to visit one of my favorite places at Headquarters. We powered down the Terraform and headed out to the wonders of the Armory.

Need I say more than its name to describe what the Armory contains? It holds a wonderful variety of magical armaments, unsurpassed in the known supernatural world. Not just wooden stakes and silver daggers, useful though those are. If there's a supernatural species out there, the Armory contains something to kill or capture it. Leprechaun traps (both the lethal and non-lethal varieties), unicorn bridles, werecat catnip, you name it, we have it. Plus all the other things you don't even know exists.

My goal was body armor. We have a wide assortment of protective gear, most of which is spelled to prevent magic from being used on its wearer. Since Scott and I knew we were going after a warlock, we had to be prepared. Luckily, the Armory contains all sorts of styles of armor, from medieval steel plate to modern bulletproof camouflage, so that no matter what situation we encounter, we can blend in. And in case you're thinking that plate mail would look out of place nowadays, have you ever had to capture an elf at a Renaissance Faire?

Scott and I snagged two sets that looked like standard human riot gear, including Kevlar vests, helmets with clear face protectors (which were also spelled to show what magic was being cast nearby), and curved rectangular shields. All magically protected, all properly labeled as FBI. Sure, it wasn't standard for FBI agents to have riot gear, but it's amazing what a badge and giant letters on a shield can do to establish legitimacy. Not many people have the stones to question a heavily armored and armed secret agent.

Next was weapons. I picked up a pistol. As you might guess, it wasn't a standard human-made gun, despite looking like one. It was more like something that James Bond would carry—it could fire a wide variety of projectiles, from troll tranquilizer to silver bullets. I loaded it with some night-night darts. Any human would immediately drop unconscious at the tiniest prick. Perfect for bringing in a warlock alive.

"Can you use one of these?" I asked Scott.

"Of course," Scott said, picking up a pistol of his own and expertly loading it.

I raised my eyebrows in disbelief—when had Scott become proficient in firearms?

He grinned at the look on my face. "Cora's been teaching me how to shoot a gun this past year."

"Well," I said, trying to wrap my head around this new information. I hadn't spent much time at HQ over the past few years, but I hadn't realized how much I didn't know about Scott's current life. How the hell did I not know about any of this? "That's good, at least. Don't need to worry about you shooting yourself in the foot. Make sure to grab some extra night-night darts."

"Grab what?" Scott asked.

"Some—" Crap, I was actually going to have to remember the real name of what I called night-night agent. "The magidormosidal ketalium darts." See why I say night-night instead? Much easier to remember, and its purpose is contained in the name. Make the bad guys go night-night.

"You could just call them M.K. darts," Scott said.

"And get them confused with manticore killers?"

Before we left the Armory, I snagged a few other items that might come in handy, including a black opal—should be part of standard field gear, in my opinion, considering how useful they are when dealing with humans. But they're rare, since it's difficult to spell an opal without shattering it, so usually it's just the cleanup crew who takes them to big incidents involving human witnesses. But because we were going to be working with Detective Marlow—and didn't want him finding out about the supernatural aspects of the case—a black opal was a necessity.

"Ready to go?" Scott asked.

I hadn't paid much attention to what he'd been doing, but a quick glance at him demanded all my focus. Scott had dressed in his riot gear, wearing everything necessary to cut an imposing figure.

Except he didn't. He looked like a ten-year-old wearing his father's suit and tie. More along the lines of adorable than intimidating. That needed to change, and quickly. More specifically, Scott needed to change.

Being a shapeshifter means that you can look like whatever you want (provided it falls within the limits of the human form). For us, our physical appearance is most similar to a human's choice of clothes—it reflects how we want the world to see us. Scott, being the definitive nerd, was a five-foot-nine gangly ginger. You know the type—pale skin that hardly ever sees sunlight, flaming red hair that looks like it's never met a comb, and the general sense that this was a person whose list of allergies could fill a pocket-sized dictionary. In other words, Scott looked like the kid who gets bullied by everyone, even the teacher.

Well, we could kill two birds with one stone. Scott didn't have FBI creds registered to his preferred appearance, but the Armory also contained a filing cabinet full of various credentials for different agencies and featuring a wide range of visages. Time to reinvent Scott.

I pulled open the drawer labelled FBI and rifled through the IDs, snagging one that looked like it would suit our current needs. Wilson Scott. Perfect—wouldn't even need to worry about name slip-ups. Besides the great name, Agent Scott was most definitely intimidating. Looked like a linebacker for the New England Patriots. The picture was of a shaved-head, strong-jawed black man, and the personal details said thirty years old, six-three, two-hundred-and-forty-five pounds of pure muscle.

"Here, use this," I told Scott, tossing the ID and badge to him.

He studied the picture for a minute and then shifted. No matter how much I shapeshift myself, I'll admit that it can be weird to watch someone else doing it. Scott shot up six inches as his sallow skin darkened to a deep sable. For a brief moment, his bright red hair stuck out boldly from black skin before retreating into his scalp. Muscles bulged where none had been before, and blue eyes melted into chocolate. His facial features reformed as if an invisible sculptor was reshaping clay. Within thirty seconds, nerdy Scott Avery had been replaced by Agent Wilson Scott. Big improvement.

"How do I look?" Scott asked in a baritone, much richer than his normal voice.

"Like you're ready to bust down doors and haul people off to Gitmo," I said. "Let's go."

Since my standard field kit was back in my apartment in Summerville, I grabbed another tracker as we left the Armory. "Is there any time limit on your tracking potion?" I asked Scott. "Or can we activate the tracker now and not worry that it's going to run out of juice?"

"We should do it now," Scott said. "And hope Newell's still using magic. We can't transfer the signal from the Terraform."

"Son of a—" I hadn't thought of that. I thought once we got the signal, we were good to go. Didn't think about the differences of stationary equipment and field devices. "Someone really needs to make these things sync. If my phone and my computer can share everything, why shouldn't our magical items be able to do the same? After all, isn't magic supposed to be able to do stuff beyond technology's capabilities?"

Scott didn't answer. Instead, he pulled out another vial of the potion and poured it into the tracker. As expected, no result yet, but we knew Newell was in Summerville at least. We could kill time in the car ride there. And then, with any luck, Newell would be in our crosshairs once again. After all, this case had thrown an overabundance of crap at me so far—surely I was due for a little good fortune. Right? Please?

CHAPTER 24

A Dead End

"GOT IT!" SCOTT'S sudden exclamation broke the mind-numbing silence of our car ride to Summerville. Since we couldn't agree on a radio station—Scott wanted to listen to classical music, of all things—we'd opted for quiet instead.

"Where?" I asked. We were a mile from the nearest Summerville exit. Perfect timing. At last, something was going right.

"Somewhere northwest of us," Scott said. "No, wait. Southeast. Huh, that's weird."

"What's weird?" I asked, overtaking a semi-truck from the right lane. Screw the whole "passing side, suicide" bumper sticker he had on the back of his trailer. If you're going to drive in the middle lane, you're going to get passed on the right side. Sure, there were three lanes of traffic here, but someone who didn't know what a gas pedal was had their minivan planted in the left lane. Quick driving tip: If you can't pass a big-rig, stay out of the fast lane.

"The tracking light is pulsing," Scott said, holding onto his seat as I quickly zipped around a slow-moving horse trailer.

Okay, I'll admit: my driving skills aren't something you should try to emulate.

"It means that Newell's currently using magic. He didn't just do one spell; this is multiple spells in a row."

"But it gives us a strong signal to track?" I asked. Had to focus on the positives.

"Yes. I just don't know what the hell he's up to. Could be preparing a trap for us."

"What exit do I take?" The first was rapidly approaching.

"I'm not sure. It's not like this thing shows streets the way the Terraform does."

I growled in frustration as we passed the first exit.

"Oh," Scott said a moment later. "I think you should've taken that one."

Suppressing a curse—Scott was doing the best he could—I took the second offramp.

"Now where?" I asked.

"Due south."

I gunned the woefully underpowered engine as we exited the curve onto the streets. A yellow light was threatening to turn red, but I ignored it and squeezed across the white line just before it changed.

"Good, keep going in this direction for a mile or so." At least the tracker had a tiny map scale on it—gave us a little more to go on.

"Still showing new activity?" I asked.

"Not for the last couple of minutes."

What were we getting ourselves into? At least we were equipped this time, both with knowledge and with superb armor. Newell wasn't going to get away again.

"Turn left here," Scott said suddenly.

"A little heads-up next time!" I shouted as the tires squealed around the turn. Horns blared behind me, rapidly fading into the distance. We hadn't hit anyone, so what were they complaining about? "Now what?"

"Slow down," Scott ordered.

I complied, easing off the gas until—

"Here," Scott said.

I screeched up to the closest curb, leaped out as soon as the keys were out of the ignition, and paused only to pop the trunk on the way out the door.

"He's close," Scott whispered as we retrieved our shields from the trunk. "Just down this alley."

Slowly, shields raised before us, we advanced into the dead-end alley. Four-story buildings rose to either side, casting the lane into perpetual shadow. Nothing to see so far, other than a couple of overflowing dumpsters and a pile of what was likely fresh vomit. I led the way—although we were equally equipped, I was definitely more prepared to face the threat than my friend was, new tough appearance aside.

"He should be here," Scott said, a note of defeat in his whispered voice.

"He is," I said, but it wasn't confidence that colored my voice—it was disappointment, with a dash of annoyance thrown in. Newell was just past the last dumpster. Or, should I say, Newell's body was. Ding-dong, the warlock's dead.

CHAPTER 25

DING-DONG

A QUICK EXAMINATION of the body showed exactly how Newell died. Sure, I know you're supposed to wait for the medical examiner to officially pronounce the cause of death, but it's difficult to argue with a foot of sharp steel sticking from a man's chest.

I ignored the body—not like he was going to jump up and attack us—and searched the surrounding area. Nothing. No signs of who Newell was fighting with. Undoubtedly the surges of magic that Scott had seen on the tracker were Newell battling with the person—or thing, can't rule that out—that killed him. But there were no obvious signs of what he'd been up against. Granted, there were a few craters in the walls of the alley, but that wasn't really indicative of anything other than a magical battle.

"Enzo, look at this," Scott said, closer behind me than I'd thought. I suppressed a jump and turned around.

"What the hell?" I exclaimed. Scott had retrieved the murder weapon from Newell's corpse and was holding a bloody, serpentine dagger. "Why'd you take that from the body? It's evidence."

Scott waved a hand impatiently. A massive hand, I might note. His new form was certainly on the oversized side of things. Almost makes you wonder . . .

"We can't leave it here for humans to find," Scott said, pulling my mind out of the gutter. "It's clearly something magical. Look at the runes on the blade."

I looked closer. Sure enough, there were markings etched along the dagger's length. Currently looked like bloody rivulets in the steel, but easy enough to see. No idea what they meant though. But more importantly, I recognized the dagger. I'd seen it before—at the apartment, when Finian used it to punch through the window. Apparently the universe has a sense of irony, for Newell to be killed by the very weapon he'd intended to commit murder with.

"Put that in the trunk," I said, handing Scott the car keys. No need for the humans to get their hands on any more magical objects.

Whoop whoop. Shit. Red and blue lights flashed down the alley, accompanied by a semi-courteous partial siren. The human police were here. No doubt some concerned citizen had called 9-1-1 when they were unfortunate witness to whatever supernatural battle had occurred in this alley. And here stood Scott and I, with a skewered corpse and the murder weapon in Scott's hand. At least we had FBI uniforms on—should be able to weasel our way out of this one.

"Put the dagger back by the corpse," I ordered Scott. Fortunately his movements were obscured by the dumpster as two figures exited the lit-up cruiser. Hands on holsters but guns not drawn, I observed. Good—a bullet wound isn't exactly a fun thing, even if you can heal from the non-lethal shots. As I put on my most ingratiating smile—nothing to see here, just a fresh corpse in a dank alley—I recognized the policemen. Hawkins and Marlow. I felt an iota of relief—at least we had a working relationship, weird though it was.

"Agent Thornton?" Marlow asked, his tone filled with an expected surprise and suspicion. "What are you doing here?"

"We tracked down Newell," I said. "But someone got to him first. He's dead."

Scott came out from behind the dumpster, hands mercifully empty of murder weapons. "This is Agent Scott," I introduced. "Agent Scott, Detective Marlow and Officer Hawkins of the Summerville PD."

"I thought the other guy you were working with was Scott," Marlow said. "The nerdy one."

"That's Scott Avery, a consultant. This is Wilson Scott, FBI."

"Must get confusing."

"Not really—I just yell 'Scott' and one of them will show up."

Cora was looking back and forth between us, a slight frown on her face. Out of the corner of my eye, I saw Scott give her a surreptitious wink, and her expression cleared. Figured out it was the same Scott.

Introductions (reintroductions?) through, it was time to return to the body. I led Marlow and Hawkins around the dumpster to where Newell's corpse lay, the dagger's hilt protruding from his chest. Dammit—I'd need to have a word with Scott later about putting the dagger *by* the body, not *in* the body. Forensics would be able to tell that it had been put back in, and they'd ask questions. At least Scott was wearing combat gloves, so his fingerprints wouldn't be found. At this point, I was more than grateful for the small blessings in life.

"What happened?" Marlow asked as he looked over the scene.

"Got an anonymous tip. Led us here. We got here five minutes before you." Time to redirect. Before I had to pile more fabrications on top of my story. My lies were shaky enough as it was. "What brought you here?"

"Neighbors called in a complaint. Said someone was lighting off fireworks in this alley. We were the closest unit, so we came to check it out."

Fireworks. More like flashes and explosions from a magical duel. And who better to fight a battle with a warlock than a witch with a grudge? Most likely Jane Doe had killed Newell. Either revenge, or merely finishing the fight that I had interrupted last week, when Newell had stabbed her.

Something niggled at my memory as I thought about the previous stabbing. Something Newell said during his interrogation. The knife he used to stab Jane Doe. He said it had protected him from her magic attack. Likely a lie, since Newell had been hiding the fact that he was a warlock. He'd probably used his own magic to shield himself. But he'd also called it a mortal blade. Said one nick, and you're dead within a week. What if he'd been telling the truth about that?

One thing was for sure: we needed that dagger. Couldn't let it fall into human hands. Time to call in some backup.

I pulled out my cell phone and dialed the FBI. The real FBI, not Protectors. I would've called my own people, but with the damned kraken situation, there wasn't enough manpower at HQ to remedy this situation.

"This is Enzo Thornton," I said. Good thing I had the direct extension to the super-secret division. Didn't need to worry about transferring calls, proving credentials, or answering time-wasting questions. "I need an investigative team to retrieve a body. ASAP. Summerville Police are already on scene." I gave them the cross streets and hung up.

"What was that?" Marlow demanded. It was the first time I'd seen him actually angry, not merely annoyed. "This crime scene is in our jurisdiction. Are you trying to take it away from us?"

"Sorry." I was surprised that I actually did feel a bit guilty. The detective was just trying to do his job, and here I was, getting in the way. If only he knew the truth. No, scratch that. Telling him the truth would only lead to more complications. "This is too closely tied to my own investigation. The murder weapon is one of the stolen artifacts I've been tracking."

Marlow opened his mouth to say more—harsh words, no doubt, about meddling federal agents—but Hawkins pulled him away, murmuring defusing phrases. Definitely nice to have someone in the know to run interference. If I had the black opal on hand, I could've easily calmed Marlow myself. But, of course, I'd left it in the car—I'd been expecting a magical fight, and I wasn't prepared for a coverup.

The real FBI agents showed up soon, medical examiner in tow. They were efficient at their job, taking photos, bagging evidence, loading the body into a van, and questioning the witnesses. The last part was mostly for show— they knew Scott and I were holding back, and that it wasn't their job to pry further. Their job was to get everything taken away so we could examine the evidence away from human police oversight.

"Careful with the weapon," I warned the ME softly as he examined the body, so Marlow couldn't overhear from his position of glowering over the proceedings. "It's more dangerous than it looks."

"Yes, sir," the examiner replied, and I watched as he carefully extracted the dagger and placed it in a steel box. No risk of someone getting accidentally cut.

I went to Marlow. "Any leads on Jane Doe?" I asked.

Irritation warred with professional dignity on Marlow's face. In the end, professionalism won. "Nothing yet," he said stiffly. "BOLO is still out. You think she did it?"

"It's looking that way," I said. Appreciation flashed on his face for the shared news, so I decided to try and take it a step further. Mend the smoldering bridge. "I'm sorry I can't tell you more, but I do appreciate your help. There are many aspects to this case that are still eluding me."

Marlow gave a short nod. "Anything else I can do for now?"

"I wish. I'll let you know if anything pertinent comes up."

Once everything was bagged and tagged, everyone went their various ways. Hawkins and Marlow back to their police cruiser. The FBI back to their headquarters—with a stop along the way to drop everything off at the Protectorate, I knew. And Scott and I went back to my spartan apartment. Task complete: find Newell. Only problem was, so far it was a dead-end alley.

CHAPTER 26

Cipher Spirit

EARLY ON SUNDAY morning, Scott—looking like his usual nerdy ginger self—and I drove back to Bay City. I love to drive, but I was definitely getting sick of this same commute. At least it was too early for traffic. I knew the freeway would be a nightmare in the afternoon, with all the mountain-vacationers heading home to the City.

When we got to Headquarters, there was an uptick in pedestrians and traffic. We'd arrived just in time for the ten o'clock Sunday service. Devout parishioners flocked toward the cathedral, blocking the entrance to the Protectorate parking lot. I appreciated the security that the holy ground gave to HQ, but the actual logistics of maintaining the holy status could be a pain sometimes. I just wanted to get in and get back to work. Find out why Newell had been killed and, more importantly, what the hell was going on in Summerville.

I'd spent the drive wishing that I had the chance to re-interrogate Newell, now that I knew he'd been lying to me. Unlikely to get the chance to talk to him again, considering he was dead, but I wasn't completely out of options. Before we started going through the evidence, I decided we needed to find Martin.

It's amazing how someone who inconveniently pops up all the time can be difficult to track down when you actually want to talk to him. Scott and I split up, both calling Martin's name as we traversed the empty Protectorate halls. No Martin. No Jake, either, but at this point I'd be happy to see my rival if Martin was at his side.

The bells tolled in the cathedral tower, reminding me of what I should've considered in the first place. Martin loved music. And, being mostly confined to the grounds of headquarters meant that his main source of songs were the celestial overtures during the Sunday morning hymns. Of course—the ghost was at church.

I texted Scott, letting him know where I was going. He replied that he'd get back to reading the grimoires. Not that we really needed that info, now that the spell-caster who'd owned the books was dead, but it didn't hurt for

Scott to continue to research. It was what he was best at, and maybe he'd dig up a nugget of information that would explain what was going on.

I slipped through a back door in the cathedral, staying out of sight of the faithful parishioners singing along to the melodic tunes resounding from the organ. Our Lady of Faith had a genuine pipe organ—one of those ancient, majestic instruments that takes up the majority of a wall, not some rinky-dink thing that looks like a piano with exhaust pipes. I climbed a circular staircase to the second floor of the cathedral, where a walkway ran around the perimeter, passing behind the massive pipes of the organ. There were literally thousands of them—I couldn't imagine how much it took to maintain the antiquated instrument. It was there that I finally found Martin, floating serenely next to the lead pipes as he listened to the hymns filling the air.

Instead of interrupting, I sat down, leaning back against the stone wall to wait. This close, the music of the organ was nearly deafening as air reverberated through the massive pipes. So I did a minor shift, preemptively rendering myself deaf, although the bass tones still vibrated through my bones. As I waited, I saw Martin stick a hand through the wall of one of the pipes, a mischievous grin on his face. A minute later, he gave a satisfied nod and removed the incorporeal hand, waited another minute, and put it into another pipe.

Knowing I wouldn't get any answers to Martin's behavior until the music was finished, I closed my eyes and settled down to wait. I was nearly asleep when my left side suddenly felt like it was plunged into a bucket of ice water—the aftereffects of a ghostly tap on the shoulder. My eyes snapped open to see Martin floating next to me. His mouth moved, and for a brief second I couldn't understand why no noise was coming out. Oh, right. I just couldn't hear it. Shifting my ears back to normal, I heard the deep, almost melodious sound of the priest delivering his sermon down below.

"I need to talk to you," I whispered to Martin.

"I'll meet you in the lab where you've been working," he replied, and then vanished.

"Dammit," I complained. "Wish I could do that." To my knowledge, nobody really knew how ghosts moved about—did they simply disappear from one point and then reappear in another, or did they travel on a different plane, undetectable to mortals, as they moved from place to place? No ghost had ever been willing to divulge the answers. Or even hint at one. Buggers.

I took the long route around, tiptoeing down the stairs so as to not interrupt the priest's message as I headed back toward the main buildings of Headquarters.

Martin was waiting for me when I got to the lab room. The contraption that Scott had set up to make the tracking potion was still there. The brownies hadn't cleaned it up. Apparently they'd learned their lesson after they cleaned out an incubator housing petri dishes. Clean could be too clean, as the brownies found out from the screeching of the lab techs when they discovered their cultivations washed down the drain.

"Odd for you to seek me out," Martin said, looking surprisingly serious considering how mischievous he usually was. Perhaps he suspected that I was after something out of the norm.

"What were you doing with the pipe organ?" I asked, delaying the real reason for my visit. I wasn't sure if I would be happier if Martin could help me or if he couldn't—ghosts could be quite enigmatic to work with, and their motivations were often difficult to decipher.

Martin's usual grin flashed. "Forming ciphers."

I frowned. "Creating codes?"

"Same word, different meaning," Martin said with an exaggerated air of lofty superiority, rising several inches higher in the air. "Time for you to learn more about the most noble of all art forms: classical music."

I fought the temptation to roll my eyes—Martin was apparently in one of his strange moods.

"In relation to pipe organs, a cipher refers to a continuous sound produced by one of the pipes when the valve is stuck open. It's usually caused by a mechanical defect. It can create quite a disharmony in a piece of music, although expert organists are able to adapt their music to the constant note, making it blend in with the rest of the piece."

"So why do you make them?" I asked. "I thought you liked music."

"I don't just *like* music; I'm a connoisseur," Martin said. "And as an expert in the art, I have a great appreciation for a true master of music. But the only way to separate a true master from one who is merely good is to set challenges for them to overcome. So I was testing the organist. She did quite well—I doubt any of the uncouth parishioners ever realized there was a change in the music. Undoubtedly, though, she will have the maintenance staff hard at work, looking for a fault in the pipes."

"And when they don't find anything, they'll all chalk it up to it being haunted, not knowing how right they are."

"Exactly." Martin smiled and nodded, then grew a bit more serious. "But you did not come to me to talk about ciphers. Why were you looking for me?"

Time to stop stalling. "I need to know if you can get in contact with a dead warlock for me."

Whatever Martin had been expecting, that clearly hadn't been it. For once, he was rendered speechless. If he could've gotten whiter than his normal translucent pallor, I'm sure he would have.

"You have no idea what you're asking me to do," he said. His blue eyes, usually sparking with mischief, were serious beneath his bushy white eyebrows, slanted in a frown. "I will not even try it. Do not ask me again."

"But—"

"I said no," Martin snapped.

The atypical temper puzzled me. "Can I at least ask why not?"

"You can ask," he said, a ghost of a grin returning to his face. "But it doesn't mean that I will answer."

"What if he's come back as a ghost?" That would definitely be easier than interrogating a corpse. "I could talk to him myself. I'd just need to track him down."

"He hasn't," Martin said, certainty filling his voice the same as if he'd said the sun rises in the east or sasquatches shit in the woods.

"How do you know?" Curiosity filled me, momentarily distracting me from the root problem of getting information from the dead warlock. Ghosts have always been extremely secretive about life beyond death, and Protectorate knowledge of them was mostly limited to what we were actually able to observe.

Unfortunately for my catlike curiosity, garrulous Martin was uncharacteristically tight-lipped in his response. "I just know."

"But how? Is there some sort of psychic memo that goes out to all ghosts when a new one pops up?"

Martin just smiled, the familiar glint of roguishness back on his translucent face.

"C'mon, Martin, at least give me a hint as to why you won't even try to contact Newell," I wheedled. I was certain that Martin knew how to do it—otherwise he wouldn't have had such a strong reaction to my request. "Otherwise I'll have to figure it out on my own. And you know how that might end up."

He studied me, eyes narrowing in thought. "Very well, I'll tell you. But only to warn you of the dangers of what you are asking. Before I say any more, you must swear to never ask me to contact the dead again. And to not ask any other ghost to help you do so either."

"I promise." Maybe this info would give me enough insight in order to form alternate plans.

"When a being dies, there is more than one plane of reality that they might enter. Most enter the realm of death. Very few enter the ghostly plane, which strongly overlaps with that of the living. It's tied to existence as you know it, but is still separate. That is why ghosts can be seen and heard but, for the most part, can't interact with the physical world. Most of our . . . essence . . . is contained on another plane, invisible and intangible to living mortals.

"The realm of death is separate from the others, and there is a barrier between it and them. The entrance is one-way, designed for souls to enter, not exit. A ghost could enter the realm of death and, theoretically, return to the ghostly plane, as they belong to neither that realm nor the one of the living. But doing so would cause damage to the barrier, with no way of knowing how severe the effects of that particular breach would be until they occurred. They could be insignificant and self-repairing, or they could cause the barrier to crumble, allowing life and death to crash into each other, with world-ending consequences."

"But how do you know that could happen?" I asked. "Surely it's all hypothetical, since such a cataclysmic event has never occurred."

"What makes you so certain that it hasn't happened before? Ever wonder what happened to the Martians?"

"Are you telling me—"

"I've told you more than enough," Martin said. "Just trust me—do not try to find your dead warlock. It will not end well for you."

Martin faded away before I had a chance to respond. I sighed in annoyance—always irritating when someone insists on having the last word. Especially when they're telling you what to do. Or not do, in this case.

The things we'd collected from Newell's house were still sitting in the lab, minus a couple of grimoires. No doubt Scott was sequestered away in a comfy chair someplace, reading through the rest of the spells. Not that it really mattered now. We didn't need to know what magic Newell was capable of anymore.

Scott's device that he used to create the tracking potion was still in place. Apparently nobody had ever taught him to clean up after himself. The cat skull, sitting in the remnants of the red liquid, caught my eye. What was it that Scott had said about it? Newell had used it to communicate with spirits? A slow grin spread across my face as a new plan began to form.

Bad idea, a small part of my brain cautioned. *Remember what Martin said about potential consequences.*

I chose to ignore that warning. Instead, I fished the skull out of the beaker and set it on a couple of paper towels to dry. Then I grabbed one of the spell books and flipped through it, no longer searching aimlessly for anything of interest. I had a purpose: find the spell that Newell used to speak to the dead.

CHAPTER 27

FLOWER POWER

AS I READ, part of me debated whether or not to get Scott involved. Two sets of eyes were better than one, I finally decided, and sent Scott a text of what to look for.

"Why?" came his quick response.

"Might be able to talk to Newell. Get more info about what's going on. Maybe find out who killed him," I texted back.

"You sure that's a good idea?"

"What's the worst that could happen?"

Good thing Scott hadn't heard all of Martin's warnings. He wouldn't have helped me if he had. But, then again, Martin was talking about a ghost crossing over to the realm of the dead. All I wanted to do was communicate with a spirit, not send anyone (or anything) across the barrier. Besides, Newell had clearly done it successfully, with no earth-ending consequences.

Two hours later, my phone dinged. Text from Scott. Three words: "Found the spell."

"Come to the lab," I typed. Just as I hit send, the door to the lab opened and Scott rushed in, his thumb holding a place in one of the thick tomes.

"What's it say?" I asked. "How long will it take to do?"

Scott set the book down, opened to a page titled, "Commuening with the Dedd: Useing Bonns to Bringg a Spirite Acrosse the Veill."

I started reading the spell, ignoring the atrocious spelling as much as possible. Thank God for the invention of dictionaries and spellcheck. Makes reading contemporary documents so much easier. At least for the most part the misspellings didn't make a difference to understanding the text, until I got to the fifth line: "Makk a circl of dryed wite flower, grownd fyne." Was that flower or flour?

Scott and I debated for a minute, then came to a consensus. It must've meant flour—otherwise, surely it would have made a difference what species of flower it was, not just the color. It figures though—the one word that was spelled right was actually a homonym.

Once we'd both read the spell, we assembled the components. It took a while—had to raid the kitchens for some ingredients, the science cabinets for others. One was a bit tricky—something that contained the essence of the person we were trying to summon. After a short argument, which I won, we decided that the cat skull counted for that, since Newell had used it to perform magic. We could use it both to channel the spell and act as an ingredient. Kill two birds with one dead cat.

Once we'd arranged everything according to the instructions, I read the incantation aloud. No, I'm not going to say what all the steps and words are—no use getting other people into trouble with spells they don't fully understand. I've learned my lesson in that regards. Just assume it was something mystical and wonderfully spooky. You know—"We stand here in reverence to summon forth a spirit of the dead." That sort of Hollywood B.S.

It's a good thing that I took a basic spell-casting course in the Academy, or I would've had a much more difficult time getting the spell to work. As it was, as soon as I spoke the last word, a gray mist arose in the flour circle we'd made on the lab floor. The mist twisted and braided itself, slowly resolving into the form of Peter Newell, warlock, deceased.

I halfway expected to hear his deep voice proclaim: "Who summons me here?" Instead, his first words were much less solemn. "Aw, hell. I thought that death meant I wouldn't see you anymore. Why can't you just leave me alone?"

I grinned, triumphant. The spell worked. Newell was here, ready or not. "We're trying to find the person who killed you," I said. "We're on your side this time. What can you tell us?"

Newell's features were blurry, like a photo taken with a fingerprint on the camera lens, but his scowl was still easily recognizable. "On my side," he scoffed. "As if. You're just trying to figure out what I was up to in life."

"That too," I admitted. "But you're dead now—it's not like it matters to you."

"Oh?" A sly tone entered his voice. I didn't like the sound. The hair on the back of my neck prickled. "Is that what you think? You would've been right, that it didn't matter to me. I was gone from this world. But then you summoned me back."

"Only to question you," I said, ignoring the sinking feeling in my gut. "Then it's back to hell—or wherever you've been."

A broad smile spread on Newell's face. "Yes, that would've been true. If you had made a proper containment circle out of white flowers. But you didn't. So now, I'm free to go."

Horror at the realization of my mistake—damn that spelling—was just beginning to surface when Newell stepped a misty foot across the white line. "Shall I say *hasta la vista?*" he asked with a smirk and disappeared.

I sat down on one of the lab stools as dismay overwhelmed me. What had I done? The question was rhetorical. I already knew the answer. I'd set a malicious dead warlock loose upon the world.

CHAPTER 28

THREE STRIKES

I WON'T EVEN begin to transcribe the swear words that were bouncing through my head when Newell disappeared. I called myself seven kinds of idiot in between cursing my impulsiveness. Granted, I hadn't destroyed the barrier between life and death like Martin had feared, but I had brought back another opponent. One that had been dead and gone and not my problem anymore. Shit.

Of all ghosts I didn't wish to see at the moment, Martin suddenly appeared. "What have you done?" he snapped, anger emanating from his intangible form. "I warned you—"

"Against sending a ghost to the realm of death, yes, I know," I said wearily. The weight of the investigation loomed over me. Had to keep going. Had to fix everything. "So I didn't. I found a spell that would allow us to talk to the dead."

"And then you botched it." Cold anger infused the words.

"Yes," I admitted. "But I'll fix it."

"See that you do. Soon. Or there will be consequences beyond your imagination."

"Can you help us?"

"I've already done far more than I should've. This rests on your shoulders now." With those final words, Martin faded away.

"Bloody hell, Enzo," Scott exclaimed. "What are we going to do?"

"Whatever needs to be done," I said, running over the investigation's checklist as I thought aloud, hoping I sounded optimistic. "Find Newell and send him back to the realm of death. Figure out who murdered him in the first place. Find the witch—she probably killed him. Find the sprite. Figure out what the hell is going on. Some sort of smuggling operation, it appears. Return the stolen dagger to the vampires." The last task seemed the most feasible at the moment—if fairly distasteful. Despite my relatively danger-free visit to Nolan Blair's coven, I still had no desire to make a return trip anytime soon. But I had to, if I wanted to fulfill all my various encumbering obligations.

I sighed, letting out my exasperation, annoyance, and frustration in one breath. In theory. But those emotions stayed lurking in the back of my head, along with impotence, incompetence, ineptitude . . . I had to stop the list there, lest I get bogged down in pessimism. That's the last thing I'll tolerate.

"I'll send a message to Blair, let him know we'll return his dagger tonight," I said. "With any luck, us bringing it back will make him feel a bit benevolent and generous. Maybe he can give us some clues to move forward in the investigation. A vampire that old has to have informants everywhere. Maybe they've heard something of interest."

Scott paled. "Are you saying that you want *me* to go with you?"

"Who else?" I gave him a half grin. "Besides, Hawkins and I came away unscathed last time. You just have to watch out for the hellhounds."

"Hellhounds?" Scott yelped. "You've got to be kidding me. I swear, this case is going to be the death of me."

"You and Hawkins should start a club. The 'Enzo is Trying to Passive-Aggressively Kill Me' Club."

"Nothing passive-aggressive about it, as far as I can see," Scott muttered sourly. "Should've stayed in the library. Worst thing that can happen there is a paper-cut."

"Well, until sunset, pretty much all we can do is continue to research. I'll send a message to the vamps, and you can look for some sort of banishment spell that we can use to send Newell back."

"I might've read something like that in one of the grimoires," Scott said. His eyebrows creased in thought, not anger anymore, as the prospect of more research distracted him. "I'm just not sure which one. I'll find it though."

We went our separate ways, Scott to his library haven, and me to the courier room. Once again, I signed my message in blood, trying not to think about why vampires, in particular, required a bloody signature on all messages sent to them.

As I headed to the library to help Scott, I ran into Councilor Ainsley. AKA the last person I wanted to see after I'd made a massive blunder. No, scratch that—seeing Jake would've been worse. I fervently prayed that Ainsley would pass by without comment but, of course, my flicker of hope was in vain.

"What's the status of your case, Thornton?" Ainsley asked.

"The warlock, Peter Newell, was murdered," I said. Start with the minor bad news. "Our main suspect is the witch, Jane Doe, who was in the initial confrontation with Newell. We recovered the mortal blade used in both fights." Yay, finally some good news. But it was an ice-cube of goodness against the Titanic-sinking iceberg of bad shit going down.

"What about the sprite you mentioned before?"

"Still no trace of him."

"So, to sum it up: You haven't found the sprite. You haven't found the witch. And one of your main suspects has been murdered. Does that about cover it?"

Yes, that's it, I wanted to say. Just taking a while to track down the bad guys. No big deal, I'll get them. But when I opened my mouth to lie, I saw Martin suddenly appear a short distance behind Ainsley. He was out of her sight, but the hard, accusing stare he gave me made my blood run cold. He knew the truth, and from the anger on his face, I knew he'd tell Ainsley what had happened if I didn't confess.

"No," I said. "That's not all. I summoned Newell's spirit back, intending to question him, but he escaped." No need to tell Ainsley about Scott's role. After all, I knew it was completely my fault, not his.

Martin gave a short nod of stern approval and disappeared back into the wall.

"You. Did. What?" Ainsley's voice was surprisingly quiet as she bit off each word individually, though a tic began in the corner of one of her furious gray eyes. "Of all the irresponsible things to do. I expected better of you, Thornton."

"I'll fix it, Councilor," I vowed.

"No, Thornton, you won't. I'm taking you off this case."

I felt like a centaur had kicked me in the gut. "But—"

"No. My decision is final. I'm putting Jonson on the case instead. You can take over his guard shifts in the dungeons."

That was too much. Put Jake on my case? I could live with my mistakes, but having Jake fix my problems was too much to bear. "Councilor, you can't!"

"I can and I have," Ainsley snapped.

I opened my mouth to protest again.

"Keep it up, Thornton, and I'll have you thrown into a cell in the dungeons instead of the guard desk."

My mouth snapped shut. I knew her threat wasn't idle. Even though I hadn't done it maliciously, I had set a dangerous spirit loose. And that was definitely a punishable offense. "Yes, Councilor," I said miserably.

"I will inform Jonson and Avery of the change in plan," Ainsley said, marching away and leaving me to my desolation.

Scott. Loyalty to my friend briefly held my pity-party at bay. Because of me, he was going to have to work with Jake. I wouldn't let Scott get punished on top of that. I quickly texted him, "Ainsley took me off the case. I told her I summoned Newell. Left you out. Don't tell her you were involved."

At that moment of my disgrace, a courier appeared, bearing a heavy parchment envelope. I broke the red wax seal, imprinted with the vampires' insignia, and pulled out the message.

"On behalf of my noble master, I am honored to invite Protectors Enzo Thornton and Cora Hawkins to his Bay City home tonight, at the stroke of midnight.—S.P." Identical to the first message from Sergio, except it mentioned us by name. I knew that fact wasn't something to be lightly ignored. The vampires would be incredibly offended—at the very least—if different Protectors showed up tonight. Well, one last thing to do on this case. At least the task would get me out of HQ. Away from Jake. Right now, I'd rather spend quality time with the whole coven of vampires than face my nemesis while humiliated. Of course, at this point, it was quite possible that I'd get the chance to do both. Lucky me.

CHAPTER 29

LAST HUZZAH

I TEXTED HAWKINS as I headed to the evidence lockup, where we'd stored all the stuff from Newell's house that we weren't actively working with. "Need to go back to Blair's tonight. Invite requested you too. You available?"

As I hit send, I debated about whether to tell her I'd been replaced on the case by Jake. And summoned a dead warlock. I wasn't sure what Hawkins would be madder about—me bringing a supernatural entity back into the case, or having to work with Jake. The latter, I guessed, although either thing would give Hawkins justified reason to be pissed at me.

In the end, I decided to wait to tell her about my massive blunder. Not because I wanted to delay the confession, but because I didn't want to risk her partner seeing a text message about a summoned spirit. With Marlow's investigative nature, and my current rotten streak of bad luck, he'd no doubt figure out that the supernatural really existed.

The Protector at the evidence lockup gave me a form when I requested the vampire dagger. Finally, something was going right. No hassle getting the blade. Just one measly paper to fill out and sign. It was all routine, of course, but I was starting to count the small blessings in life. After all, they were all I had at the moment.

My phone dinged as I waited for the Protector to return with the dagger. "Does it have to be tonight? You have any idea what traffic is like going to the city on a Sunday?"

"Sorry," I typed, knowing I was going to be using that word a lot in the near future. "Can't ignore an invite from Blair. Don't want to offend him. Midnight meeting again."

"Fine. Be there when I can."

I checked the time. Nine p.m. Even with the decline of traffic as the evening wore on, Hawkins would have to leave now if she had any hope of making it on time. Meanwhile, I had a couple of hours to kill, hopefully managing to avoid Jake during that time. I couldn't bear to face him now. Not until I'd figured out some way to redeem myself.

With that thought, I realized that I would keep working. Keep trying. I wouldn't give up at this setback, even if it was a major blow to my case, career, and confidence. I'd find some way to make up for my error. I had to. The alternative was unthinkable, so I wouldn't dwell on it.

Of course, it's hard to move on when your past mistakes are constantly thrown in your face. I rounded a corner (why do we say "rounded" when corners are square?) and came face to face with Jake. A victorious sneer spread across his face.

"So, Enzo the Bozo, I hear from Councilor Ainsley that a competent Protector is needed to replace you," Jake taunted. "Looks like I'm going to have to clean up your mess."

"But you just said Ainsley was looking for someone competent," I retorted. "That rules you out."

Jake laughed derisively. Both of us knew that my insults currently held no power. "If I'm incompetent, and I was chosen to take over for you, then what exactly does that make *you*?"

I itched to punch that smug look off his face. But I knew that would just get me into further trouble, undermining my efforts to redeem myself. "The person who's going to solve this case," I snapped.

Jake snorted. "Good luck with that. You're benched. You're not going to solve anything from the dungeon guard desk. Now, I have to go. Some of us have *important* work to do, fixing other people's screwups." He sauntered away, his stride exceedingly jaunty.

Grinding my teeth in frustration, I headed the other direction. Away from Jake. Away from my problems—I wished. No. The only way to fix my mistake was to confront the issue head-on. I needed to study the grimoires some more, try to find a way to banish Newell.

I found Scott and the pile of spell books in the mostly empty library (I would say "totally empty," but Scott was there). Taking a deep breath to brace myself, I opened the door.

Scott jumped, a brief moment of fear flitting across his face before recognition filled his eyes. "Enzo! What in bloody hell is going on? Jake was just here, grilling me on the case. He said he's my boss now."

"No," I said empathetically. "Jake's replaced me on the case, but he is *not* your boss. If anything, you should be in charge, since you've been on the case longer." I would *not* see my best friend acting subordinate to his lifelong bully.

Scott shook his head slowly—denying something, although I wasn't sure what. "But why's Jake on the case anyway? He's no more of a field agent that I am, even if he *did* pass his tests. You have more experience than the two of us combined."

"Yeah, but I also have more mistakes," I admitted. "And summoning Newell was a huge one. Ainsley was right"—the words were bitter in my mouth—"I shouldn't be on this case anymore. I've just made everything worse."

The depression that I'd been keeping at bay crashed over me like a tidal wave. Overwhelming. Inescapable. Who was I to think that I could fix anything, after all the mistakes I'd made?

"Shut up," Scott snapped. I stared at him, mouth slightly agape in shock. I'd never heard Scott use that tone before. "Quit feeling sorry for yourself. If anyone has a right to complain now, it's *me*. I'm the one who has to work with Jake. And work on a case that I have neither the training nor experience for. But you don't hear me whining about it. And I'm not going to take that crap from you either. So either shut up and help me, or go away and leave me to my work."

Scott turned his glare back to the grimoire he'd been reading. I sat down across the table from him and, stunned from his outburst, pulled a book to me.

It was several minutes before I could focus on the words, though, as I tried to process my emotions. Scott was right—I couldn't wallow in self-pity. I'd told myself that already, but it's one thing to know what you should do, and another to work despite uncontrollable emotions. After all, nobody can change how they feel just by wishing it to be so. But we can control our actions. Make the choice to keep trying, no matter what. Even when you'd rather crawl under the covers and not emerge for a week.

We read in silence for a couple of hours, the only sound the turning of the pages, until my phone buzzed. Hawkins had arrived. Checking the time, I realized that we needed to leave now in order to make the midnight meeting with the vampires. "Be right out," I texted Hawkins, then told Scott, "Gotta go."

"Where?"

"Return the dagger to Blair."

"But you're off the case. Shouldn't Jake do it?"

I gave a half smile at the thought of sending Jake to the vampire coven. Better him than me. Except this time, when I was returning Blair's stolen dagger. No way I was letting Jake get the credit for that, the one thing I'd been successful at in this case.

"Hawkins and I were invited specifically," I said instead.

"Okay. Be safe."

"Aren't I always?"

"No."

I laughed as I left Scott to his continued research.

Hawkins was waiting in the parking lot, car idling by the curb.

"How'd you get in the lot?" I asked as I slid into the passenger seat.

"Hello to you too," Hawkins muttered, then began sarcastically miming different voices. "'How was the drive?' 'Horrible, actually. It took two and a half hours to get here.' 'Oh, sorry to hear that. Thanks for coming on such short notice.' 'No problem—I just *love* visiting vampire covens.'"

Great. She was already in a bad mood. I'm sure breaking the news that she would be working with Jake would do wonders to improve her temper. I could only hope she didn't try to bite my head off—literally.

"Sorry," I said contritely. Or, as contritely as I could manage. Can't completely change my nature overnight. "Thanks for coming. I really appreciate it. Couldn't do it without you."

The streetlights above allowed me to easily see Hawkins roll her eyes. "Laying it on a bit thick, aren't you?" she asked. "Anyhow, I come here every month to change, remember? My DNA's authorized on the scanner."

We started driving in silence, though, for me at least, it wasn't a peaceful one. I was torn with an internal debate as to whether I should tell Hawkins the bad news.

"I got kicked off the case," I finally blurted out. "Jake's replacing me."

"What?" Hawkins's hands clenched on the steering wheel, jerking the car into the oncoming lane. Thank God it was so late. No traffic, so we didn't get the chance to experience what a head-on collision felt like. She slid back onto the right side of the road as she demanded, "How the hell did that happen?"

I confessed in a rush, the words tripping over my tongue as they spilled out. When I finished, the only noise over the purr of the engine was Hawkins's fingers angrily tapping on the steering wheel. I waited for her recrimination, her justified accusations.

"That was a stupid thing to do, there's no denying it," Hawkins finally said, less fury in her voice than I'd been expecting. "But why did *Jake* get chosen, of all people? Isn't there someone, anyone, else who could do it instead?"

"All the local Protectors are at sea, busy with a kraken relocation," I said.

"Krakens exist?" Hawkins asked in surprise. Sidetracked. No anger in her voice. Good. "I thought they were just myths."

I laughed. "As mythological as werewolves."

"Touché," she said. "But give me a break. I've only known about all this for a year. How am I supposed to know all that's true or fake? I mean, Scott told me that the Tooth Fairy is real but the Easter Bunny isn't. How can I know the difference? They're both myths told to human children."

I shrugged. "Just learn as you go, I guess. Most mythological creatures are real, or at least heavily based on real beings."

"But why don't humans know they're real?" Hawkins asked. "I mean, if there are stories about supernatural beings, those stories had to come from somewhere. So what keeps humans from knowing the truth?"

"They used to," I said. "That's where all the ancient stories come from. Back then, people knew they were real. But after the Concealment Pact of 1456, all supernatural creatures went into hiding, and any time a human saw one, we covered it up."

"Why go into hiding though?"

"The advancement of weaponry. Guns, to be specific. Humans became powerful enough to slay many supes, and they were determined to become the dominate sentient species on the planet. They started killing indiscriminately, driving many peaceful species, like unicorns and winged horses, toward extinction. Even the creatures who could fight back were taking massive casualties. A werewolf can't outrun a silver bullet, after all. So the sentient supernatural races made the pact to disappear from human reality, to be known only as myths. It took a few generations, but in the end, almost every human scoffed at the idea of the supernatural. Only a few small pockets of believers remain worldwide, and even those who do believe have a skewed view of what the supernatural is. They're the ones responsible for witch killings, for example, although nearly all their victims are innocent humans."

My long-winded recital of supernatural history was thankfully interrupted by Hawkins pulling up to a curb and shutting off her engine. We'd arrived. Back for another visit to one of my favorite supernatural species. Bring on the bloodsuckers.

CHAPTER 30

PROMUS PROMISE

AS WITH OUR last visit to the vampire coven, the hellhounds disguised as Chihuahuas came out yapping in force when we entered the wrought-iron gate. This time, however, Hawkins didn't make fun of their diminutive, non-threatening appearance as they sniffed our shoes. One brown hound grabbed the hem of my pants and gave a small tug, shaking his head back and forth. I gave silent thanks that his strength matched his size. For the moment, at least. I'd seen firsthand how quickly they could transform.

"Crinitus, is that you?" I asked, remembering the beast inappropriately named "Fluffy." Hellhounds are quite intelligent, and able to understand almost anything said around them. No matter the language. Nobody knows how, though, as any biologist who's attempted to study them has been subsequently eaten.

Luckily for me, the dog just dropped the end of my pant leg and sneezed in response.

"Can you let Sergio know we're here? He invited us."

Crinitus sat down, tipping back his head to let out a high-pitched howl. I don't know what's worse: nails on a chalkboard or the rest of the hellhound pack joining in on the wailing.

The door to the mansion flung open, revealing Sergio. He was dressed in an immaculate black suit with a pattern of magenta and silver flowers. Once again, a bold fashion statement, and once again, Sergio pulled it off flawlessly. Well, it would have been flawless, but the effect was somewhat spoiled by Sergio's fingers stuffed in his ears as he grimaced against the yelping noise.

"Enough, enough!" he cried out. Mercifully the pack fell silent. Sergio dropped his hands and brushed invisible specks of dusts from his sleeves. Reorienting himself, it seemed. Then he gave a wide smile and flourishing bow. "Welcome, welcome, Protectors! My noble master is expecting you. Please, come in."

After submitting to another pat down and disarming—I was allowed to keep the vampire blade, at least—we were led back to the throne room on the second floor.

More vampires were in the room this time. Nearly thirty. Though surprised by the number and, naturally, tense from being completely surrounded by immortal killers, I affected an air of nonchalance. After all, before there had been more than enough vampires to kill both Hawkins and me, disarmed as we were. What were the extra vamps going to do? Kill us again?

After Sergio presented us and we made our bows to Blair, I pulled out the obsidian dagger. "Lord Blair, it is my pleasure to return your stolen item to you."

A satisfied smile spread across Blair's face. Close-lipped smile, so Blair's handsomely sinister image wasn't ruined by revealing his braces. To my surprise, he stood, descending the two steps from his throne to take the dagger from me personally.

Running a finger down the length of the blade in a creepy sort of caress, he asked, "And the thief?" Braces flashed as he spoke, but I'd been expecting them, so I didn't laugh or let my amusement show.

"Dead."

I saw disappointment in his eyes, but only because he was so close, and I was looking for it. It quickly disappeared as he expertly hid his dissatisfaction with the terminal conclusion. No doubt that he'd been hoping for a chance of torturous vengeance against the person who dared to steal from him.

"I should congratulate you on a job well done, then, Protectors."

"Thank you," I replied, though I'd noticed that he hadn't actually congratulated us. I decided to let it slide, hoping that if I kept Blair in a good mood, I'd be able to get more information from him. "However, there are still a few things that are open in the case. Like why the blade was stolen from you, and how."

Blair's eyes narrowed. This close, they looked like the depths of a glacial cave of molten ice. For the first time, I truly comprehended Blair's centuries of immortal life—and his ability to enact cruel vengeance on those who crossed him.

But I stood my ground, meeting his gaze. Our staring contest was interrupted by another voice. "Protectors?" a male voice nearby asked. He looked like a faded photo—pale blue eyes, white-blond hair, and the unnaturally pallid skin of his sun-deprived race. "That's Protec*tors*? Plural? But one of them's a *dog*." The last word dripped with scorn.

"You got a problem with me?" Hawkins snapped. My mouth quirked in a half smile as I realized she was repeating one of the first things I'd said to her.

"The beast speaks!" the blond vampire said with sarcastic incredulity.

"Enough, Larkin," Blair snapped. "These are my invited guests. And need I remind you, they brought my blade back? The one you swore to recover."

"Yes, my lord," Larkin replied with a bow. Evidently cowed, but I didn't buy it.

Blair returned to his throne and sat, twirling the dagger between his fingers. All he needed to do was let out a malicious "Mwa ha ha ha" at that moment to perfectly fit the bill as a stereotypically cheesy B-movie villain.

"The lapse in security has been handled," he finally said, as though the interruption had never happened. Looking at the hard set of his jaw, I knew that someone had died over that security breach. "The Protectorate need not concern themselves with that. As to why it was stolen—this dagger is rare, one of five identical blades. Therefore it's invaluable. What more could a thief want from it?"

He was lying. I was certain of it, though nothing in his words, tone, or body language indicated anything other than complete honesty. But there was no way that someone would steal something so precious—and so easily identifiable—from a powerful vampire with no more motive than greed. There had to be something else going on, but I knew Blair wouldn't tell me what it was.

"I'm glad to hear that your security issue was resolved." Two could play the lying game. "And that we were able to recover your property."

"You have done me a great service, Protectors," Blair said. "I owe you a debt. If there is anything I can do for you, within reason, just say the word and I will see it done."

"Thank you, that is very generous," I said, giving a short bow. "I cannot think of anything at the moment, but I will be sure to call on you if something arises."

I saw a brief hint of anger in Blair's eyes at my response, although he quickly masked it in a wide smile and a gracious nod. Undoubtedly it galled him to be in the debt of a Protector. Would've preferred to pay it off immediately, instead of having it called in on a future date.

Sergio escorted us back downstairs and returned our weapons to us. Before we left, he handed us each a personal business card.

"My master always pays his debts, and I am authorized to act upon his behalf during the daylight hours. If you need anything, please, call me."

I glanced at the card and read the elaborate script with Sergio's name and phone number, Flipping it over, I saw a company logo for Promus & Sons, Executive Assistants, Blair Enterprises.

"Family business?" I asked, amused.

"Of course, of course. Founded in 1284. Proudly and loyally serving Lord Blair ever since."

"Is there anything that you can tell us that would help us help him with this investigation?" Hawkins asked. I admired her twist of logic when I saw Sergio take a breath, hesitating. "We are still pursuing suspects who have connections to the one who had the dagger. Any information might help us catch them more quickly. And end any potential threat to your master."

Sergio glanced around nervously. We were alone. Leaning close to us, he whispered, "My grandfather told me that when he was a very young child, the infamous witch Henrietta tried to steal the dagger. She failed, but she escaped. My grandfather didn't know why she tried to take it, but perhaps you will find out. It might be related to the current theft, somehow."

With that enigmatic answer, Sergio ushered us out with a bow.

"What do you make of that?" Hawkins asked once we were in her car.

"No idea," I said. "But now I know what to research while I'm stuck at the guard desk." Nothing like ending the night on a purely optimistic note. I wish.

CHAPTER 31

In the Slammer

THE FOLLOWING MORNING, after a dismal breakfast and acidic coffee at the Protectorate cafeteria, I reported to the dungeons for my first shift of guard duty. Geoff was manning the desk when I arrived.

"Welcome, Enzo," Geoff said cheerfully. "I'll show you around before I go."

"Sure," I replied sullenly, trying to not take my anger at this assignment out on Geoff. After all, it wasn't his fault I was stuck underground. It was Ainsley's. And mine. A bit.

It didn't take too long to get acquainted with my new duties. There were only three prisoners at the moment. The banshee, who was taking a nap when we did our tour. Apparently her nonstop wailing had finally tuckered her out. And there was a pair of kleptomaniac dwarves who'd been caught tunneling into human homes, emptying the liquor cabinets, and stealing single socks.

All I really needed to do was keep an eye on everything, be prepared to check in any new prisoners, and let the kitchen staff in with food—for me and the inmates—when they arrived. Easy. It had to be; after all, Jake did it all the time. My biggest risks were dying from boredom or bleeding out from a paper cut from the grimoire I'd brought to read.

Once Geoff left, I settled down at the guard desk in the soundproof box and started to read. Two hours later, I slammed the book down in bored frustration. Nothing useful. The guard cubicle was starting to feel claustrophobic. I was meant to be out in the field, doing my job, not stuck in a squeaky office chair.

I pulled out my phone to text Scott, see if anything new had come up in the case, but I had no reception. Too far underground. Great. Cut off from the investigation in every way possible. Just perfect.

I stood up, planning on pacing the length of the cell blocks to work off my excess energy. But when I opened the door to the guard shack, I was immediately assaulted by the wailing of the banshee. Dammit. Didn't want to listen to that. I slammed the door and paced behind the desk instead. Three strides before I had to turn. Now I know what a caged lion feels like.

Had to get out of there. But there was only one way to do that—redeem my name by solving the case. I plunked back down in the chair and started reading again.

Six hours later and I was free. For the evening, at least. I'd have to be back the following day for another shift. I wanted to go home to my apartment, get away from HQ, but I couldn't stand the thought of battling commuter traffic each way. I'd practically have just enough time to sleep in my own bed before I'd have to leave again to get back in time for round two of hellish boredom tomorrow. But I couldn't stay at HQ all evening. Couldn't face either Jake or the cafeteria food—breakfast and lunch had been as much as I could tolerate for one day.

An epiphany suddenly hit me. I knew exactly the place to go. Great food, good drinks, and, even better, supernatural patrons. Maybe I'd be able to find out something that would help in the case. At the very least, I'd get a decent dinner. Maybe even get pleasantly drunk to drown my current sorrows.

I thought about inviting Scott to come along, but then realized that I'd risk him accidentally saying something to Jake. And I'd rather give a bath to a sphinx—they hate water even more than mundane cats—than give Jake any leads in the case.

I quickly got changed—showing up in a Protectorate uniform would probably cause half the patrons to flee at first sight. Out of uniform, they'd still know what I was, but at least it would look like I was off the clock. Not nearly as alarming. Once I was dressed in street clothes, I headed off to Saint Paddy's Leprechaun Bar, hoping the luck of the Irish would be with me.

CHAPTER 32

Luck of the Irish

SAINT PADDY'S LEPRECHAUN Bar is the go-to watering hole for supernatural beings in the Bay City area. To keep any humans from accidentally stumbling inside, it's covered in an ingenious chameleon spell. It doesn't make the building blend in—rather, it makes anyone who looks at the bar see the type of establishment they hate the most. To homophobes, it looks like a gay bar, whereas to the gays it appears to be a local chapter of the Westboro Baptist Church. You get the idea.

To me—well, to me, Saint Paddy's always looked like a funeral home. Feel free to psychoanalyze me as to why that may be. I've never given it much thought.

I pulled open the front door and stepped into the entryway. The second level of security was there—a burly cyclops, wearing sunglasses that hid the fact that he was monocular. His job was to kick out all the masochistic humans who saw their most hated place and decided to enter anyway.

"Don't want any trouble tonight," the cyclops bouncer warned me when he realized what I was.

I flashed an impish smile. "Not interested in trouble."

"Hmph."

Amazing how one grunt can contain so much skepticism and caution in one noise. But the cyclops opened the second door, the one leading to the main bar, for me.

As it was a Monday night, Saint Paddy's wasn't too busy. A group of goblins in one corner, a dwarf couple cuddling in a booth, some werewolves raucously making toasts and slamming beer steins together at a long table.

I went to the bar and sat at a stool. Wanted to get a feel for the crowd before I approached anyone. Didn't want to give off too many "cop" vibes. Also wanted a drink. A stiff one. Make that many drinks.

"I'll have an Arctic Twister," I told the leprechaun behind the bar. He wore a scowl and a bright green suit and top hat. Brass buckles on hat, belt, and shoes, a four-leaf clover pinned to his lapel. I recognized him from an earlier visit—well, to be honest, it was actually a raid.

"Don't want any trouble tonight." The bartender repeated the bouncer's warning as he added various ingredients to a mixer and vigorously shook it. Almost as if he wished his hands were throttling my neck instead.

"Can't a shifter just drink in peace?" I asked plaintively.

"Not when it's you, Enzo," he said grumpily, pouring my drink and sliding it across the bar. "Last time you were here, you arrested half my patrons."

"You should be thankful that I didn't nab you too," I snapped. "Those pixies were selling their dust to your other patrons. That's a Class-C banned substance." I took a breath—wouldn't do me any good to get kicked out for disorderly conduct before I found out any useful intel. "Anyhow, I'm not here on Protectorate business tonight. Just a personal night out." True enough, even if I *was* here to investigate.

I picked up my glass, its rim crusted with blue frost that sent minuscule, otherworldly snowflakes drifting into the air. Most of the drinks at Saint Paddy's had a minor magical effect. When I sipped the frigid, minty cocktail, I experienced a brief flash of sensations: an icy, refreshing breeze on my face, the muffled crunch of snow underfoot, and a hint of pine and woodsmoke in the air.

While I drank, I flipped through the menu, ordered some food, and surreptitiously studied the other bar patrons, trying to decide which—if any— of them might be worth approaching. None looked particularly promising.

My food arrived, and I dug in. Chicken strips and fries, all coated in Paddy's special seasonings. I didn't know what the various spices were, just that they weren't something you could find in a human store. And that they were absolutely delicious.

As I was finishing the basket and starting on my second drink, the front door opened again. I turned to see who entered. A thin, short female, with a wild tangle of brown hair, and brown skinned. No, not brown skin—she was covered in a fine layer of flexible bark. Almost looked like full-scale psoriasis. She was a wood sprite.

I kept a triumphant smile off my face with great difficulty and forced my expression to remain neutral. Didn't want to look like a major creeper. But she was exactly what I'd been hoping for. If only she would be willing to talk to me.

The wood sprite climbed onto a barstool a few seats down and ordered a nut-brown ale. I was surprised to see one of her kind here—all sprites are naturally nature-lovers, usually avoiding cities. Then again, I'd seen the water sprite Finian in a ghetto, so maybe I needed to reevaluate my preconceived notions about sprites of any kind.

I signaled the bartender for another drink and wracked my brain for a conversation starter that wouldn't make it seem like I was a random barfly hitting on her, but all my brain was offering me were cheesy pickup lines. Luckily for me, I was saved from the effort of coming up with a satisfactory opening line.

"Not often I see a Protector in a place like this," the wood sprite said, smiling at me. Her voice was low and husky, a shock after the high-pitched squeaks from Finian.

"You come here often, then?" I asked, turning the question back on her as the leprechaun slid another Arctic Twister across the polished bar-top.

"Oh, I wouldn't say *often*, but it's nice to get out of the woods every now and then."

"The woods? You mean like Silver Arch Park?" I asked.

She laughed. I thought I heard rustling leaves in her laughter. An interesting sound. "Those aren't woods. Not *real* woods at least. They're tame. Civilized, you might say, but I'd call it conceited. Just look at the sprites living there. Every one of them sporting Gucci and Armani. I wouldn't be caught dead living in a place like that. Too snobby for my tastes. Although, I will admit that I enjoy visiting the City on occasion."

"Where do you live, then?" I asked.

"Over near Summerville."

Excitement spiked. Perhaps she could help me find Finian.

"Really? I live in Summerville. I'm Enzo, by the way."

"Brin," she said, extending her hand for a shake. I took it, feeling the odd texture of her skin-bark. It was rough yet smooth, if that makes any sense. Brin slid over onto the stool next to me. "Nice to meet you. I've never met a shapeshifter before."

"Yeah, most supes try to avoid us. We kinda get a bad rep from our jobs. You're the first wood sprite I've met. Not the only sprite though—I saw a water sprite last week." I hesitated, debating whether I was showing my hand too soon. Maybe I'd scare her off, not get any more info from her. But I needed to take the gamble. The risk was worth it, and the alcohol was making everything seem like a great idea at the moment. "His name was Finian."

"I hope you were arresting him," Brin spat, anger smoldering in her eyes.

I grinned and raised my glass in a toast. My shot in the dark had paid off. "I was trying to. But he escaped. Any idea where I might find him?"

"Somewhere in or near Summerville," she said. "I stay in the woods up in the hills, but I've heard he's a real city boy. Ran into him myself about a year ago. Him and a couple pals. I decided to steer clear of Summerville ever since. Don't want to run into those creeps again."

"Pals?" I asked, my interest piquing. "What sort of pals?"

"One was a warlock. Middle-aged white guy, brown hair and eyes."

Sounded like Newell. That was one accomplice already accounted for. Sort of.

"The other was a werewolf," Brin continued. "White female in her early twenties. Short, dark hair."

I started having a sick feeling in my stomach. Her description matched Hawkins. Had I been wrong to trust the werewolf after all?

Brin's final words confirmed the identity. "The were had just been turned. Still had healing wounds from the attack. Looked pretty gnarly."

The timeline fit. The description fit. What had Hawkins been doing with Newell and Finian?

CHAPTER 33

BURNING BRIDGES

I STAYED AT Saint Paddy's for a few more hours, but didn't learn anything else of interest related to the case. Brin didn't have any more useful nuggets of info, although she did give me her number and extract a promise from me to give her a call so we could go out for celebratory drinks once I caught Finian. Nice to have someone who believed I could do it.

Since I'd had such a late night, I slammed the snooze button on my alarm clock when it blared in the morning. Far too soon, it screeched again. Bam! Meant to hit snooze, but I accidentally turned the alarm off, because the next thing I knew my phone was ringing.

"H'lo?" I muttered groggily.

"Enzo, where are you?" Geoff's irritated voice sounded from the speaker. "You were supposed to be down here ten minutes ago."

Shit. I looked at the clock. Where had the time gone? "Sorry, overslept. Be there soon."

I got dressed in record time and then rushed to the dungeons. Geoff was standing in front of the guard station, tapping his foot impatiently.

"Sorry," I said. Was saying that word too much lately. "Won't happen again. I'll buy you a drink to make up for it."

Good thing Geoff was a fairly laid-back guy. "I'll hold you to it," he said with a small smile, before leaving me to another eternity of boredom.

First things first, though: call Scott. I needed to let him know what I'd found out about Hawkins. Didn't matter that it might give Jake a break in the case—I needed to warn my friend. She was playing him. I didn't know how, but I did know that my unsuspicious friend was in danger.

Since my cell phone didn't work underground, I used the landline in the guard booth.

"I need to tell you something," I said without preamble. "I found out last night that Hawkins knows Finian and Newell somehow, but she hasn't told us about it. She's hiding something."

"No way," Scott immediately replied, adamant. "She would've said something. She's not involved in this."

"Don't be so naive!" I snapped. Perhaps a little too harshly, but I had to get it through to him that Hawkins wasn't as innocent as he thought. "How well do you really know her? She could be lying to you."

"She's not lying. And she's not involved. Besides, where did you get your information? How do you know that *you* weren't lied to?"

Sudden doubt assailed me. What if Brin *had* been lying to me? Had the alcohol clouded my judgement more than I'd thought? Maybe she and Finian were in cahoots. They were both sprites, after all, even if they were of different affiliations. It wouldn't be the strangest thing to happen in this case. She could've been a plant, purposely feeding me false information.

I soldiered on anyway. "But what if I'm right? Hawkins has been in on this case since the beginning. Maybe that's why we haven't made any progress. She's been a spy in our midst."

"She's not," Scott replied. Just as stubborn as me.

"But—"

"This is just about your prejudice against werewolves, isn't it?"

"No!" Great, now that was coming back to bite me. Scott wouldn't believe anything I said if he thought I was just being biased. "You have to consider—"

"No, I don't." I'd never heard Scott's voice sound so cold before. "If that's all, I'll talk to you later." Without waiting for a reply, he hung up.

I slammed the handset back into the cradle. "Dammit!" I growled in frustration. How could I get Scott to listen to me? I wracked my brain for answers, coming up empty. Nothing left to do but keep forging on. Alone. Abandoned in the dungeons. But I would do it. I had to. I picked up the grimoire, determined to find answers.

The rest of the week proceeded in similar fashion, other than my tardiness on Tuesday. A shift in the dungeons, reading grimoires, followed by information hunting (and dinner) at Saint Paddy's. True to my word, I took Geoff there the next night. It was enough to mollify him, but that was where my luck ran out. I found no more useful tidbits from talking with various bar patrons throughout the week. Although, on a plus side, I was on good enough behavior that by Thursday evening I was no longer greeted with a scowl and a warning from the barkeep.

Finally, Friday rolled around. Freedom. I skipped the bar, heading straight home to my apartment in Summerville. Screw the traffic—it was worth dealing with to not have to spend one more night at Headquarters. I needed the weekend to myself, away from it all.

Scott still wasn't talking with me after our last phone conversation. I'd tried once more to convince him to keep an eye on Hawkins. That conversation had gone over like a lead balloon. Even Martin, usually good for a laugh, had given me the cold shoulder every time I saw him floating down hallways.

Still mad that I'd set Newell loose, even though I felt I was being more than adequately punished for that mistake.

I finally arrived home, ready to unwind and relax after a tough weekend. I settled down in front of the TV with a cold bottle of Guinness and put on *Planet Earth*. Sometimes nice to see the beauty of nature sans the deadly supernatural freak show that I had to deal with on a regular basis. Just as Sir David Attenborough's soothing voice came on air, my phone rang.

I checked the caller ID. Hawkins. Shit. So much for a magic-free evening. Why in hell was she calling me? Could there actually be a break in the dead-end case?

CHAPTER 34

PLAUSIBLE PAWS

"YEAH, HAWKINS?" I asked. Not sure whether to be feel excited about a potential break or irritated about having my quiet evening interrupted.

"There's been a kidnapping. A human girl, eight years old." Straight to the point. Apparently neither of us were in the mood for pleasantries.

"Why are you telling me?"

"I think it might be related to the case."

I smirked at the thought of her calling me instead of Jake, but then was suddenly flooded with misgiving. Could I really trust Hawkins? What if this was a trap?

"How do you know?" I asked.

"Meet me on the corner of Fifth and Oak. I'll explain there." *Click*.

Damn. I briefly considered staying home, just to show the werewolf that I wasn't at her beck and call, but immediately dismissed the notion. I couldn't let pettiness stop me from saving a kidnapped girl. I quickly threw on my working uniform—black, long-sleeved shirt and black pants, both concealing numerous blades—and grabbed a couple of other artifacts that might come in handy.

My apartment was on Eighth Street, and Oak was only about a half mile away, so I decided to jog rather than bother with an Uber.

Officer Hawkins was waiting a short distance from the corner when I showed up, pacing agitatedly at the mouth of an alleyway. "We need to hurry. Marlow will notice I'm gone soon."

"Hurry with what exactly?" I stopped a short distance from the alleyway. Seemed like a good spot for an ambush, and I was far from over my suspicions of Hawkins working with Finian and Newell.

"A little girl was snatched out of her bedroom an hour ago. It's critical we find her fast, before the kidnapper gets too far away."

"Why do you think it's tied to our other case?"

"I told her it was," a familiar, deep voice said as Newell's spirit materialized in the shadows of the alley.

I jumped backward with a muttered "bleep" of my own, drawing my daggers—one silver, one titanium—and settled into a fighting crouch. Not that I would likely be able to do much against an incorporeal spirit, but it was all I had, and I wasn't going to go down without at least attempting to fight.

"Truce!" Newell said, to my shock. "Finian kidnapped the girl."

"And why the hell should I believe you?" I snapped.

"No time to explain. You need to find her. Quickly—before it's too late." And then, just as abruptly as he'd appeared, Newell vanished.

"What's going on, Hawkins?" I demanded. "Are you working with Newell?"

"No," she said. "He just appeared. Said he knew the girl's life was in danger. And I need your help to track her. You need to cover for me. Talk to the police."

"What?" I had the strange mental disconnection of understanding every single word, and yet not having a clue as to what had been said.

"I can track the girl," Hawkins repeated. I gave her a blank stare. "As a wolf."

"You've got to be shitting me!" I shouted, then glanced around. Nobody was nearby, but I lowered my voice anyway. "What the hell makes you think that I would condone a *werewolf* running around near humans? You could kill someone!"

Hawkins gave me a look of utter disdain. "It's only during the full moon change that we lose control of ourselves. When we choose to change, our minds remain intact. Surely you know this."

"Yes, but—come on! It's dangerous. Not to mention it will be difficult to explain why there's a wolf running around in the suburbs." And not to mention that Hawkins could do some serious damage to *me* if she wanted to, even though I did have a silver dagger. With this sudden reappearance of Newell, I trusted Hawkins about as far as I could throw a unicorn.

"I'm sure you'll think of something," she said. "Now quit arguing with me. The longer we spend here, the less chance there is of us finding the girl."

"But—" My protest died when I saw how pointless it was. Hawkins had ducked into the shadows of the alley and was already unbuttoning her uniform. I went around the corner of the alley and stood on the street, out of view, both for modesty's sake and to keep a lookout for any passersby. A minute later, I felt the shiver in the air from her transformation.

I watched the alley entrance, silver dagger held at the ready in case of an ambush. A large black wolf emerged, staring at me with dark brown eyes. As she walked by me, it took every ounce of willpower to not strike out. As much as I thought that Hawkins wouldn't attack me in this public location if she was in collusion with Newell, I'd been in too many bloody fights with werewolves for my instincts to not be screaming that danger was prowling past.

The wolf stopped and looked back at me, jerking her head in a beckoning gesture. Wanting me to follow. Gritting my teeth, I sheathed my daggers and jogged after her as she trotted down Oak Street toward Fourth. Once we reached the corner, I saw police cars parked halfway down the block, lights illuminating the street like an early Christmas. A few officers were putting up crime scene tape and examining the area around one of the cookie-cutter houses of the development.

I slowed to a walk. "Follow my lead," I told Hawkins. She stopped and glanced back over her shoulder at me. "If you want to pull this off, you need to act like a trained dog."

She lifted her lip in a silent snarl, and I quelled the urge to draw my silver dagger.

"Don't give me that shit," I said. "You called me for help, remember? Now come walk next to me and listen to what I tell you."

She looked back toward the police officers and then, with a resigned sigh, padded to my side and we continued to the crime scene and stopped at the taped barrier.

Officer Marlow was nearby, speaking to a civilian. Probably interviewing a neighbor. They looked as if they were wrapping things up, so I waited until Marlow turned away from the woman to get his attention.

"Enzo!" Marlow said in a tone of surprise. "What are you—Jesus Christ! Is that a wolf?" He eyed Hawkins nervously.

"Half wolf," I said. "She's my pet dog. We were just going for a walk."

Hawkins growled softly, too quiet for Marlow to hear, at the word "pet."

I fought the urge to smirk. "What's going on here?" I put my hand in my pocket and drew out my black opal. It was by far the most useful tool I'd checked out from the arsenal, allowing me to sway the minds of humans, even to the point of altering memories. For now though, I just used it to encourage Marlow to be open to my plan. I felt the connection to the opal in my mind and knew my eyes were glowing with a soft blue light. I didn't worry about anyone noticing the change, though—part of the opal's power is to prevent a person's conscious mind from noticing the effects and realizing it was being manipulated.

"Kidnapping," Marlow said.

"My dog is former military service animal," I said. "She knows how to track scents. Maybe we can help find the kidnapping victim."

Marlow shook his head. "Sorry. Against regulation."

I increased the pressure from the opal. My eyes shone brighter; I could see the blue light reflecting in Marlow's eyes. I didn't want to damage his mind by overwhelming him with the power, but I pushed to the point that he began to waver.

"I know it's unusual, but I think we can help," I said softly, gently persuading.

I saw the moment when the opal overcame Marlow's desire to do everything by the book. "I guess we can use all the help we can get. I don't want anything bad to happen to the little girl." Marlow looked around. "Where's Hawkins, though? She should come with me."

"I'm sure she's more useful wherever she is," I said.

"You're probably right," Marlow agreed.

Damn, I love that opal. Makes bullshitting so much easier.

I ducked under the police tape, wolf Hawkins at my heel. I felt a little more relaxed in the police presence. I couldn't imagine why Hawkins would attack me in front of them. Even though they weren't armed with fatal silver bullets, I knew regular bullets would still hurt a werewolf like hell. If this was a trap, this house was unlikely to be the place where it would be sprung.

With Marlow by my side, no other policemen challenged me as I went through the front door and to the girl's bedroom. The big black wolf sniffed around, taking in the girl's scent for the hunt. I scanned the room, looking for anything the human police might have missed. First floor, open window. Easy access for an intruder, magical or otherwise. Typical little girl's room (at least, I think so). Lots of stuffed animals, Barbie dolls with a plethora of accessories, and horse pictures, figurines, and plushies everywhere. Is it true that every little girl loves horses? Looking at this girl's room, I'd say that's a fact.

Hawkins gave a small *wuff*, bringing me back to the task at hand. Find the little girl. Then, without warning, she leaped out of the open window. Must have a scent. I dove headfirst after her, rolling to my feet as I landed. "Come on!" I shouted to Marlow. Hawkins was already racing out of sight, following whatever scent had caught her interest.

Marlow exited the window a little more delicately that I had, one foot after another before he straightened his tall frame, but it didn't seem to slow him down much. It was amazing how agile he was for his height. But the moment his feet hit terra firma, he was off.

"This way!" I shouted, to give him a directional bearing as I raced after Hawkins.

"Wait for me!" he called back, feet pounding the ground. "You aren't authorized to make an arrest."

"Authorized, shmauthorized," I muttered. "What do you know?" But I slowed down a bit, giving him a chance to catch up. You never know when policemen and their flashy uniforms and big guns might come in handy. No need to reveal my powers and weapons if the human police could do the dirty work for me. And a bullet would take down a sprite just as easily as a human.

Though, if Marlow saw our blue kidnapper, I'd have to alter his memories. At least I had my opal.

Hawkins paused in the middle of the street, casting back and forth. Good thing it was so late in the evening—not much traffic on the streets. After a few seconds, she set off again at an unfaltering trot.

I kept at a slow, steady run, Marlow at my side. Luck was on my side, since he was a marathoner. I did not want to be slowed down too much by a human, and who knew how long we'd be chasing after the kidnappers.

Hawkins stayed in the center of the lane as she followed the scent. Fortunately, what few cars we saw pulled to the side when they saw the two men, one of them a policeman, chasing a large black wolf down the street. A small part of me secretly hoped for roadkill werewolf, but I tried to quash it—she's doing the right thing, she's helping people instead of eating them.

Every so often, Hawkins paused at an intersection, sniffing about to determine which way the girl had been taken before trotting off again. Not gonna lie, I was getting a wee bit jealous of the werewolf's super senses. But the cost still outweighed the benefit, in my opinion. I couldn't imagine losing complete control of myself one night a month. (Losing control during a booze-fueled Spring Break is a different story, of course.)

After a half hour of steady running—eight miles per hour, at my best guess, minus the sniff stops—I suddenly recognized the neighborhood. Or, should I say, I recognized the slums? Rusty park with no swing seats. Empty basketball court. Dingy apartments.

Hawkins suddenly veered off the road, halting at a white-panel van. After giving it a thorough sniff, she continued down the sidewalk to a dilapidated building. Damn. It was the apartment where I'd lost Finian the first time. So either Newell had been telling the truth, or we were about to walk straight into a trap. Well, I've never been one to shy away from danger. And it's my opinion that it's far better to go into a trap knowing that it's there. Better than being blindsided.

CHAPTER 35

A REALLY SHITTY INVESTIGATION

WHEN I HELD the door to the apartment complex open for Hawkins, she immediately bounded up the stairs to the third floor, just like I knew she would. Apartment 312. I was starting to get a serious sense of déjà vu as Marlow and I followed her up the stairs, both prepared to draw our weapons. But when we got to the apartment, Hawkins just briefly sniffed the door and then continued down the hallway, nose to the floor, clearly still following the scent.

"Wait for a moment," I told her.

She paused, giving me a glare of irritation. *You're wasting time, I know she's not in there,* her look clearly stated.

"We don't have a search warrant," Marlow said, when he saw my intention of entering the apartment.

"I have one from before," I lied—I knew I'd be able to weasel out of any human repercussions, since I knew a supernatural creature had been in the apartment before. The Protectorate would back me up, warrant or no.

I tested the doorknob. Unlocked. Unexpected. Either empty or booby-trapped. Marlow shadowed me as I entered cautiously, wary for any magical surprises, but a quick search revealed nothing more than the same dilapidated furnishings from before.

We returned to the hallway. "Lead on," I told Hawkins.

She immediately beelined for the opposite staircase, leading us outside and halfway down the block at the rear of the building. Oh God, no. Not the sewers.

But the trail led straight to the manhole cover. Hawkins barked and pawed at the closed steel plate.

"The sewers?" Marlow asked, disbelief filling his voice. "Why the hell would a kidnapper take a little girl into the sewers?"

"I have no idea," I said, though my stomach was churning at the thought of following the sprite down into the wet tunnels. Well, at least if he'd brought the human girl along that meant that there was breathable air down below.

"Are you sure that your dog is right? That this is the place he took her? Couldn't she be following a different trail? A city worker, or something?"

Hawkins barked, apparently offended that her judgement was being questioned. I, on the other hand, couldn't blame Marlow's skepticism—he had no idea what he was truly dealing with, both allies and enemies.

"I'm certain," I said, giving Hawkins a covert slashing hand gesture to shut up. No need for Marlow to have any more suspicion that anything nonhuman was going on. "We need some hazmat suits."

"Enzo, I'm sorry, but we can't just go rushing down into the sewers. We need to follow protocol. We need to call in waste management workers from the city, people who are familiar with the sewer systems."

I sighed. "I'm sorry, Detective. But I can't wait. Every second is vital." I reached into my pocket for my black opal, drawing its power into me. "Please call the police station and have them bring a hazmat suit and ventilator here. Immediately."

"Of course. You're right. We need a hazmat suit."

Marlow made the call on his radio, and fifteen minutes later, a confused-looking patrolman pulled up. "Detective Marlow, you called in for a hazmat suit?" he asked as he exited the car and popped the trunk of his cruiser to reveal the requested items.

"Yes, thank you, Officer," Marlow said. "Enzo, what's the plan?"

I saw that his normal grasp of reality was returning. "Detective, return with this patrolman to the scene of the kidnapping. This lead was a dead end. My dog was following a false trail. Once we realized that, I went home and you decided to go back to the crime scene."

"Yes, of course. False trail," Marlow said. "I'll go back and work with Cora."

"She has the night off, remember?" I said, pushing harder on his mind with the opal. "She isn't there."

He gave a rueful laugh, shaking his head. "Of course, how could I forget that? She isn't on duty tonight. Officer, take me back to Fourth Street."

"Officer," I said, capturing the patrolman's attention with my opal. "You came to give Detective Marlow a ride. Nothing more."

"Of course, sir. I just came to take him back to the crime scene. Nothing more."

I pulled the hazmat suit and regulator out of the trunk. "See you later."

The two policemen climbed into the car and drove away. Once they turned the corner, I looked at Hawkins, bracing myself for an attack. If she was double-crossing me, now would be the time to do it. No police, no witnesses, and a perfectly convenient sewer for disposing of my corpse.

But the look Hawkins gave me was one of puzzlement and impatience. A look that stated, "Well? Get on with it!"

So I donned the suit—basically a full-body condom—and asked, "Ready to go for a swim?"

She gave me a look of disgust but nodded in agreement.

"Here goes nothing," I said, and dragged the manhole cover off the sewer entrance, thankful for the greater-than-human strength of my kind. A foul wave of air rose from the dark hole, hitting my nostrils like a wrecking ball. Was Hawkins going to be able to follow the scent through that stench? I glanced at her and saw the resolution on her canine face.

Well, nowhere to go but down. I put on the regulator mask and swung down onto the ladder, slippery with an unidentifiable slime. Quite frankly, I didn't want to even think about what substances I would encounter on this trip underground. I did my best to ignore the sights around me.

At the bottom, I turned on the flashlight that I'd retrieved from my pocket before donning the rubber suit. A quick look in either direction showed an empty tunnel stretching out into the darkness. Well, empty of large lifeforms at least. I didn't want to consider the slurry of fluids and soft solids that I was standing calf-deep in. At least the tunnel was tall enough to stand in—about seven feet in diameter. Hopefully we wouldn't come across anything hanging from the ceiling.

Aboveground, the air shivered, and a moment later a naked Hawkins climbed down the ladder. I averted my eyes as she descended. "This is the most disgusting thing I've ever done," she said as I heard her step down into the muck. A moment later, there was a small *splash* as her front paws landed in the sewage and the wolf let out a mournful whine.

"Too bad they don't make dog-sized hazmat suits," I said, my voice distorted by the mask I wore. "Can you pick up the trail?"

Hawkins gave an experimental sniff in either direction, sneezed twice, and then set off down the tunnel to the left, splashing sludge on the walls as she went.

I followed, shining my light ahead into the seemingly endless tunnel that stretched before us. We walked in silence, save for the wet, squishy sounds of boots and paws rising and falling in the unidentifiable, horrendous glop. Our tedious trek was occasionally interrupted by a side passage—smaller tunnels joining the main one we traversed—but at each intersection, Hawkins continued straight.

I was grateful. Some of the smaller tunnels were only a few feet in diameter, and I wasn't sure I could shift to a small enough form to fit down them. I would've had to crawl, and even with the protection of the hazmat suit, that was an experience that I was definitely eager to avoid.

After a timeless amount of trudging—could've been ten minutes, an hour, or a day—we reached a part of the tunnel that was decidedly incongruous with the rest of the polluted concrete mess. A rusty iron door was set in the wall, decorated with loops and swirls of ancient runes. I shined the light on them, trying to decipher them, but could make no sense of their message.

Too bad Scott wasn't with us. Although I doubted that love, money, or fear of death could get Scott to descend into this dark, slimy hell.

Hawkins sniffed urgently around the door, whining softly. So, the girl had been taken through here. The wolf pawed at the iron, then yelped as a spark struck her. Damn. It was magically warded. But exactly what kind of wards were they?

I reached for the handle, prepared for a sting. Sparks jumped when my gloved hand made contact, but I felt nothing. Momentary confusion cleared up when I realized that I was wearing non-conductive rubber boots. I wasn't grounded, so I wasn't getting shocked. I grinned—I loved it when magic was forced to operate within the laws of nature.

Yanking on the handle, I received another surprise when the rusty door opened without a groan. The hinges swung smoothly, recently oiled, and the sloppy grunge moved away from the base of the door, held at bay by a magic barrier.

Hawkins immediately jumped out of the sewage and into a mercifully dry tunnel. I followed, just in time to get splattered by filth as Hawkins shook out her coat.

"Thanks," I said. "I didn't have enough crap on me already."

It turns out that wolves can roll their eyes, as Hawkins demonstrated quite expressively. Amazing how easy it can be to communicate with a non-verbal creature. She was clearly saying, "At least you're wearing a protective suit. That gunk got in my fur—I'll never feel clean again."

I grinned, shut the door behind us, and shined my flashlight around our new settings. The tunnel we were in was dirt and rock, rough and unlined with any sort of brick, concrete, or smooth stone. It reminded me a bit of the tunnels of Shelob's lair, minus the webs, and I hoped that we weren't going to encounter a giant spider at the end of it.

Hawkins trotted down the tunnel, nose moving from side to side as she took in the scents. So. Still on the trail. But where on earth could this tunnel be leading us? And why would someone (or some*thing*) drag a kidnapped girl down here? It just didn't make sense.

I jogged after Hawkins, my damp suit and boots making an annoying *squelch squich squolk* as I moved. Not exactly stealthy. "Hold up," I hissed at Hawkins, pulling off the regulator. Foul air assaulted my nose, but at least it wasn't as pungent as the sewers themselves. I took shallow breaths through my mouth as I stripped off the rest of the full-body condom. No need for it here. Stealth was more important than bacterial protection.

The black wolf shifted impatiently while I took off the outer layer. "Ready," I whispered, and we were off again. I checked all my various weaponry as I jogged. Everything was still in place. Ready for—almost—anything.

A few minutes later, Hawkins slowed to a walk, ears pricked intently forward. I matched her pace, listening for whatever she'd noticed. As we crept forward, the smell grew more pungent. The stink of rot and feces increased, despite the greater distance from the sewer tunnel, but it wasn't the only thing assaulting my nose. Sage and lavender filled the air, perhaps trying to mask the fouler odors. Unsuccessfully—the mixture of scents only served to overwhelm me, causing my eyes to sting and my nose to run. I wondered how Hawkins, with her sharp wolf senses, could stand it.

A hundred yards later, I heard what Hawkins's ears had picked up: a woman's voice chanting rhythmically, echoing down the rocky tunnel. At the same time, I saw a faint light ahead, around a bend. I clicked off my flashlight and stuck it back in my pocket. No need to give away our position. Side by side, the wolf and I stalked forward, intent on our prey.

As we peeked around the corner, a terrible sight met our eyes. In the center of a large, candlelit cavern was a flat, rectangular altar with a small figure tied down on top. I couldn't see who it was, but I knew it had to be the girl we were tracking. Standing above her, chanting and wielding a wickedly curved blade, was Jane Doe.

CHAPTER 36

So Close, Yet So Far

HAWKINS BOUNDED FORWARD with a snarl. No more doubt whose side she was on. I was hot on her heels. "Stop!" I yelled as the witch lifted the knife high in the air, pointed straight at the girl's heart.

The witch spun abruptly. I could only imagine what went through her head at that moment—a huge black wolf, teeth bared and bearing down on her, followed by a dagger-wielding Protector. She threw up one arm, holding her hand out in a command to halt. There was a sudden flash, and Hawkins slammed into a translucent barrier with a yelp. The impact threw her to the ground, but she was quickly back on her feet, growling and patrolling the edge of the protective shield the witch had cast, which ran the width of the cavern.

"Surrender now. There's no escape." I filled my voice with confidence, although I was silently berating myself for leaving all my supernatural body-armor at my apartment. This was the exact situation that I had requisitioned it for.

"Who's going to stop me?" Jane Doe sneered. "A little slayer and his tame pup?" She chuckled. No, not an evil witch's cackle. Just a grating, derisive laugh.

"What are you doing with the girl?" I asked. Had to keep her talking. Stall for time. Even a powerful spell-caster couldn't keep a protective barrier up forever—she'd burn herself out if she tried.

"Wouldn't you like to know," she taunted.

I saw movement behind Jane Doe, and a blue figure materialized from the shadows. The water sprite, Finian, aka the kidnapping delivery boy. His naked blue skin was covered in muck from knees to webbed toes. A quick glance at the witch showed that her clothing was clean— no trudging through the sewers for her.

Which meant there was another entrance to this cavern. No doubt it was on the other side of the magical barrier from us. Crap. She wouldn't need to burn out her power. She could just leave the shield up and escape through the back door. I needed to figure out a way to get her now, before she got away. Again.

A flash of inspiration—my opal. I paced the barrier, hoping that my body would prevent the witch from seeing me reach into my far pocket. I drew on the opal's power. "None of this is necessary," I told the witch. "I'll be able to help you if you surrender yourself and let the girl go."

Jane Doe just laughed. "You think your little parlor trick will work on *me*?"

"Didn't hurt to try," I said nonchalantly, then turned my glowing blue gaze on Finian. "Get her."

The sprite leaped forward and wrapped his arms around the witch. The cavern went black as all the candles extinguished at once. I fumbled for my flashlight, hardly able to believe that my mad plan had actually worked—the opal was designed for use on humans. It was a shot in the dark to think it would work on the sprite.

Speaking of shots in the dark—I heard another canine yelp. What happened to Hawkins? I finally got my fingers around the flashlight—it had been stuck in a fold in my pocket—and yanked it out. Shining it to where I'd heard the yelp, I saw Hawkins, teeth bared in a silent snarl, looking at the translucent barrier. So, it was still up. She must've tried to get through it again, thinking it disappeared when the candles snuffed out.

I swiveled the light toward the altar. Nobody there, except the girl tied on top. A thorough scan of the rest of the interior of the cavern showed no sign of either Jane Doe or Finian.

Growling in frustration, I kicked the magical barricade, receiving a sharp shock for my loss of control. "Ouch!" As I rubbed my stinging leg ruefully, Hawkins padded up to me, eyes luminous in the beam of light. "Any ideas?" I asked.

She shook her head.

"Yeah, me neither. Want to change back?"

Hawkins pawed at my pant leg.

"Right—no clothes. Well, I guess we'll just have to wait until this barrier fades. Shouldn't take too long."

We explored our part of the cavern while we waited. There wasn't much to see—rough stone walls and a hard dirt floor. Hawkins sniffed everything, although what odors she could pick up over the general scent of the nearby sewers, I had no idea. After a minute, she gave a quiet bark to catch my attention.

I crossed the width of the cavern to where she stood by the far wall. The stench of rot and sewage grew stronger as I approached. I shined the flashlight around and realized that what I'd taken for just a rocky protrusion was actually hiding the entrance to a smaller cave. I peered inside, wrinkling my nose against the stench.

The chamber was roughly twelve feet in every direction, and the floor was covered with various rags, fiberglass insulation, and empty burlap bags, forming a giant bed or nest of some sort. When I pointed my light at the floor of the entrance, I saw footprints, roughly humanoid in shape, although humungous and with massive bunions. Troll tracks.

So, this was a troll lair. Thank God the trolls weren't currently in residence. An encounter with trolls was always unpleasant, to say the least. With gray-green skin, lumpy teeth strong enough to crush rocks, and faces that looked like they'd had an encounter with the grill of a speeding semi-truck, trolls were nauseating to look at. It was hard to keep your gaze focused on their piggy little eyes instead of counting the glistening hairs curling out of their pug noses.

The smell, on the other hand, was somewhere along the lines of garbage dump meets wastewater treatment facility. The only baths trolls ever took were when they accidentally fell into a river or lake (or were pushed in by a good Samaritan trying to de-pollute the rancid air). And even then, the troll who found himself unexpectedly clean (ish) would generally immediately seek out some sort of refuse heap to roll about in and reestablish his vile odor. Trolls must consider stench to be an attractive perfume or something. The stinkier, the better.

For all other species—except for merpeople, who have no nostrils and, therefore, no sense of smell—an encounter with trolls is greatly improved by the use of a nose plug. The last time I had a scheduled meeting with a troll, I spent several days in a hospital's emergency room, sitting as close as possible to all the coughing, hacking, disease-riddled human patients. My plan worked—by the time I met with the troll, my sinuses were so plugged up that I could barely breathe, let alone catch wind of the overpowering troll stench. The 103-degree fever, all-night spewing from both ends, and rasping cough that lasted a month were totally worth it, in my opinion.

Now the question was: did Jane Doe chase the trolls away, or was she somehow working with them? Normally trolls wouldn't associate with other species—correction. Normally other species refused to get within smelling distance of trolls. But then again, sprites were usually solitary as well, and Finian was somehow connected to both Jane Doe and Peter Newell. Couldn't rule anything out at this point.

I heard a soft fizzing sound behind me, like a shaken soda spewing forth from a cracked lid. Hawkins and I whipped around, ready for battle. And saw nothing. Heard nothing more. I frowned, puzzled at the source of the noise, then realized the answer. There was nothing there—the barrier was gone.

We rushed toward the altar where the kidnapped girl was, still on guard in case the witch had left behind any nasty surprises. Not that we could do an awful lot about them, but it always sucks to be taken completely unprepared.

And maybe the slowest one to dodge would be the one to get hit by the curse. You know what they say about hiking in bear country—make sure you can outrun your slowest friend. Although with Hawkins's werewolf reflexes against my Protector reactions, I wasn't entirely sure who'd be quicker.

The girl was unconscious, hands and legs bound in a spread-eagle position atop the flat stone slab, but she appeared to be unharmed. I'll admit that I was somewhat grateful she was unconscious—kids can be annoying to deal with. Oh, and she wouldn't have the horrible memory of nearly being sacrificed. That too.

I drew my silver dagger and put it to the mundane task of cutting through the ropes. They easily parted under the razor-sharp blade. Before I picked her up, I used my flashlight to do one last sweep of the cavern, looking for obvious evidence, halfway hoping the witch had dropped the sacrificial knife. No such luck, though I did spot the exit tunnel in the cavern's dark recesses. I'd have to come back later and do a more thorough investigation. After I took care of the girl.

Hefting her into a fireman's carry, I headed toward the exit, Hawkins trotting ahead of me, keeping just within the beam of light. The tunnel was rough stone, with an uneven dirt floor. Thank God for my flashlight, or I would've twisted my ankles a dozen times in the first hundred yards. But then we had to stop, faced with a dilemma. The tunnel split, branching off in two different directions. Hawkins sniffed at the entrance to each, finally trotting down the left-hand tunnel.

"Wait," I called out.

She stopped, looking back at me impatiently.

"That's the way they went, right?"

She nodded.

"Are you sure we should go that way? I mean, we aren't exactly prepared to fight them right now. And we have this girl to take care of."

Hawkins gave a loud sigh of annoyance and returned to me. I understood the feeling. Quarry so close, but unable to pursue. But the witch and the sprite would have to wait to be captured another day.

"Can you tell if this tunnel leads to the surface?"

Hawkins sniffed the air of the right-hand tunnel, then gave a shrug. It was definitely an odd gesture—I had no idea that wolves were even physically capable of shrugging.

"Well, I think we should check it out. At the very least, we won't have to worry as much about the witch leaving behind magical booby traps for us."

Hawkins nodded again, setting off once more at the edge of illumination cast by my flashlight. I followed, carrying the unconscious girl.

A short ways down the tunnel, Hawkins stopped, whining softly. I tensed at the surprisingly fearful tone—what had her super-sharp senses detected?

Should I run, or stand my ground and fight? I hesitated, torn, but then I heard the sound of deep voices echoing off the rock walls, accompanied by an unmistakable stench of sewage, garbage dumps, and rotting carcasses combined. I knew what we were facing. Trolls.

Carefully, I set the girl down near a rock outcropping. She should be safe enough there. Out of immediate view, and in a spot that shouldn't get accidentally trampled. Then I stood and faced the approaching voices, Hawkins at my side. Ready for whatever came around the bend. Or so I hoped.

CHAPTER 37

Maternal Monster

I CRINGED AS the voices of the trolls grew louder, readying myself for the sight—and smell—of the underground denizens. I had a marginal advantage this time—after mucking about in the sewers, my nostrils were already somewhat prepared for the abusive odors. Undoubtedly the sewer access was one of the reasons the trolls had made their lair in the cave. Great place to add to their stench, and also good hunting grounds for rats. Not to mention the occasional fish carcass from an aquatic pet's porcelain burial at sea. That was like caviar to trolls.

A pair of trolls lumbered around the corner. One male, one female—I think. It's difficult to tell with a race of creatures so ugly that they've been known to crack magic mirrors just by looking in them. But one of the ten-foot brutes had a set of snow chains draped like a necklace, and I've never known a male troll to wear any sort of jewelry, so I assumed that one was female.

The trolls stopped when they saw me. Clearly startled, although it was only a moment before they recovered their dim wits and resumed their advance, stopping a nose-destroying three feet away to hulk over us.

Hawkins snarled, baring gleaming white fangs.

"Easy," I muttered quietly to her. "Trolls are usually peaceful."

"Usually" being the operative word. But still, so far the trolls had shown no sign of aggression. And believe me, they had no qualms about immediately squashing anyone who annoyed them. And we were well within squashing distance, yet still unharmed. So I had to assume these trolls were peaceful. Peaceful enough, at least.

I craned my neck to look up at them. From my low vantage point, most of what I could see was nose hair. Lots and lots of nose hair that was slick with yellowish-green boogers. I swallowed convulsively, forcing back the rising bile in my throat.

"I am Protector Enzo Thornton," I said formally. Breathe through the mouth, not the nose. Oh God, I could taste the stench. Do not vomit, do not vomit. "This is my partner, Cora Hawkins."

"Midget thorn, hawk-wolf," the male troll grunted. "Me Drog Nash. Woman Glask Norp. What shundbuk want you, hrekfast?" No, you don't want to know what those words mean. Let's just say they aren't PG-rated and leave it at that.

"We are trying to find a way to the surface," I said, fighting to keep my voice even and my stomach from heaving. "We tracked a witch to the cave behind us."

"Witch!" Drog Nash bellowed, preventing me from continuing. "Bukhin magicman take our cave. Make freskin hurting sparks and chase us away. Shulpan witch." Then his piggy eyes narrowed ominously. "You midget thorn friends of that guldbag?"

"No, no, not at all!" I vehemently protested, taking a step back and holding up my hands placatingly. It didn't take a seer to know that the wrong answer would quickly get us pummeled. "She's a bad witch. Shulpan! Very shulpan. We were trying to catch her, but she escaped."

"Hmph," Drog Nash grumbled, then he and his . . . wife? . . . had a brief conversation in trollish. I couldn't understand them, even though I do know some trollish swears—I'll admit it, curses are my favorite part of any foreign language. Especially trollish. And German. There's just something satisfying about shouting a guttural "Scheisse!" It even beats "Hrekfast!"

"Why you chase witch?" Glask Norp finally asked in English. Besides not swearing the way Drog Nash did, she had a slightly more feminine voice. That is, if you can consider the sound of an avalanche more feminine than a pure rockslide. Let's just say neither troll was going to be auditioning for musicals on Broadway anytime soon.

"She's broken the law," I said. "She killed a man, and kidnapped a girl, intending to sacrifice her."

"He try to kill girl?" Glask Norp roared. If I can say one thing positive about trolls, it's this: They certainly have strong maternal instincts, no matter the species involved. Despite the fact that their grammar isn't all that refined.

"Yes," I said. "But we saved her."

I gestured with my flashlight to the unconscious girl near the wall. Big mistake. A massive hand grabbed me around my waist, lifting me eight feet in the air before I could react.

"Girl no alive!" my captor, Glask Norp, yelled. "You kill her!"

"She's fine!" I gasped, struggling to breathe with her fingers tightening around my body. My arms were pinned, leaving me helpless to fight back. Not that stabbing the troll would've done anything but piss her off even more.

Hawkins was snarling somewhere below me but hadn't attacked. Apparently she, too, realized how completely overmatched we were. The only way to get out of danger was to talk my way out of it. Good thing I'm an expert at verbal bullshit. On the downside, though, I could barely speak with the troll's hand squeezing like a python. "She's just asleep!" I fought to take another breath. "We're taking her to the doctor! Healer. Will fix." The last words barely wheezed out.

The overwhelming pressure slackened, and Glask Norp set me down. I coughed violently, spending a few minutes just being grateful for every lungful of air, no matter how foul-smelling.

"How long has the witch been coming down here?" I asked when I finally regained my breath.

"No time questions," Glask Norp grumbled. "You take girl healer now."

"Okay, okay, we will," I said. Didn't want to endure another troll tantrum. Even though it meant I'd have to come back later to question the trolls. And endure their stench again. "Does this tunnel lead out?"

The trolls nodded.

"Very well." I picked up the girl again and hefted her over my shoulder. "We'll be back later."

"You catch bukhin witch," Drog Nash ordered. "He bad shulpan."

"I will, I promise," I vowed. And not because I was afraid of retaliation from the trolls. Jane Doe and Finian had crossed the line, kidnapping and trying to sacrifice the human girl. I would make sure they paid for their crimes. No matter what it took.

CHAPTER 38

Body Dump

THE TROLL TUNNEL emerged behind a pile of rubble in an abandoned industrial complex. The scene was dimly lit from nearby streetlights. Big warehouses, rusting steel machinery, plenty of graffiti. There were fading "Keep Out" signs on the surrounding chainlink fence, which was topped with barbed wire and filled with gaps from where vandals had snipped the wire. Perfect setting for a horror movie.

Of course, it was right at this moment that the girl stirred on my shoulder, starting to wake up. Crap. Couldn't have her as a witness to anything supernatural. I suspected (well, hoped) that she'd been rendered unconscious before she'd gotten a look at her blue, gilled kidnapper. Even if she'd seen Finian, who'd believe her?

I fumbled in my pocket for night-night powder, but before I reached it, the girl asked, "Mommy?" in sleepy confusion. Her head was behind my back, so she couldn't see my face. But that also meant that I couldn't get a headshot with the night-night powder either. I rubbed a handful onto her leg, silently praying it would take effect quickly.

Then I felt the girl tense. She drew in a breath, letting it out in a single screamed syllable: "Wolf!"

Shit. She'd spotted Hawkins. Why couldn't she have made the mistaken assumption that Hawkins was just a big dog? My bad luck, that's why.

The girl wriggled violently to break free from my grip, but I held on tight. Thankfully her defiance only lasted a few seconds. The night-night powder finally kicked in, and the girl went limp across my shoulder once more.

But now what was I going to do with her? I didn't want a human to spot me at the moment. Creepy location aside, I knew it didn't look good—some guy carrying an unconscious girl.

It would be best if I could anonymously call 9-1-1, but I didn't want the call to be traced back to my phone. Too bad pay phones were a thing of the past. Although, speaking in advances in phones these days. . . .

I set the girl down and patted her pockets. Bulge in the left front. I carefully reached in and pulled out her cell with a grin. You wouldn't catch me complaining about kids these days all having phones.

As I dialed, I shifted my vocal cords to those of a young girl.

"9-1-1, what's your emergency?" the operator asked.

"I need help," I said, my voice high-pitched and feminine. "I don't know where I am."

"Are you hurt?"

"No, but I'm lost. Please come get me."

"I'll send a police officer to your location," the operator replied. "Stay on the line with me. Are you in a safe place now?"

"Yes. I think so." I added a little sniffle to make it seem more realistic. "I'm all alone."

"What's your name, honey?"

Shit. I hadn't gotten that info. Well, might as well just ignore that question. "Please come soon. I'm scared. Do you know where I am?"

"Yes, I have your phone's location. An officer is on the way there now."

Good. No need to keep the charade up anymore. I hung up the phone and slipped it back into the girl's pocket. No need to worry about DNA or fingerprints—human DNA tests aren't sophisticated enough to recognize supernatural DNA, and I'd erased the ridges from my fingers before I'd picked up the phone. Benefits of being a shapeshifter.

I picked up the girl and moved her to a brightly lit area alongside the deserted street, where the responding officers could find her quickly. Then Hawkins and I melted into the shadows where we could observe without being spotted.

Soon a screeching siren announced the arrival of the police. A black-and-white cruiser, light bar ablaze, came wailing around the corner and stopped near the unconscious girl. Detective Marlow got out and knelt next to her.

Perfect. She was in safe hands. And the night-night powder would naturally wear off in an hour or so. I'd have Hawkins check on her later, make sure that she didn't remember anything supernatural. Other than the werewolf sighting, of course, but since a werewolf looks identical to a normal wolf, there was no worry that any human would jump to the supernatural conclusion.

Girl taken care of, Hawkins and I left the industrial complex through the back, away from Marlow. Once we were in the streets, I oriented myself to where we'd come aboveground. Maybe a mile from my apartment.

"Want to come to my place, get cleaned up?" I asked. I didn't particularly want a sewage-splattered wolf in my apartment, but I couldn't let Hawkins roam through the city in wolf form. Someone would call Animal Control. And she couldn't shift without some clothes. Plus I had some questions for her, and I wanted to get them out of the way sooner rather than later.

Hawkins nodded, so I set off at a brisk jog. She kept up easily, trotting by my side. On the way to my place, I made a brief detour to the alley where

Hawkins had stashed her clothes. They were still there, luckily, but her weapons belt and badge weren't.

"I hope you put your valuables somewhere else," I said.

She nodded again, only this time it was accompanied by an eye-roll and a sigh. I could practically hear her saying, "Duh, Enzo. Do I look like a total amateur to you?"

I contented myself with merely replying "Good" as I gathered up her clothes.

We soon arrived at my apartment complex, but didn't go inside right away. Instead, I led Hawkins to a hose. "Need to get the worst of the gunk off first," I told her. "But I swear, if you shake water on me . . ."

I left the threat unfinished. Hawkins bared her teeth in a wolfish grin.

It took over fifteen minutes to get Hawkins passably clean. The muck had embedded itself deep in her thick black fur, and the amount of time that had passed since we'd traversed the sewers caused it to dry in matted clumps. At last, though, I'd finally gotten the majority of it off, and Hawkins went a short distance away to shake off the excess water.

Of course, who would come out right then, at that time of night—my landlord. He stared at the large, wet wolf in the courtyard. "Hundred dollar deposit for pets," he said. "And I need proof of vaccinations. Fifty pound weight limit, too, for all dogs."

Both of us eyed Hawkins—in wolf form, she was at least triple that weight. "She's not mine," I said. "I'm just watching her for a friend for a couple of hours. She won't even be spending the night here."

"If I see her in the morning, I'll add the deposit to your next rent."

"Swing by anytime, and I'll be happy to prove she's not living with me," I said with a smile. My landlord gave me one last suspicious look before wandering off. Thank God. As if my life needed more complications.

I dropped Hawkins's clothes on the bathroom countertop and pulled out a towel for her once we finally made it back to the comfort of my spartan apartment. "Don't use up all the hot water," I said as I closed the door. A moment later, I felt the strange shiver in the air that meant that she'd returned to human form.

I left her to her shower and focused on priorities: food. The thrill of tracking a kidnapper and then finally, finally, getting face-to-face with Jane Doe, only to have her escape again, had left me tired, a bit cranky and, most importantly, hungry. Fortunately for me, there is a large college in Summerville, which means a lot of late-night munchies, so it was easy to order a pizza despite the fact that it was pushing one in the morning.

When Hawkins emerged from the bathroom, human-shaped and rubbing a towel through her short black hair, I gratefully changed places with her for a shower of my own. Despite the fact that I'd worn a protective suit for the worst of the sewer adventure, I still felt dirty to my pores—now there's a girly feeling for you. Sue me. It's perfectly fine for a man to take pride in personal hygiene.

The pizza arrived just as I left the bathroom, clean and feeling like a new man. Hawkins and I ate in silence for a few minutes. Only once the hunger pangs abated, and I was nibbling merely for the sake of enjoyment, did I broach the subject that had been bothering me all week.

"I met a local wood sprite," I informed Hawkins. "She told me she saw Newell and Finian about a year ago. With a new werewolf."

As I spoke, I studied her expression. Curious at first, then guarded. Cautious. Worried. Emotions I might expect to see from someone who'd been lying to me from the beginning. I forged on. I needed to get to the bottom of this—Hawkins's actions tonight were at odds with her being associated with the magical beings I was trying to capture, despite Newell's appearance tonight, but Brin's description had been spot-on of Hawkins. And her facial reactions to my statement was so far only lending more weight to my suspicions.

"The wood sprite described the werewolf to me. It sounded exactly like you. And the timing fits—it was right after you were turned." My voice was quiet at first, but anger built as the questions that had been nagging me all week bubbled forth. "Why didn't you tell me you knew them? What's your role in all of this?"

"It wasn't me," Hawkins said softly. I was surprised by her tone. I'd been expecting defensive, angry. Instead she sounded . . . sad?

"How can I believe you? How can I trust you? If not you, then who was it?"

"I know who it was. Julia." Hawkins paused. "My ex."

"You're gay?" I asked. Scott would be devastated when he found out that Hawkins wasn't just out of his league, she was playing for another team entirely.

"I'm bi."

Still hope for Scott then. If Hawkins wasn't a lying traitor. Needed to refocus on priorities.

"A year ago, Julia and I were dating. We decided to go for a moonlit hike in the woods. Thought it'd be romantic. Naturally, we picked the night of a full moon because we wanted to be able to see without using flashlights. When we came across the boundary to the werewolf sanctuary, Julia convinced me to sneak in. All the 'Keep Out' signs just added a spice of danger for her. Maybe we'd get caught. Of course, we thought it would be only humans who might catch us."

Her voice suddenly hitched, and I realized with a start that tears filled her eyes. Sadness, regret, despair—those were emotions that were disconcerting to see on the face of someone who I normally thought of as tough. Resilient. Unflappable.

Hawkins took a breath. "Biggest mistake of my life. When the pack found us, they attacked. I'm not sure how we survived. All I remember is the pain. And the screams. Mine. Even worse, hers. But we were close enough to the fence that we somehow managed to climb over and escape. We spent the rest of the night just lying there, waiting for death. But werewolf bites heal quickly, and so we survived."

Hawkins paused, then pulled out her phone and showed me a picture. Two happy, smiling women with their arms around one another. Hawkins and Julia. There was definitely a resemblance. Both short and athletic, with close-cropped black hair. They had different facial structures, but if I had to describe them, the only real defining difference was Julia's green eyes versus the brown eyes of Hawkins.

"So it was Julia that was with Newell and Finian," I said slowly. "Do you know why?"

She shook her head. "No. We broke up not long after the attack. Something changed between us. I'm not sure if it was her or me that was more different. But she wasn't the person that I thought I knew."

"Did she join the pack?"

Hawkins shook her head. "They approached us the morning after, offering for us to join. We both declined. They told us about the Protectorate, warning us that your people would punish us if we were unconfined during the full moon transformation. That's what gave me the idea to contact the Protectorate for help, which is how I met Scott, who arranged it so I could turn in the cells. I told Julia about it, even though we'd already broken up. She told me she'd made alternate arrangements. That was ten months ago, and I haven't heard from her since."

A glimmer of hope and excitement was beginning to bloom in my chest. It looked as if Brin had been telling me the truth—she had actually seen a new werewolf with Newell and Finian. It just wasn't Hawkins. I was surprised by how much relief I felt over that news, but my suspicions still weren't totally alleviated. "But what about Newell giving you the tip tonight?"

"I swear, I have no idea why he showed up. I'm not working with him, and I never have. He must've had some sort of ulterior motive."

I weighed the facts of the case and Hawkins's actions so far. Could I trust her? My gut told me she was telling the truth, but I'd been wrong before. Finally, I made my decision.

"You busy tomorrow?" I asked Hawkins.

"No. I get weekends off. Why?"

I flashed a mischievous grin at her. "Want to come with me to see your ex?"

CHAPTER 39

BACK ON TRACK

I GOT UP early on Saturday morning, despite the late night. Had to get as much work done over the weekend as I could, before I had to return to my punishment guard duty at Headquarters. I knew at some point, I would have to fill Jake in on everything that was happening. After all, it was technically his case now. But I wanted to delay that bit of unpleasantness as long as possible.

Instead I called Scott. "You were right about Hawkins," I said when he answered. "She wasn't involved. But there was another werewolf. Her ex, Julia."

"Told you Cora was innocent," Scott said.

"Yeah, but I had reason to be suspicious of Hawkins. How was I supposed to know that there was another werewolf out there that matched her description? Maybe I should've listened to you more, but I had to be sure I could trust her." That was as close to an apology as I could bring myself. After all, my actions were justified. "Anyhow, that's not the only reason I called."

I quickly filled Scott in on the events of the night before. "Any idea why Jane Doe would be trying to sacrifice a little girl? And why Newell would clue us in?"

"Actually, I think I know." Excellent—having an ultra-knowledgeable friend was paying off again. "One of the spells in the grimoires was to protect against malevolent spirits. It was a nasty spell. Required the sacrifice of a virgin on a stone altar."

"She was trying to protect herself from Newell," I said. And Newell had been using us to protect himself from her. It was hard to be angry at him for manipulating us—after all, his actions had allowed us to save a life. Instead, guilt rose up in me. That little girl had almost died because of what I'd done. "And she had to pick someone young, to ensure she was a virgin. No telling what kids these days get up to."

"That's what I was thinking."

A sudden, horrible thought occurred. "What's to prevent her from trying again?"

The deafening silence on the line gave me all the answer I needed. The only way to prevent her from killing someone was to catch the witch before she could.

"Scott, I need you to find a way to banish Newell back to the realm of the dead," I ordered. "If we can get rid of him, it'll buy us some time with the witch. Hawkins and I will see if we can track down the werewolf. Hopefully that will lead us to Jane Doe and Finian."

There was one more thing that needed to be done. The altar needed to be kept under guard, in case Jane Doe returned. If so, we could prevent her from being able to attempt it again. Unfortunately for me, it would require far more manpower than just Hawkins, Scott, and me. We needed backup. Time to face the inevitable.

"We'll need to set up a round-the-clock guard shift at the altar," I told Scott. "I'll call Jake, let him know. Ainsley too. Maybe she can pull in some outlying field agents for this."

"Good news on that count," Scott said, surprising me. Was some good luck actually coming my way for once? "The kraken was successfully relocated. Everyone who was dealing with that situation is on their way back. Should be here sometime tomorrow."

Excellent. We'd have the needed manpower. But until they got back, we'd still be shorthanded. I said goodbye to Scott and briefly debated who I wanted to call first. Jake, I finally decided. Get that nuisance taken care of.

"What do you want?" Jake answered rudely. "I'm busy. *Some* of us have important work to do."

I bit back the nasty retort that tried to spring from my lips. For once, animosity would do me no good. Instead, shortly and concisely, I filled Jake in on what had happened and what I'd learned, conveniently forgetting to mention that I'd spoken to Brin early in the week and hadn't told Jake about the pertinent intel she'd given me.

"You let them get away?" Jake asked accusingly when I'd finished. "No wonder Ainsley kicked you off the case."

Grinding my teeth in frustration, I replied, "At least we know where they might come back to. Anyhow, what have you done to progress on this case?"

"I don't need to tell anything to you," Jake said, which I took to mean that he'd gotten bupkis this week. That put a small, satisfied smile on my face.

"Well, no matter. We need to guard the sacrificial altar in case she tries again."

"That's for me to decide, not you," Jake snapped.

My smile broadened. Jake had just backed himself into a corner by trying to assert his authority. It would be giving me even more of an upper hand now, if he agreed to my course of action. And he'd have to agree—there was no way the altar could be left unattended at this point. I knew it, and I knew Jake knew it.

"So you don't want the altar guarded?" I asked slyly.

"I didn't say that. But I'm in charge. You go there now and wait for me to arrive. I'll take the afternoon and evening shift. Then you can come back and take over for the night."

The smile slid from my face like water from a dragon scale. Of course Jake would stick me with the crappy night shift. And I would have to do it—Ainsley had put him in charge after all. Dammit. If only I hadn't blown it by summoning Newell.

"Fine," I said, refusing to let my extreme irritation show.

After I hung up with Jake, I called Ainsley in order to fill her in on what had happened. I was definitely getting bored with repeating all the details, but I didn't want Jake to take any credit for what I had found out.

"This is disturbing news," Ainsley said when I finished. "There hasn't been a witch practicing sacrificial magic in this area for over a hundred years. We need to catch her soon. Have you told Jake about this?"

"Yes."

"Really?" Surprise filled Ainsley's voice. "That was very . . . mature of you, Enzo, to not let your silly rivalry get in the way of what's important." She paused, and I tried to overcome my shock at being complimented by Ainsley. "Considering that you are based in Summerville and familiar with this case, I am reinstating you as a field agent."

"Yes!" The exultation escaped from me. Free of the dungeons, and back in the field at last.

"However," Ainsley continued briskly, ignoring my outburst. "This is a probationary reinstatement. You set one toe out of line, and I will make sure you are permanently assigned to the dungeons."

"Yes, Councilor," I said in my most polite and well-mannered voice. "I won't let you down." I couldn't—there was no way I'd survive if I was forever banned from working in the field. It was what I was born to do, was trained to do, and loved to do. I couldn't mess up this one slim chance.

After I ended the call with Ainsley, I checked the clock. Almost time to meet up with Hawkins. I gathered all the gear I'd need for guard duty in the cavern. No leaving behind my body armor this time. I wasn't going to be caught unaware by a magic user again. Even though I would definitely attract the attention of any humans who saw me in my FBI-emblazoned battle gear.

Scott had left his armor behind after we'd found Newell murdered in the alley, so I loaded it in the trunk of my car. It would be oversized on Hawkins, but it was better than nothing. No use in me being protected if my partner wasn't.

I drove to Hawkins's place. It was in a nice neighborhood. The houses were somewhat older and on the small side, but they all looked clean and well-maintained. Decent place to live. As I pulled up in front of her address, Hawkins came out. Must've been watching for me out the front window.

"I found Julia's new address," she told me by way of greeting. Then she frowned at me, puzzled and confused. "What are you wearing that getup for?"

"Brief detour before we go find Julia," I said. "We need to make sure that the witch doesn't try and use the altar again, so we're setting up guard shifts. Since we're closest, we're the lucky ones who drew first shift." No need to mention that we (okay, yes, I was including Hawkins in my assignments) had also gotten the lousy graveyard shift as well. "Armor for you is in the trunk."

We pulled up to the abandoned industrial complex a short while later. I popped the trunk so Hawkins could arm up, then pulled out my phone and shared the address with Jake—I hadn't made a note of it the night before—and gave him the instructions to find the hidden troll tunnel. Thank God we'd found this way to the cavern. I had absolutely no desire to ever enter the sewers again.

Hawkins quickly donned her protective gear. Unlike Scott, she didn't look comical in the large armor. The expression on her face was too fierce for that. Instead, she looked like she could go toe-to-toe with an ogre and come out unscathed.

After she was properly girded, we made our descent through the tunnel entrance. Fresh air was quickly replaced by the underlying foul troll and sewage stench, but at least it was fairly faint, not overpowering.

When we reached the intersection, I paused—What was down that other tunnel? But my curiosity would have to wait. We needed to secure the cavern against the return of the witch.

The smell was more suffocating when we reached the main cavern. The trolls had apparently resumed their residence. I heard the movement of large bodies in the shadows near their lair. Lifting my shield, in case I was wrong, I called out, "Drog Nash? Glask Norp? Are you there? It's me, Protector Enzo Thornton. And my partner, Cora Hawkins."

"Tiny thorn, hawk-wolf," came a rumbled reply as a hulking form detached itself from the shadows. "What kuldnak you do here?"

"We're here to make sure the shulpan witch doesn't return," I said, slipping a bit of troll swearing into my speech. "Have you seen the guldbag since we were here last night?"

"Grashknap no come back," Drog Nash said with a smile that was hideous to behold. Chunks of unidentifiable gristle were stuck between his huge, uneven yellow teeth. "Tiny thorn scare grudbnug away."

"Good," I said, trying to breathe as shallowly as possible. Too bad my riot helmet didn't come with air filters. I'd have to see about getting that added on as an upgrade. "We're here to make sure she doesn't return."

"Glask Norp and Drog Nash go hunt now," Glask Norp said, lumbering up next to her mate. I wasn't quite sure if she was informing me of a fact or telling Drog Nash what to do. "We go find tasty food in magic tunnels."

Of course the trolls would think the sewers were magical. All sorts of amazing smells and delicious foods. Thinking about what they might find to munch on, I repressed a gag as we watched the trolls lumber off into the foul darkness.

Once they were gone, I did a more thorough examination of the altar. It was old, that was for sure, but whether it was a hundred years or a thousand, I couldn't tell. The rectangular stone slab was about three feet high, a little wider than that, and maybe seven feet long. Four-inch runes were carved along the upper edge of the base.

"You know what these mean?" Hawkins asked, her fingers tracing one of the curling runes.

"No," I said. "Must've been created by magic, though, to get such smooth curves in the stone." I studied them carefully, hoping that their purpose would become clear, with no success. Frustrated, I left the altar and paced around the cavern, looking for any clues, anything that Jane Doe or Finian might've left behind. There was nothing, except the ropes used to bind the girl to the altar, and there was nothing special about them. Just plain rope you could buy in any human hardware store.

I knew where the next answers might lie: down the tunnel branch that we hadn't searched yet. But we couldn't leave the altar unguarded, in case Jane Doe decided to return via one of the different routes while we explored.

However, there were two of us here. This time waiting for Jake to replace us didn't have to be a complete waste. Divide and conquer. Kill two birds with two stones.

"You stay here," I told Hawkins. "I'm going to go check out the other tunnel."

"Shouldn't you wait for backup?" Hawkins asked, making far too much sense. "In case you run into trouble? Or in case the witch shows up here?"

"Just shoot her with that gun," I said. "It's full of night-night darts."

"Full of *what*?" Hawkins asked with puzzled skepticism.

"Magical tranqs," I said. "Don't worry, it'll be fine."

"Enzo, I really think you should wait," Hawkins admonished, but I was already heading down the tunnel.

"Howl if you need help!" I called.

"It's not me who's going to need it!" Hawkins shouted back, her voice echoing as I rounded the bend.

CHAPTER 40

A Bitch of an Ex

I KEPT GOING at a slow trot down the rough stone corridor, turning left when I reached the intersection. Holding my magically reinforced riot shield in front of me, I advanced more slowly as I continued down the unfamiliar tunnel. Didn't want to be caught by surprise in any magical booby trap. Or suddenly come face-to-face with the witch as I rounded another bend.

My right hand held my flashlight, sending a bobbing beam along the corridor. Before long, I noticed that it wasn't the only source of light. I clicked it off, using the dim ambient light coming from the tunnel entrance to guide me as I crept forward at a walk. .

Slowly peering around the final tunnel curve, I saw the interior of a small wooden shack, sunlight shining through thin, dusty curtains on two of the three walls. The third wall was occupied by a plank door. There was no fourth wall—just the rocky outcropping that contained the tunnel entrance. Apparently this building had been erected for the sake of concealing the underground passage.

Nobody was inside. Carefully, I approached one of the curtained windows and peered out. A small meadow surrounded the front of the cabin, bordered by gnarly oaks and scruffy pines. I knew I had to be near the southern edge of Summerville—the tunnel had been too short for me to have gotten far from the city, and I knew that bordering the city was a wildlife preserve, filled with hiking trails, trees, and a significant amount of poison oak. I'd been there once, tracking down a lost faun kid, and I could painfully attest to the abundance of poison oak in the area.

Since the area appeared deserted, I left the old cabin and looked around. No obvious trails led away from the meadow, to my disappointment. No doubt whoever knew about this entrance wanted to keep it hidden, so that humans wouldn't unsuspectingly stumble across it. Come to think about it, how had Jane Doe found it in the first place? Magic? Or had Finian led her here? I doubted the latter scenario, considering Finian was a water sprite, and Blue Lagoon was a fair distance away, but then again, I'd been surprised to see him in the ghetto apartment.

When I turned back toward the cabin, finished with my brief reconnaissance, I saw Hawkins standing by the door, in wolf form. "I thought I told you to stay and guard the altar," I said, somewhat surly as I walked toward her.

She cocked her head to one side, staring at me with bright green eyes.

At that moment, my phone beeped. "Just a sec," I told her, pulling it out and reading the text message. It was from my least favorite person. "Jake's at the industrial complex," I said, even as I began typing a reply. "Idiot's having a hard time finding the tunnel entrance."

A moment before I hit the send button, realization slammed into me. Green eyes. Hawkins's eyes were brown.

Instinct took over and I raised my shield, just in time for a huge body to slam against it, knocking me off balance. Instead of futilely trying to stay on my feet, I moved with the force, tucking and rolling to come back up in a defensive stance, shield held between me and the snarling werewolf.

"Julia, I presume," I said in a mock friendly voice, drawing my silver dagger with my free hand.

She growled and lunged forward, but I used the shield to thrust her body aside as I slashed with the silver dagger, hearing a shrieking yelp as the sharp blade scored her ribs. I grinned, adrenaline pumping through my veins. Now this was what I was made for: a one-on-one, no-holds-barred fight to the death with an aggressive supernatural creature.

The knife cut was but a scratch, but there was still a very real possibility that the werewolf could bite my legs off. Even though she'd been wounded by a silver dagger, it was by no means a deadly cut. Sure, silver was one of the only things that could kill a werewolf, but it still had to be a lethal wound to do the job.

Wary now, the werewolf circled me, fangs bared threateningly. I pivoted with her, shield held high, dagger at the ready. "You don't have to do this," I said. "Surrender now, and I'll make sure your sentence is light."

A menacing growl was the only response.

"Suit yourself," I said, and leaped forward on the offensive. I thrust my dagger forward and stabbed deep into the wolf's left shoulder as I kept my shield between me and the snapping fangs.

Julia yelped as the dagger bit into her muscle, jumping back with surprising agility despite her wound. I lunged again, but she twisted out of the way and fled into the woods with a pronounced limp.

Tempted as I was to follow, to finish the job, I restrained myself. I needed to get back to the tunnels, make sure that this hadn't been a double-pronged attack with Hawkins as another target.

I ran back down the rocky tunnel, footsteps echoing on the uneven walls.

"What's wrong?" Hawkins asked as I skidded around the final corner, alert for any danger. Her eyes locked on the bloody dagger I was holding. "What happened?"

"I think I just met your ex," I said.

Hawkins paled. "Did you kill her?" she asked, her voice devoid of emotion.

"No, just wounded her. She ran off." I suddenly remembered Jake's text message. "Have you seen Jake?"

She shook her head. I pulled out my phone to send the message with directions, only to see that I had no service. Dammit. I'd have to go to the surface and guide the asshole down here.

"I'll be right back," I told Hawkins, then jogged back up the tunnel, taking the right-hand turn this time.

There was no sign of life when I reached the abandoned industrial complex. At least I had cell service though. I sent the text, then sat down to wait for Jake. And wait. And wait. Was the bastard making me kill time on purpose, as petty revenge for my delayed response to his message? Finally I called him.

A noise sounded around the corner from where I sat. A ringing phone. At least he was close by. "Over here!" I called. No answer. The phone continued to ring. The hair on the back of my neck started to prickle. This wasn't Jake being Jake, this was something else. Something had happened.

Wary of a trap, I followed the sound around the building and saw a phone sitting on the ground. The gravel road nearby was scuffled. Signs of a fight. Crap. Something had happened to Jake.

Just to be sure, I picked up the ringing phone and saw that the caller ID said, "Asshole DNR." Wasn't sure if that meant "Do Not Reply" or the classic "Do Not Resuscitate." Either one would make sense for how Jake might label my number.

I silenced the phone and shoved it in my pocket. The course of action was clear: I needed to rescue my lifelong foe, despite the temptation to leave him to a (hopefully) grisly fate. The Protectorate really should give me a medal for this.

CHAPTER 41

Risky Rewards

I RETURNED TO the altar cavern. "Jake's been taken," I informed Hawkins without preamble. "Can you track him down?"

"Sure," she said, stripping out of her armor as she talked. "What happened?"

"No idea. Must've been the witch. I can't imagine a sprite being able to overpower him. I found his phone near signs of a struggle."

"Shouldn't we call for backup?" Hawkins asked.

"Good idea, I'll do that as soon as we get aboveground," I said, then realized that Hawkins was about to pull her shirt off. I turned my back to her for privacy. "But it'll be at least an hour before we can expect anyone. Probably more. So for now, we're on our own."

Feeling the strange shiver in the air that marked a werewolf's transformation, I turned back to Hawkins. Her brown eyes stared at me out of the black wolf's face.

"Ready?" I asked.

She nodded, bounding past me to take the lead down the tunnel. I followed at a sprint, and shortly we burst out into open air.

"Hold up," I said, pulling out my phone to call Ainsley when we reached the place I'd found the phone. Hawkins sniffed around the area as I dialed.

"What's happened, Enzo?" Ainsley asked. Either she was very pessimistic or highly intuitive about why I might be calling her so soon after our last conversation.

I filled her in on the situation as quickly as possible. Despite my efforts at brevity, I was still apparently taking too long for Hawkins. She finished canvassing the immediate area and stood watching me, impatience filling every line of her body.

"The kraken relocation team is almost back. I'll send reinforcements as soon as possible," Ainsley said when I finished. "Do not take any unnecessary risks."

"Yes, ma'am," I replied, and hung up. Of course I wasn't going to take unnecessary risks. I never did. I only took risks that were essential and unavoidable. "Let's go," I told Hawkins.

She immediately trotted off, nose questing through the air for whatever scent she had picked up, leading me deeper into the industrial complex.

"Can you smell the witch?" I asked. "Or Finian?"

She nodded her answer to each question, not bothering to slow down or look back. Great. Well, at least this time I was prepared to face a magical opponent.

Hawkins stopped at the side door to one of the smaller warehouses. Nearby, a white van was parked. Seeing it made me realize that I had let yet another thing slip through the cracks—I'd seen that van on the hospital surveillance tapes, picking up Jane Doe, and then again at the apartment complex as we tracked the kidnapped girl. The second time, I'd been so focused on finding the girl that it had completely slipped my mind to have the police investigate the van. Not this time though.

"Just a sec," I whispered to Hawkins, in case our perps were nearby. I drew one of my daggers and slashed both the passenger-side tires. Easy way to ensure that the van would still be waiting for us when we were done rescuing the helpless maiden. I mean Jake. Plus, it would keep anyone from being able to use the van as a getaway vehicle.

Task complete, I went to stand next to the door with Hawkins. No windows on the building, except for a row about fifteen feet off the ground, so there was no way to see what was going on inside. I pressed an ear against the door. No noises.

"Hear anything?" I asked Hawkins.

She shook her head, then let out a low whine.

"What's wrong?" I asked. It wasn't like she was whining over the possibility of Jake being hurt or killed while we took our time.

She shrugged, giving another soft whine, and sniffed the air.

"You smell something weird but don't know what it is?" I guessed, receiving a nod in return. "Great." I sheathed my dagger and pulled out my pistol instead. As I checked the ammo, I realized that I only had night-night darts, which were great for humans but basically useless for any supernatural creature. Well, they'd work on Jane Doe, at least.

Resettling my shield on my left arm, I reached for the door handle. "Ready?" Hawkins nodded, and I quietly opened the door, ready to see what awaited us on the other side.

The warehouse was brightly lit by the upper windows. Wooden crates of various sizes were scattered and stacked around the interior in a somewhat haphazard fashion. On the far side of the warehouse were some interior rooms—office space, I suppose. I guessed that was where Jake had been taken.

The fact that he had been snatched rather than killed outright made me believe that they were planning on interrogating him. Good—it wasn't like Jake had much useful information stored in his tiny brain. They could continue that exercise in futility for as long as they wanted, in my opinion. But, if I wanted to keep my status as field agent, I needed to rescue my fellow Protector, no matter what my personal feelings were. So together Hawkins and I entered the warehouse and crept toward the office rooms.

It was a good thing we'd taken the stealthy approach. We weren't halfway across the room before I heard a scraping sound across the concrete floor. Hawkins and I ducked behind the nearest crate, keeping it between us and the noise. I peered around the edge of the crate to see what faced us next.

I immediately wished I hadn't. Lumbering across the room, its scaled belly brushing the floor, was a dragon.

CHAPTER 42

CALLING IN A FAVOR

CRAP. THEY HAD a dragon. And not just any dragon—an ironscale. Although ironscales weren't a particularly large species of dragon, rarely exceeding twenty feet from snout to tail-tip, they were formidable. Not because they're highly aggressive—they're surprising docile, as far as dragons go—but because of the incredibly thick and hard gray scales that give them their name. They basically have an organic suit of plate armor, strong enough to withstand a 50-caliber bullet or a shaman's lightning.

I ducked back behind the crate, hoping the dragon hadn't spotted me. Though dragons were difficult to train, when properly handled they made excellent "guard dogs." You know all the dragon-living-in-a-cave-of-treasure stories? Well, there's definitely some truth to them. The mistake is believing the dragon is guarding its own riches, because in reality it's protecting someone else's gold and jewels. I mean, think about it—what possible use could a giant flying reptile have for that sort of thing?

My breath sounded loud in my ears, filling the quiet air of the warehouse. I tried to breathe softer, straining to catch any sounds made by the dragon. Had it seen me? Was it quietly approaching our meager hideout, waiting for the right moment to roast Hawkins and me in a torrent of flame?

Silence. I must've escaped its notice, for the moment. I glanced over at Hawkins, who was watching me with a puzzled look on her wolfy face, head cocked to one side. She still didn't know the beast we faced. I mouthed the word "Dragon" to her and saw fear in her eyes. Great. That made two of us.

But I needed to figure out some way to rescue Jake, and the only way to reach the offices was to get past the dragon. I did a quick mental inventory of all the weapons and magical gadgets I'd brought along. Nothing that could defeat such a powerful beast.

I chanced a quick peek around the edge of the crate. The ironscale was curled up in the center of the warehouse, its eyes closed. Hopefully sleeping, but I've heard of some dragons pretending to be asleep when they are actually alert and listening for any intruders. Couldn't risk trying to tiptoe past the great gray beast. Not unless I wanted to attend my own funeral as a charcoal briquet.

Even my magical armor was limited when confronted with a dragon. Sure, it could keep me from getting roasted for a while, but with each fiery breath, the spells would be slowly burned away. And with no way to defeat the dragon, it would only be a matter of time before I succumbed. If only I'd loaded my gun with deathspell darts—one prick, and any living creature would die. Of course, due to their overwhelming lethality, they were strictly controlled.

One thing was for sure: we needed backup. Something to even the odds between us and the bad guys. Fortunately for me, I knew just who to call. There was one particular species of supernatural that was superbly equipped to deal with fire-breathing dragons. And luckily for me, I had a favor to cash in.

I looked at Hawkins and jerked my head toward the entrance. Slowly, carefully, making no noise, we crept to the door, keeping crates between us and the (maybe) slumbering beast. The scattered arrangement of the crates finally made sense to me—the dragon had arranged them to its liking, creating a lair. But what was inside them? That answer would have to wait until the scaly creature had been dealt with.

Easing the door open with the utmost care—and thankful that the hinges had been oiled recently, so we weren't given away by groaning rusted metal—I slipped out of the warehouse, Hawkins following at my heels. I decided to move a short distance from the warehouse before making my phone call. Didn't want to alarm the guardian dragon.

But as I neared the corner of an adjacent warehouse, I heard soft footsteps in the gravel. Someone trying to approach stealthily, but being thwarted by the noisy rocks underfoot. I paused, leveling my gun, then was startled when Hawkins suddenly nudged my side. I glanced down and saw her shake her head. So, this newcomer was known to her. But who could it be?

Detective Marlow rounded the corner, pistol held steady in both hands. He saw me and Hawkins and frowned in confusion, but lowered his weapon as I did the same.

"What are you doing here?" we hissed simultaneously.

I shut my mouth, determined to wait Marlow out. Not because I didn't mind lying to him, but because, for the life of me, I couldn't straighten out which lies would make sense at this point.

"I got a lead on the van that picked up Jane Doe at the hospital," Marlow finally said, after the silence had stretched an uncomfortable length. Perfect. Honest police work was finally paying off, at exactly the wrong moment. "But why are you here? Your colleague, Agent Jonson, said you were off the case."

I surpassed a wince at hearing Jake being referred to as my colleague, even though it was technically correct. "I was, but I'm back on it now," I said simply, following the KISS rule. "Long story."

"What's happening here?" Marlow asked, eyeing my riot gear.

"Jane Doe is in the next warehouse," I said. "Come and see."

Marlow walked forward and peered around the corner. "Where? I don't see any—"

Psst. The night-night dart made a small hissing sound as it shot from my gun and embedded itself between Marlow's shoulder blades. He immediately collapsed, although I was close enough to grab him before he crashed to the ground.

As I slowly lowered him down, Hawkins growled softly at me. "What was I supposed to do?" Not like she could answer. "He can't know the truth about what's going on."

Another soft growl answered me as I stashed Marlow in the shadows behind a stack of pallets. Didn't want him to be caught in the crossfire. Fire being literal in that sense.

Once the human was placed out of harm's way, I pulled out my phone and called Sergio.

"Blair Enterprises, this is Sergio," the flamboyant voice answered on the second ring.

"Sergio, it's Protector Thornton—"

"Enzo! It's so good to hear your lovely voice. What can I do for you?"

"You know how you said you owed me? I'm calling in the favor." I quickly outlined my dragon dilemma and my plan.

"He'll be there in ten minutes," Sergio said when I'd finished.

"But the drive from Bay City's an hour, at least!" I protested.

"True, but he's not driving. Ten minutes," Sergio said. "Good luck!"

"Thanks," I muttered to the suddenly dead line. This plan was certainly going to need a lot of that.

CHAPTER 43

DOGUS EX MACHINA

TEN MINUTES TO the dot after the call with Sergio ended, I heard the sound of tiny claws on gravel. A heartbeat later, and a brown Chihuahua trotted around the corner, tail wagging happily.

"Hello, Crinitus. Thanks for coming." Always a good idea to be polite to a creature that can instantly transform into something that can literally bite your head off.

The hellhound barked, a sharp yip that was such a contrast to his hidden power, I had to hide a smirk. Then he greeted Hawkins, sniffing her in the fashion common to all canines, mundane and magical. I couldn't help snickering at the indignant outrage on Hawkins's wolf face, though I muffled the laugh in my elbow to keep anyone from realizing we were there.

Once all meetings were finished, Crinitus looked at me expectantly. "You ready to fight a dragon?" I asked.

The tiny growl that emanated from his throat was one of the most vicious sounds I'd heard in my life—never mind the puniness of the actual sound. It was the rage and promise of destruction that sent shivers through my spine, not the volume of the snarl.

"Good," I said, leading the way back to the dragon's warehouse. I opened the door, and all hell broke loose.

Crinitus bounded forward, rapidly expanding into a ferocious black-and-red beast as he barreled straight toward the ironscale. He barked—well, more like roared—a challenge, and the dragon bellowed in response, sending a white-hot streak of flame toward him. Undeterred, Crinitus continued his charge, running straight through the flame as if it meant nothing to him. After all, it didn't. One of the hellhounds' magical abilities—they were completely impervious to flames.

"Come on," I whispered to Hawkins as the two behemoths came together in a snarling clash. The hellhound was maybe a sixth the weight of the dragon, but that didn't stop his ferocity. There was a reason hellhounds chose Chihuahuas as their mundane disguises. So much viciousness trapped in such a tiny body.

Growls echoed through the warehouse as the battle was properly joined, although that was not my problem. I stayed focused on the office rooms, though I was still careful to keep crates between me and the battling dragon and hellhound. Didn't want to get accidentally swept into that fight. Hawkins stayed by my side, alert and ready for action.

The door to the second office suddenly flew open, no doubt in response to the sound of the battle raging in the warehouse. Finian and Jane Doe emerged. Could it get more perfect than this? I lifted my gun and fired at the witch—the night-night darts wouldn't work on the sprite—and held the trigger until the gun was empty, expecting her to collapse immediately.

Except she didn't. The darts hit an invisible shield that she'd apparently cast before the door had even opened. Dammit. I hate a clever enemy. But I love a cowardly one. Finian took one look at us—I knew we had to make an imposing scene, with me decked out in full battle gear and Hawkins snarling at my side—and fled, leaving Jane Doe to stand alone.

"Get him!" I yelled at Hawkins, then jumped forward toward the witch.

She cast a spell. I don't know what, because it hit my shield and shattered like a dropped chandelier. Thank God for protective spells. I bulled onward, intent on finally taking her down.

That was when the ground disappeared beneath me. I had a brief flash of admiration for the witch. She had seen that spells would be useless against me, so she directed them against my surroundings instead. That admiration quickly vanished when I hit the bottom of the pit she'd created, wind driving out of my lungs in a forceful rush. I lay there, gasping, trying to catch my breath as I held the shield above me, hopefully protecting myself from any more nasty surprises.

None came. I stumbled to my feet, looking up at the rim of the magic-created crater. It was approximately twenty feet deep, the walls a layered, uneven mess of concrete, dirt and rock. Scaling them would have been easy, without my armor to contend with. As it was, it was slow progress. I had to keep my shield above my head, in case Jane Doe decided to send any more unpleasant spells my way.

As I climbed, the battle roars of the two great beasts continued overhead. I glanced behind me when the noise grew louder—Crinitus was backed up against the opposite rim of the pit, the ironscale forcing him back inch by inch. The dragon's face had several long gouges in the scales, leaking dark blood, though it seemed that the wounds angered the giant reptile more than actually harmed it.

I suddenly realized that if Crinitus fell in the hole, I would be an easy target for dragon fire. I scrambled upward and dragged myself and my armor over the edge and back onto solid ground, using the last bit of momentum to roll into a crouch, shield raised defensively. No one was in sight.

A sudden yelp behind me. I turned just in time to see Crinitus fall into the hole I'd just escaped from. The dragon roared in triumph, blasting flames after the hellhound, filling the entirety of the hole so that it looked like an entrance to the fiery underworld. Then it lifted its head, fixing me with a murderous red stare. Crap.

My shield deflected the next blaze of fire to either side of me, though it couldn't completely suppress the heat. Sweat sprang from every pore in my body, only to be immediately evaporated in the furnace surrounding me.

But even a dragon can't breathe fire forever, and when the dragon drew in its next breath, I took the chance to sprint behind the nearest pile of crates. Not that they would do much good against dragon fire, but they were better protection than nothing as I desperately tried to think of a plan. I had no weapons that could kill it, and my armor wouldn't be able to withstand an actual physical assault from the behemoth. I had to keep moving, not let the dragon get close enough to maul me.

On the other side of the crates, the dragon roared in frustration. Surprised that it hadn't already engulfed the wooden boxes in fire, I chanced a peek around the corner. The dragon was circling the pit, snarling in rage.

Could it be? The dragon had been trained to guard these crates, and so it wasn't willing to destroy them in order to get to me. But what was actually in them?

I knew I had only a moment to act. Dragons may be slow on the ground, but there still wasn't much distance for the dragon to cover to get to me. I jammed the blade of one of my daggers under the lid of the nearest crate and pried open the wooden top. It's times like this that I'm thankful my kind is gifted with supernatural strength—a human would've needed a crowbar to open the crate.

Inside, separated into individual compartments, was an assortment of crystal balls of varying hues and sizes. I grabbed one that was about the size of a baseball and made of obsidian. Perhaps the fact that it was created in a volcano would mean that it could damage a magical fire creature. It was my only hope—the dragon's bloody face had just appeared around the corner. I hurled the obsidian ball at it, striking the gray scales between the dragon's eyes.

The obsidian shattered against the rock-hard scales, and the dragon roared in annoyance. Flames flickered deep in its maw, and I ducked to the other side of the stack of boxes, then raced back around the pit toward another refuge.

Not quick enough. The dragon's snakelike neck whipped around, and it sent a torrent of fire at me as I ran. I deflected most of the blast off my shield, but I felt the hem of a pant leg burst into flame as I ran.

I dove behind the next crates, then rolled and patted the fire out. My leg was red and blistered under the charred, ragged hem, so I quickly shapeshifted the wound away. It took a fair bit of energy to heal such a nasty burn, but it was worth every calorie—I needed to be in top health to stay out of the dragon's range.

Chancing a peek around the crates to see how close the ironscale was, I instead saw a welcome view. Crinitus had clawed his way out of the pit and was renewing his attack. Bellowing in anger, the dragon turned to face his persistent foe.

I used the reprieve to pry open some more crates, hoping to find some sort of useful weapon. It was clear as I opened them that this was the site of a major magical smuggling operation. So, Newell had been telling the truth about that after all. This find would definitely keep me in Ainsley's good graces. If I managed to survive, that is.

But everything I found appeared to be useless against such a formidable foe. A bunch of magical amulets—didn't have the time to figure out what they did—filled the second crate. It was followed by a box full of dreamcatchers, another with stacks of grimoires, and then one full of carefully packaged potions. Now that had some possibilities. I rifled through the bottles, picking each one up long enough to read the label and then returning it to its padded compartment. Who knew what sort of concoction might brew if the glasses broke and the potions mixed.

Love potion, love potion, skin de-ager, weight loss, super weight loss, extra weight loss, blemish remover, love potion, acne cleanser, love potion— all things that most women would fight over, and definitely worth a lot of money, to be sure, but they were completely useless to me at the moment. I gave up on that crate and opened another. More potions. I was about to continue on, considering the potions as a lost cause, when a label caught my eye. Deathsleep. Hmm. Might be interesting.

I pulled the bottle out, using even more care than normal. The potion within was black and wispy—hard to tell if it was liquid or gaseous. It seemed to shift between the two states. Unfortunately, there were no directions printed on the bottle. Just the name.

"Nothing to lose," I muttered, then stepped out from behind the crates and hurled the bottle toward the dragon. I'd been aiming for its mouth, in case the potion needed to be ingested, but the ironscale's head was a moving target as it snapped and snarled at Crinitus. The bottle of Deathsleep hit it on the side of its jaw, shattering on impact.

Thick black smoke billowed from the broken glass, enveloping the dragon's head. But it didn't stop there. It spread in a rapidly expanding cloud, blossoming into a dense, foggy sphere ten feet in diameter, obscuring the front half of the dragon and all of the hellhound. Oops.

The dragon collapsed in a heap, shaking the ground with the weight of its fall. I watched, waiting, anticipating, as the smoke cloud slowly dissipated. When it cleared, it revealed both combatants limp on the warehouse floor. Asleep or dead?

I approached cautiously, prepared to retreat if I caught the whiff of anything unusual. A sudden rumbling noise made me jump, lifting my shield defensively as I searched for the source of the sound, which had taken on a rhythmic quality. A broad grin split my face when I realized what the noise was: dragon snores. Both the ironscale and Crinitus were fast asleep. I knew the hellhound would probably be furious with me for drugging him when he came to, but for now I was just grateful that the dragon was out of commission.

I warily circled the slumbering beasts and went to the office room that Finian and Jane Doe had come out of. Opening the door carefully, ready for any magical booby traps, I saw Jake chained to a chair in the middle of the room. His head whipped around when the hinges squeaked. Outrage filled his eyes when he saw that it was me who was rescuing him.

Smirking, I entered the room and looked around. The office had clearly been used recently. A couple of computers sat on desks against the far wall. Likely this was the headquarters for the smuggling operation. A key gleamed on one of the desktops, out of reach of the chained Jake. I picked it up and unlocked the padlock binding his chains.

He got up, rubbing his wrists. "Took you long enough," he muttered.

Rolling my eyes, I replied, "You're welcome."

I hadn't seen Hawkins since she'd gone chasing after the sprite. Leaving Jake behind in the office, I went to the door on the far side of the building, the direction I'd last seen her running. When I exited the building, wondering how I was supposed to track her down, I realized that I didn't need to. She was walking toward me, Finian's arm in her mouth as she led him forward. He was disheveled looking and sported a couple bleeding nips on his bare skin—luckily for him, only humans are subject to the werewolf curse—but appeared mostly unharmed. Even the arm that Hawkins held in her sharp teeth was unhurt. She used just enough pressure to maintain her grip.

"Good job," I told Hawkins as I pulled out my magi-cuffs and slapped them around Finian's wrists after she dropped his arm.

The crunch of gravel and the grumble of engines filled the air. Before I had a chance to shove Finian out of sight—hard to explain a blue sprite to humans, without revealing the truth of the world—four cars came around the corner, sliding to a stop next to us. The doors opened, and Protectors exited, armed and ready for battle. Reinforcements, arrived at last.

I would complain that it was too little, too late, but there was still the matter of cataloguing all the magical items in the warehouse. And dealing with the unconscious dragon. The battle may have been over, but Protectorate work was just beginning.

CHAPTER 44

DREAM CATCHING

I WAS SURPRISED to see that Ainsley was in charge of the reinforcements. She hadn't operated in the field for as long as I could remember. I suppose it shouldn't have been that much of a shock—no doubt she wanted to personally keep an eye on me, instead of relying on reports.

"The witch escaped but, as you can see, we captured her accomplice. We also found a hoard of magical items that appear to be smuggled," I said as I led the other Protectors into the warehouse. When they spotted the dragon, everyone went into immediate defensive mode. "Don't worry," I said nonchalantly, flashing a broad grin. "I knocked it out."

"Wow," Zoanna whispered in the deafening silence. "Good job, Enzo."

My heart swelled with pride at the praise, and my smile widened until my cheeks ached.

"Yes, well done." The words coming from Ainsley sounded painful in their delivery. Definitely not happy about giving me any praise. "It's too bad the witch got away, but you've done better than expected."

My grin turned slightly sarcastic at her double-edged praise. I gave a short, mocking bow. "Thank you, Councilor." I curbed my sarcasm enough that I couldn't be reprimanded for insubordination. "Just doing what needed to be done."

Ainsley flashed me a sharp look, but she let my behavior slide. Good. She was finally seeing my merits.

Then, with his epically perfect timing, Jake showed up. "Don't worry, Councilor, we have everything under control. Dragon subdued, villains either captured or scared away. We have everything handled."

I sputtered, laughed, then finally exclaimed, "That is absolute bullshit!"

Jake glared at me, but I forged on. No way I was letting that moron take credit for my big win. "Yes, that is all true. But Jake had nothing to do with it. I rescued him!"

But it was too late. Jake's story was the one she wanted to hear. Turning to the other Protectors, she started calling out orders for dealing with the crates and the unconscious beasts. I was tempted to argue the point but decided to leave her to it—that work was the type of drudgery I avoided at all costs—and instead gestured to Hawkins for her to bring Finian into the office room.

I thrust Finian into the chair that Jake had been chained to. "Where did she go?" I demanded fiercely. "Tell me, or so help me, I'll . . ." I left the threat unfinished as the sprite quailed before me. He knew that he would receive no mercy from the Protectorate.

"I don't know!" he exclaimed. "Please, you have to believe me! I'll tell you anything you want, but Mistress Henderson tells me nothing of importance."

I grinned victoriously. Finally, a real name, instead of that stupid pseudonym she'd been hiding behind. I knew that Jane Doe was too blatantly false to be real. But what about her real name? Henderson had a ring of familiarity to me, though I couldn't pinpoint where I'd heard it before.

I continued questioning Finian, who was surprisingly forthcoming. Henderson, aka Jane Doe, had been heading a super-black-market smuggling operation, getting magical potions and artifacts into human hands. And making a killing at it, when she wasn't killing people herself. Or nearly getting killed.

"What about Peter Newell? What was the relationship there?" I knew it had to be juicy. How could it not, with him stabbing and failing to kill her and then her stabbing and successfully killing him?

Finian's eyes narrowed. "My testimony here will get me a reduction in my sentence, correct?"

"Yeah, sure. Of course," I replied easily. I neither knew nor cared. I supposed I could get a few years knocked off his sentence if I felt like it. At the very least I could get him in a cell away from the banshee. "Now tell me what you know."

"They were partners, at first. Henderson procured the objects, and Newell distributed them."

"And you?" I interjected.

Finian shrugged. "Go-fer, whatever they needed. Helped make contact with other supes, helped with the shipping. Whatever they needed."

"So what happened, then? Why did they fight?"

"Why do you think?" Finian snorted out a burst of derisive laughter. "Money, of course. What else do humans fight about? Henderson thought that Newell was holding out on her. Keeping some big scores for himself. So she decided to remove him from the partnership, only he was quicker on the draw than she was. Then you picked him up, so he was safe for a while, but as soon as you set him free, she was waiting to finish the job."

"And the werewolf? Julia?"

"Just extra muscle. Henderson hired her to guard the tunnel entrance out in the woods."

No matter—she was involved in a serious breach in magical security, not to mention the attack on yours truly. Now that I had reinforcements, I'd send a team out to pick her up and question her.

My line of questioning was suddenly interrupted when Scott came bursting into the room. "Enzo, I figured it out! I know how to banish Newell."

"How?" I asked, jumping to my feet.

"It was in one of the spells I read," Scott replied, taking forever to get to the point. I fought down the urge to tell him to hurry along. "It said something like, 'to catch a spirit one must catch a dream, for both are intangible and unique to each person.'"

I stared at him a minute. How the hell was this gobbledegook going to help us get Newell? Then it hit me. The crate of dreamcatchers. "What do we need to do?" I asked Scott, following him out of the office. "Watch the sprite," I told one of the nearby Protectors. Only when he went into the room with my captive did I continue after Scott. No need to let Finian escape while my back was turned. Not this late in the game.

"Well, I can't remember the exact wording of the spell, but I know that a dreamcatcher with the right spells on it will draw in the spirit that is named. There was other stuff, too, but I can't remember it all."

"That's okay, you don't have to," I said, striding to where a pair of Protectors were examining the crate of dreamcatchers. As I approached, I saw proof that my luck truly was turning for the better—one of them was Zoanna.

"Hey, Enzo," she said with a smile. Her skin was more bronzed than the last time I'd seen her, no doubt as a result of her recent adventures on the high seas. I wanted to ask her how the kraken relocation went, but taking care of Newell was too pressing at the moment.

"Hey, Zoanna," I said. "Scott and I need to take those dreamcatchers back to Headquarters."

"Why?" she asked, although her tone was curious, not hard.

"Long story. But, without confessing to anything, it's possible that I may or may not have accidentally set a malevolent spirit loose in the world. And Scott found a way to get rid of it using those dreamcatchers."

Zoanna shook her head in disbelief at the abbreviated version of my story. "I swear, Enzo, one of these days your impulsiveness is going to catch up to you in a bad way."

"It already did." I flashed her a cheeky grin. "Ainsley took away my field agent status. But I was a good boy, so she reinstated me."

Zoanna just rolled her eyes and handed me a clipboard with an evidence form she'd been filling out. "Here. Take care of this, and the dreamcatchers are yours."

Hawkins—dressed and in human form—showed up just as Scott and I were loading the crate in the trunk of my car. Good thing it was one of the smaller crates, because, as it was, it barely fit. "Here's your armor back," she said after greeting Scott, who looked a little moonstruck. Hawkins tossed the riot gear onto the back seat. I decided to follow suit—not like I'd need it right now, with all the nearby threats taken care of.

"I led some of your guys down into the altar chamber," Hawkins continued. "They're examining the altar stone now."

"Good, let them figure out those runes," I said. "We're going after Newell. Want to come?"

"I would, but I need to take care of Marlow." I felt a guilty twinge; I'd completely forgotten that I'd left Marlow unconscious behind a stack of pallets. "Any advice on what I should say to him?"

I grimaced and stalled for time by rummaging through my potions kit. "Here," I told her, handing her a vial of sleep-no-more. "Put three drops of this on his tongue when you get away from here. It'll wake him up. As for what to tell him . . . keep it simple. We got ambushed, but then the feds arrived and took over the case. They made you leave."

"So you want me to lie to my partner?" Hawkins demanded.

"You got a better idea?" I shot back. "We can't tell him the truth. It's too complicated."

"And all these lies aren't?" she muttered. When she saw me about to answer, she shook her head. "I know, I know. It just sucks to have to lie to someone that I respect. I'll do it though, don't worry."

"All right, well, good luck," I said, slamming the trunk shut and getting in the driver's seat. Scott had a brief conversation with Hawkins—I couldn't overhear what was said over the noise of the starting engine—then slid into the passenger side.

"Let's go catch a ghost," I said with a grin.

"Technically, Newell isn't a ghost," Scott replied as we started driving. "He's a dead spirit summoned from the realm of the dead."

"Close enough." I switched on the radio. "Highway to Hell" was on. Awesome. I cranked up the volume and gunned the gas. Time to banish a ghost. Evil spirit. Whatever.

CHAPTER 45

WHO YOU GONNA CALL?

WHEN SCOTT AND I got back to HQ, he went in search of the grimoire that contained the spirit-catching spell, while I lugged the crate containing the dreamcatchers into the lab where we'd been working. I thought it was fitting—capture Newell in the same place where we'd originally botched the spell and set him loose. Everything was coming full circle.

Scott finally arrived in the lab and together we looked at the spell. Seemed simple enough, although I double- and triple-checked everything for any homonyms that might trip us up. Didn't want to make the same mistake as last time we tried our hands at witchcraft. At least this spell book was more modern than the other one—much easier to read—and the only item it required was a dreamcatcher. Specifically, one with nine points connecting the web to the circle because three by three was an extra-magical number.

It wasn't until we started sorting through the dreamcatchers that I realized exactly how many different designs they came in. Eight point, ten-point, too-many-to-count point. Finally, though, we found a nine-pointer. It was a particularly pretty one, in my opinion. Black circle with teal cords forming the web, and the eyes of three peacock feathers hanging from the bottom. I grabbed a piece of twine from the supplies cabinet and hung the dreamcatcher from the ceiling, using a push pin to fasten the twine to the ceiling. The dreamcatcher swayed and twirled at the end of its makeshift hanger.

"Ready?" I asked Scott.

"No," he said. "But let's do it anyway."

I read through the spell one last time, making sure that I understood all the phrasing, then began to chant. And no, I will once again not say what the words to the spell are. This one would be way too easy for a naive reader to replicate. It finished, however, with the words: "By the power woven in these cords, I call thee, I bind thee, and I banish thee from the world of the living."

Scott and I stared at one another when I said the last word. At first, nothing seemed different. The dreamcatcher spun slowly on the end of the twine. Suddenly, it froze, quivering slightly. A breeze picked up—not something you'd expect indoors with all the windows closed—and I heard a faint noise, getting louder by the second.

As the sound increased, I realized it was a deep, human voice. Newell. "No, no, no, no!" he protested. His transparent shape suddenly flew through the wall, being dragged along by the increasing wind. When he saw me, his protests changed to curses. "You! You son of a—"

Before he could finish the insult, Newell's misty body made contact with the dreamcatcher. Bright blue light flashed, temporarily blinding me. When I blinked away the stars in my eyes, Newell was gone. All that was left was the dreamcatcher, glowing with a faint blue light.

"We did it," I said, sitting down in a lab stool abruptly, with relief. "We actually did it."

"Well done, boys," Martin said as the ghost floated through the opposite wall. Scott yelped in shock, knocking over the stool he'd been perched on and crashing to the floor.

As I gave my friend a hand up, I asked Martin, "So, does this mean you forgive my mistake?"

"Have you learned your lesson about dealing with things in the spirit world that you don't understand?"

"Yes."

Martin smiled and shook his translucent head. "The fact that you used that spell to capture Newell's spirit means that you haven't truly learned the lesson yet."

"So, damned if I do, damned if I don't?" I asked. "What else was I supposed to do? Leave him loose to wreak havoc until I understood everything?"

"No, I didn't say that," Martin said patiently. "But in the future, do not meddle in the spirit world."

"I won't," I vowed. "I don't want to deal with anything like this again."

"I've got my eye on you, Enzo Thornton," Martin said, then drifted back into the walls. Gotta love a preachy ghost who has to have the last word.

"What do we do now?" Scott asked after a moment of silence.

"Four easy things." I grinned. "One: Find a witch. Two: Catch her. Three: Lock her up, and finally: Throw away the key."

CHAPTER 46

For Whom the Bell Tolls

FOLLOWING THE LEAD that I'd gotten from Finian, I searched the Protectorate database using the keywords "Henderson" and "witch." Bingo—Henrietta Henderson. Witch and conjurer extraordinaire. Known brewer and distributor of illegal potions. Suspected thief. Confirmed user of sacrificial magic.

Then I saw the personal details. Residence: Summerville. Born 1865. Deceased 1904. Shit. Wrong Henderson. The witch I was pursuing was probably her descendant, working with the same spell books that her great-whatever Henrietta had used. As I dug further into the information, I saw a detailed sketch of Henrietta's residence. It was the cabin in the woods that hid the entrance to the tunnel. No wonder the modern witch knew how to find the underground altar.

But, as interesting as this information was, it didn't help me at all in tracking or capturing the present-day Henderson. Even the manner of death for the ancient one wasn't useful—killed by a pack of goblins when she cheated them on a deal. Goblins are fairly magic-resistant. It'd be a stupid witch who pissed them off.

Sudden exhaustion hit me like a steamroller. I'd done enough for one day. Defeated a dragon. Dueled a witch. Detained a sprite. Well, technically Hawkins did that last one, but I helped. And, lastly, captured a malevolent spirit. This case could wait until morning. At that moment, all I wanted was my own little apartment, and my own bed. The pull on my heart toward home was almost a tangible thing. I logged off the computer, waved goodbye to Scott, who was still entranced by his own research, and left Headquarters, heading back to Summerville.

I let my mind drift as I drove, paying more attention to the lyrics of the songs on the radio than I did to where I was driving, taking my exit automatically and driving through the familiar sights of suburbia. Only I didn't live in one of these sprawling ranch-style homes. I couldn't afford something like this. Newell did, though. I blinked, suddenly realizing that I wasn't driving toward my home. I was headed to Newell's. Why had I done that? Suspicion crept into my mind.

Just to be on the safe side, I shapeshifted. I'd only seen the human form of Julia in a photograph, but that was enough for me to be able to mimic her. As I shrank to her size, I realized that I should've pulled the car over first. My legs were now much too short to reach the pedals, but I managed to slide the seat forward while driving without crashing. The small blessings in life.

Pulling up in front of Newell's house, I felt a tug to go inside. Further confirmation of my suspicions. I considered donning the armor that was still in the backseat of the car, but realized that I couldn't. Not if I wanted to sell this disguise. And this disguise was all of the advantage I had.

Exiting the car, I walked to the front door of Newell's house, doing my best to appear confident and nonchalant, while my senses hummed with the adrenaline pulsing through my veins. I had one shot at this. No going back. No failures.

I opened the unlocked front door and walked into the house. Jane Doe/ Henderson was in the middle of Newell's family room. She'd shoved the couch out of the way to make room for a giant pentagram she'd drawn on the floor. She stood in the middle, chanting a spell. The urge to go to her increased, but I resisted. Barely.

"What are you doing here?" Henderson demanded. "I thought you ran off with your tail tucked between your legs."

"I'm not that easy to scare," I said, slowly approaching her. "What are you doing?"

"Summoning that interfering, idiotic Protector," she snapped. I feel the raw need to go to her. To help her. "He's going to pay for messing up my operation." A slight frown creased her brows as she looked at me. Thinking. Wondering. Suspecting.

Now or never. Fighting against the desire to protect the witch, I drew my silver dagger and lunged across the space between us before she could react. With one thrust, I buried the blade in her heart.

She collapsed like a puppet with its strings cut. No staggering around, Hollywood-style, or slowly sinking to her knees. Just instant death.

I stared at her unmoving corpse for a minute. I'd done it. It was over. Although, I half expected a bunch of Munchkins to suddenly pop up from behind the couch and sing their trademark song. But, of course, none did.

And so, in the end, the case finished the way it had begun: with the stabbing of Jane Doe.

EPILOGUE

SO THERE IT is. My first tangle with an investigative case, without a simple directive of "arrest this dwarf" or "kill that minotaur." Despite all my many blunders in getting to the bottom of this mystery, I'm still not sure which I like more. Granted, life was a lot simpler without humans involved. But if I hadn't gone out with the intent of finding human villains, I would never have stumbled upon this major supernatural smuggling operation. And I never would've found—despite all my efforts to prevent it—a friend who happens to also be a werewolf. In the end, I think I'm a better person for it. Even Ainsley agrees, and that's saying something.

Sure, not all the loose ends of the case were tied up. But that's life. It's not wrapped up with a pretty bow on top. Julia is still on the loose. Both mundane and magical BOLOs haven't found her so far. It will be interesting to see which gets wind of her first.

Jake, to my disgust, has taken an interest to solving cases. Hopefully a wyvern will eat him on his next investigation. Granted, he doesn't have the innate talent of my left pinky, but still he's an annoyance.

Marlow has gotten even more suspicious as time has passed. Oops. Apparently, a kidnapped young girl told him she saw a big black wolf. Unfortunately, Marlow was smart enough to associate that wolf with my wolf, aka Hawkins. I guess we won't be able to go undercover anytime soon. But, after all, what are mistakes?

People (including me, I'll reluctantly admit) fail sometimes. But that's okay. In the end, I think it's the perseverance that really matters. The determination to set things right, no matter the cost. Or, perhaps, to pursue that special girl for as long as is necessary.

In that respect, have I succeeded? You be the judge.

Donec iterum conveniant.

Protector Enzo Thornton

L. M. Filarsky graduated from Point Loma Nazarene University with a degree in Writing and a minor in Biology. She is the author of a children's book series, *The Star Horses*. Lauren lives in Northern California, where she divides her time between writing and riding.

For more information about Lauren's upcoming projects, visit thestarhorses.com and laurenfilarsky.com.

www.ingramcontent.com/pod-product-compliance
Lightning Source LLC
Chambersburg PA
CBHW020803310726
48969CB00002B/679